For my wife, Krystle.
Happy five-year anniversary!

HER FINAL VICTIM

NJ MOSS

Windsor and Maidenhead

www.bloodhoundbooks.com

Print ISBN 978-1-914614-41-5

ALSO BY NJ MOSS

All Your Fault

1

MILLICENT

Once upon a time the hours and minutes leading up to the kill filled me with light. It would expand inside of me until all the darkness – all the pain – was squashed into dim corners. I wouldn't have to face it, constantly, the never-ending maelstrom of leering faces and glinting eyes and untrue promises.

Now there's a pit in my belly, grotesque and ignoble. I feel as if I'm a mindless animal waiting in the dark, gripping a rock, scanning the pathway as I wait for my prey to come ambling along.

I haven't done anything differently. I've made sure the park doesn't have CCTV, and the surrounding roads are quiet and unmonitored. I'm wearing a hair net and a hood and a mask and gloves. Even shoe-wraps. There isn't a single uncovered part of me, except for my eyes. They must glint in the dark: the eyes of a jaguar suddenly appearing at the fringes of a fireside.

I never choose my prey beforehand. Selection leads to patterns, and patterns are the police's favourite toy. The only concession is that the quarry must be men, because men are evil down to their core. They might pretend otherwise, grinning in public, but once doors close they become savage beasts. They rape and molest and twist little girl's minds. If I had my way they'd all be rotting in a mass grave.

I picked up the murder weapon when I entered the park half an hour ago, at one o'clock in the morning. It's the sort of haphazard weapon the police will ascribe to a spur-of-the-moment crime.

The jagged edges of the rock bite into my palm as I squeeze, even through the glove.

But I don't feel *it*. There's no expansion. There's no certainty.

It's because this victim – whoever he ends up being – is not *the* victim. He's not the man who will be my last. I know it's dangerous to think like this. I've been careful over the years, establishing myself as a respected copywriter, wearing human faces to convince people I'm as trite and milquetoast as they are.

But the fight is becoming harder and harder to win. The pull is too strong.

Finally, the gate rattles. We're in a rundown part of the city, and the lights in here are either broken or not switched on. The moon is forced to send the shadow of the gate across the concrete, iron-blue as it whines open.

A man walks down the pathway.

I smile. This is good. This is very good.

He's dressed in a full tracksuit and sports trainers, with a gold chain glinting in the low light. The primary giveaway is the satchel slung across his midriff.

It is so courteous of drug dealers to wear uniforms. Courteous and stupid, but I suppose I shouldn't expect much from pathetic troglodytes who spend their days intimidating people on high streets and getting children hooked on their filth.

I stalk forward as he swaggers in, doing that disgusting thing where he has one hand stuffed down his trousers. I'll never understand why some men feel the need for this. Are they afraid they'll forget they have cocks if they're not constantly waggling them?

This one is going to be easy to get away with. Even easier than the others. I'll leave the murder weapon behind, like a junkie would.

I walk out in front of him, head bowed but eyes raised so I can watch him. It's too dark for him to make out any details of me, but I note his shoulders relax when he sees I'm a woman. He thinks it makes me weaker. That's exactly what I want.

"All right, darling," he says, waving his hand, the one not fiddling his prick.

I stop and tilt my head, the same way a hunting animal does.

I just wish I *felt* it, bone-deep: the light, the whispers before the release. There's nothing and yet I'm too far down the road to turn back.

"You all right?" His voice is abrasive and stupid-sounding. He could be lowing as much as talking. "You want me to call you a taxi?"

"What's in the bag?"

He flinches. He can hear the predator in my voice. I'm top of the food chain.

Fearing me is the smartest thing this waste of skin has ever done.

"None of your business. Why are you dressed like that?"

I walk forward, reaching up to tug down my mask. The darkness melts to reveal our faces to each other. I see a man with a teardrop tattoo under his eye – it's supposed to make him look tough, but he just looks sad and lost and ready to die – and a receding hairline and some fuzz around his chin. He sees a woman in her mid-thirties with innocent eyes that scream, *I mean no harm.*

"You know what I think, little lamb?"

3

"I ain't got time for this shit, sweetheart. Look, I've tried to be nice—"

"I think you're going to use those drugs to make innocent women compliant. I think you're going to force them to do things they don't want to do. I think you're a monster. I think you broke me. I cried. I *cried*. Why didn't you?"

The man raises his hands, finally letting his worm go. His mouth falls open. He looks at me like I'm mentally diminished. A different form of light flares awake inside of me. It isn't the kind I covet, but I'll take rage over apathy any day.

How dare he look at me like I'm insane?

"Relax. Don't be stupid. I'm happy to call you a taxi—"

"Like to rape little girls, do you, you druggie *fuck*?" I snarl, letting the beast out between my teeth.

"Fuck this."

He walks around the pathway, onto the grass, giving me a wide berth. I face the sky and drink in the stars and beg for some of their heat and power to cascade into me. But there's nothing. I'll have to do this cold. Maybe this is a sign.

The man's footsteps are soft on the grass, and then they become louder when he returns to the stone path behind me.

Gripping my rock in an eagle's talon, I swivel and judge the distance.

He's shaking his head. He thinks he's better than me.

I spring forward and bring the rock down as he spins at my approach. It crunches into his forehead and he stumbles and then I do what is necessary.

If I didn't fall upon him and hit and keep hitting – if I didn't bring the rock up and down, up and down in mechanical efficiency – if his blood didn't cast a rusty pallor to the night air, I know exactly what this man would go on to do. He'd use women. He'd hurt women.

He's a monster. He left me. He broke me.

I perch atop him, straddled like a lover. This is the closest I will ever get to intimacy, and I'm fine with that. Let the worm-fiddlers dupe other women, women who don't know how to fight back.

But even now, there's no rush. There's no certainty.

I let the rock tumble onto his belly. "What a disappointment you are."

Standing, I reach into my pocket, taking out the digital camera. The buttons are chunky and easy to use in the gloves. It's why I chose this model. For a brief moment, the flash illumes what I've done: the petal of blood blooming across the pathway and congealing in the grass, his stupid and surprised face, his seeping forehead.

Darkness returns, and I pocket the camera. "You're not doing it. It's time. This proves it. Why aren't you making me *feel*?"

I lean down and unzip his satchel. I won't ingest whatever drugs this devil is peddling. I like to keep my wits sharp. I'll dump them far away from the murder scene, leading the police to comb the area for any junkies desperate enough to kill a man for a few hours of amnesia.

Not that I blame the junkies. I'd like to forget too, if I could.

I reach inside the bag and take out his wallet, his keys, his phone – things a crackhead would steal – and then root around for the clear plastic bag that will contain his wares.

Instead, I find a small box. I flip it open and stare down as the cheap-looking engagement ring glints in the moonlight.

This doesn't complicate matters much. The man still *looks* like a drug dealer. The police will come to the same conclusion. And if he'd proposed to some poor gullible woman, and if she'd accepted, he would have made her life miserable. He would have worn her down, belittled her: shattered her so he could rebuild her in his desired shape. I've done her a favour.

If the law didn't make it so tricky for me to tell her, she'd thank me.

It's time for me to leave. I'll clean myself of this man's blood, change into cattle clothes, and then I'll burn my killer's uniform and keep his corpse's image close to my heart.

But first: one last look. Perhaps, just maybe, something will flare to life inside of me.

I glance at the silhouette in the inky pool... and nothing. My heart is cold.

This lack of sensation proves it. It's time I began the hunt that may end in my death.

I kick him in the side, feeling his ribs give a shiver under the force. I kick him again, again, and again, until my leg tires and I have to accept no amount of violence is going to provoke what I need. I stamp on his face to be sure, caving in his cokehead nose, but nothing, there's nothing.

As I walk toward the lonely tree where I've stowed my exit bag, I imagine a pair of emerald eyes watching me. They belong to my final victim, and they are beautiful, and they are hateful. They are eyes whose brightness I will steal.

2

JAMIE

I'm sneaky for such a big bloke. Wearing socks helps, and Lacy's boiler is loud. She won't hear my footsteps if I need to change position. She won't hear my breathing over the boiler's hum.

She's on the other side of the door, in her bedroom, drying her hair as she gets ready for bed. She sings along to a pop song, only catching half the lyrics. Her voice is dog shit, but the effort's what counts. It's ten o'clock and she's settling down for the night.

I've been in this detached bungalow many times. She doesn't feel like she has to keep her voice down because she doesn't share any walls. She lives alone. She's perfect.

Tonight is the first time I've stayed this long without her knowing about it. We've fucked and watched Netflix and ordered takeaways, but even so, I know she'd probably overreact if she knew I was here.

Not that it matters.

The fuck am I going to do, leap out and shout *surprise*? I grin at the thought, almost laughing.

The final nights are always my favourite. The main event will be happening soon.

Once her hair is dried, her footsteps tell me she's walking toward the boiler room, which connects her bathroom and bedroom. I flatten myself as she opens the door, holding my breath. I don't move an inch. I could stay like this for several minutes if I had to.

Lacy walks into the bathroom. Her music comes with her and her voice rises. She sounds sexy and confident, and my cock gets stiff. Singing wouldn't do it for me in any other context. But there's something about her lack of self-consciousness that really gets me going.

She pisses in the dark, which is helpful. Some women turn on all the lights as they pass through their homes, especially if they live by themselves. Even if they know nobody's lurking in the dark, they have to be sure. My grin widens. Nobody's lurking in the dark... except me.

Over the last few weeks, I've made it my goal to learn as much about her as I can. I know she prefers crunchy peanut butter to smooth and she only drinks green tea and she still hates her secondary school history teacher. I know she owns two vibrators and she's ashamed of both of them. I know she was married and she has a daughter, but she was tricked into believing she'd be happier as a strong independent woman, and now look at her: alone, singing so she doesn't have to think about the life she gave up.

She's too old to start again, and that excites me. It makes me stiff. The tension almost hurts.

She's proved how desperate she is every time we've been together, doing any depraved thing I ask her, grateful a younger man is showing her some attention. But they're *always* grateful. The older they are, the hungrier they are to let me fuck their throats, their arses, finishing on their faces or their tits or inside of them.

She could be reading her daughter a bedtime story, but the silly bitch didn't even fight for custody. She abandoned her child.

What's wrong with her?

She returns to the bedroom and gets herself set up for bed, moving her desk chair so she can place her laptop on it. I build a mental picture of her based on the sounds she makes. A little sigh: maybe she's seen something on social media that's upset her. Shifting sheets and noisy pillows: she's restless, maybe wishing she was out doing something instead of hunkering down for a night of TV.

She watches a *stupid* amount of reality TV. That's probably one of the reasons she chose this sad life, separated from her family. She thought it would be glamorous. I can't stand to listen to it, but it's not like I've got a choice. Five episodes in a row – into the early hours of the morning – these women rant and bitch and make problems out of nothing. It almost makes this not worth it.

But just as my patience is wearing thin, the show cuts off mid-argument. She fell asleep mid-episode and now she's shut the laptop in her sleep. She did that once when I stayed over, snaked her arm out of the covers and slammed it loudly.

I won't go out yet. I'll let her get used to the sounds of the house settling. I love that phrase. *It's the house settling.* It makes it much easier for my footsteps to go unnoticed.

I'm proud of how cleanly this one went. Getting her into bed was easy. All it took was buying her some drinks and nodding in the right places. Hooking her was even easier. Tell her she's beautiful, tell her she's talented, tell her she's whatever she wants to be, and she was mine. Once she thought she knew me, it was a simple matter of stealing and copying her key and watching her type in the code of her security alarm.

I wait until I hear her breathing get heavier. There's a difference between shallow and deep sleep.

When I'm sure she's not going to wake up, I slide around the edge of the door and walk carefully into her bedroom. She's conveniently left the boiler room door open. I don't have to worry about creaking wood giving me away.

My blood is pumping hot. I'm rock-hard. I have to fight the urge to grab myself. That's for when I'm alone and reliving this moment. I won't do anything to wake her. I've slipped up in that way before.

Her bedroom is a mess. Clothes are spread everywhere, three—no, *four* plates on her desk. Three mugs. It's interesting to see how much effort she puts in when I come over. Normally her bedroom is spotless.

I walk to the edge of the bed, resting my elbow against the back of her computer chair.

Oh, God, she's there, right there.

I could reach out and touch her if I wanted.

She's lying on her side, her back to me, which makes it even better. She doesn't have to be Lacy anymore. She could be any woman.

She's kicked off her blankets and she lies with a pillow stuffed between her legs. Her pyjamas aren't the sexy silky things she puts on for my visits. She's wearing a loose-fitting tank top and tatty old bottoms with a hole in the arse. She shifts in her sleep, stretching her legs, sticking her hips out. Her brown hair cascades across the sheets, with streaks of tempting grey in it.

Does she know what she's doing to me?

I bite down to stop from making any noise. I have to leave soon. I've got what I needed. A drum beats in my head. I never experience this certainty at any other time in my life. Maybe I seem certain to other people. Maybe I'm a good pretender. But I never *feel* it.

Here, I don't have to stress. Because she's right there. I could climb into bed and press myself against her. I could reach up between her legs and rub her like I've rubbed her before. And, in the moments before she remembers she's supposed to be afraid, she'd like it. She'd grind against me. She'd moan and she'd shiver and maybe we'd fuck. I'd cradle her face in my hands.

"You're right here," I'd tell her, and she'd smile. Because she'd know how true it is.

She murmurs and rolls onto her back, exposing her throat, a few lines hinting at the wrinkles that aren't far off.

Hurting this woman doesn't interest me. I needed to see her. That's all.

I head for the door, picking my footsteps carefully. The tension in my groin is becoming too much to handle. No porn is as good as this, even if they made some proper realistic virtual-reality stuff. I feel pre-cum leaking and my teeth throb from gritting them.

I move down the hallway – there are no pets to bother me – and to her front door. My shoes are where I left them, neatly arranged next to the welcome mat. There's a certain thrill in leaving them here, like I've been invited to visit. I arrived late, so there wasn't much chance of her wandering to the front door and spotting them. After priming the alarm, I slip them on and let myself out, locking the door behind me.

HAZEL

I like to dance around the studio as I work, holding my paintbrush like a weapon. I fling it at the A3-sized canvas. Droplets of rose-red flare across the upper part of the work, joining the nature-greens and the big swathe of sun-yellow I added earlier this morning. Paint flecks my cheeks and my denim dungarees, but I don't care. I feel alive. This is awesome.

I step back, studying my work. It's leaning toward an abstract nature scene, with lots of vivid colours and personal expression in the piece. I wipe my hands on my dungarees – I love these things, messy from a dozen other paintings – and go to a table in the corner and grab my phone.

There's an art to selfies most people will never understand.

I could have a full face of make-up and my hair could be worked into a gorgeous weave, but if I was standing against a grimy prison backdrop, it'd hardly matter. Although... yeah, maybe I could post something like: *I'll never let prison make me forget how beautiful I am.* Okay, fine, but that doesn't mean I'm wrong. It means I'm really clever when it comes to social media.

I stand with the corner of my painting just about in view, with the window showing a slice of our garden. The garden's a bit of a mess beyond this specific window, but I've made sure it's sublime from this angle. I've put a trellis with interwoven vines out there, making the light hazy.

I take a few with a broad smile. Then a few artistic serious ones. I take a few where it's mostly my face and then I get my stick and arch my back and give the suggestion of sexiness. I'm not being gaudy about it though. When I'm done, I've got one hundred and two images to choose from. I always like to hone it down to one or two, because then I know they're the absolute best.

There's nothing better on a sunny spring morning than expressing myself through my art. Whoever you are, remember: you MATTER, I SEE you, I HEAR you. If I can do it, anybody can.

I add hashtags using a website I subscribe to. They generate the best ones for me, and then I'm done. I reward myself with a quick scroll.

I try not to let myself care about how little my follower count has increased lately. I started my Instagram account in my early teens, but I only really began to put effort in four years ago. Since then, I've gained eighty thousand followers, for a total of almost a hundred thousand. I know it's not as many as some people, but I'm proud. The only problem is I've been getting dribs and drabs lately. I haven't had a day where I've lost followers yet though, so that's something.

I end up on Kirk Hope's profile.

He's an influencer I've been following since I was like fifteen. I used to be obsessed with him because we're the same age and we have the same birthday.

He started with pranks and comedy sketches and now he does a little of everything. I try not to come here too often – I'm committed to Jamie – but sometimes I can't help it. In recent years, Kirk has gotten *ripped*. His teeth are straight and shiny and white. His hair is tousled and blond. He's exactly twenty-two years, two hundred and thirty-five days old.

"Coffee?" Jamie says from the doorway.

I look up. My husband always seems a little tired and deflated when he returns from Cardiff. He works as a manager at a recruitment consultancy company and spends two weeks at the Cardiff office and two here, in Bristol. Sometimes he commutes back in the evenings and weekends, but mostly he stays up there, too exhausted from his long hours to come home.

"No, I'm okay."

He walks into the room, yawning. His hair is spiky from sleep, his jaws covered in a matching black beardy shadow. His dressing gown is open to show his Calvin Klein boxer shorts. He's got a different sort of body to Kirk Hope: thicker, stronger, less pretty-boy-ish. "Come here, H."

I slip my phone into my pocket and walk over to him, wrapping my arms around his broad shoulders. His aftershave and his sweat and his just-Jamie scent washes over me. I smile up at him. My man really is handsome, especially with his bright green eyes.

Lots of people comment on how striking Jamie's eyes are.

He smooths his hand up my back and pulls me close, leaning down and placing his lips against the top of my head. He inhales and lets out a satisfied groan. "Goddamn, I missed you."

I hug him tighter. "You always say that."

"I say it because it's true." He slides his hand down my back toward my bum, and I move with him, shaping my body to the path his touch takes. I can feel him getting excited, and I feel an answering song inside of me.

A memory hits me, annoyingly. I want to enjoy this moment.

Mum got way too drunk once when Dad was at sea. I lurked outside the living room, ear pressed against the door, as she ranted down the phone at one of her friends. She wouldn't talk to *me*, obviously, because I'm only her daughter. *A woman has to please her man. That's what this younger generation doesn't understand, with this do-it-yourself nonsense. Keep your man happy and you can have a simple life, an easy life, a comfortable life.*

I push my mother's voice away. This isn't the same as her and Dad. Jamie and I are happy together... mostly, even if there are a few niggling issues, a few things I'd rather he didn't do.

I study him. I could draw this man's face from memory in a hundred years. I'm certain of that. I'm lucky we have such an excellent marriage. I don't regret marrying young one bit. I repeat the sentiment in my mind, making it true.

I. Don't. Regret. Marrying. Jamie.

"You have to say it." I moan, making my voice breathy and high-pitched, the way he likes. Does that make me like Mum, changing my voice to fit my husband's desires, or does that make me a loving wife?

His hands make deeper impressions through my dungarees, making my skin hungry for more. "I see you, Hazel Smithson. I see all of you. You're never invisible with me. Everything you do, everything you are... I'll always be watching."

It's my favourite quote from our wedding vows – we did our own – and it always makes me crazy for him. I leap up and wrap my legs around him. He chuckles and stumbles backward, slamming against the wall.

"You're crazy, H."

I bite his lip, not quite hard enough to draw blood. "As if you'd have it any other way."

4

MILLICENT

As the pit inside of me grows deeper and more demanding – as the days collapse into each other and I'm forced to accept the time has come – I try to console myself with work.

My current contract is copywriting for a shower gel company. It's exactly the sort of anaesthetic I require. They ask for a perky upbeat tone, and yet they also want it to be professional and businesslike. They seem utterly ignorant that these requests are dichotomously opposed. But that's the way with people. They are both sinners and saints, evil and good, dead and alive.

He walked away – his back, the shape of his shoulders, he kept walking.

I push myself away from the desk, spinning in my chair with the engagement ring clutched tightly in my fist. Closing my eyes, I try to imagine what it would be like to truly clasp such a lofty item. If my imagination was more adept at sinking to the level of the sheep, perhaps I could see myself with some nice man: the sort of man who'd never hit a woman, belittle her, use her, reshape her.

But the ring feels like cold metal, nothing else. I don't know why I still have it.

The news hardly covered the drug dealer cosplayer. There were a few articles here and there, but the city where I slew him is big and tumbling into fresh events endlessly. There isn't time to care about a man in a tracksuit who was killed for some loose change and a cheap piece of jewellery.

I'm in a different city now. I rarely stay in one place for long. I use websites where foolish people rent out their homes to strangers. My work makes moving easy. Perhaps there will be a day when some clever detective pieces together these unsolved murders with the wanderings of a freelance writer. But it hasn't happened yet.

I slide my hand across the keyboard, caressing the keys, and then to the edge where my memory stick waits for me. But what's the use? I could peruse my past achievements in the vain hope something would erupt to lighted life inside of me, and yet I know it won't. That epoch of my life has passed.

I'm a wanderer now, truly: my soul as much as my profession.

The shape of his back, the broadness of his shoulders, the back of his head – his footsteps...

Clip-clip-clip, so loud on the concrete.

How were they so loud? Am I remembering it wrongly? No, my perceptions are sharp, knotted around me like barbwire, honed to a level the bleaters cannot even imagine.

I sigh, I sigh, I sigh.

I am so fucking bored of sighing.

Clicking away from Word, I navigate to Instagram, to Hazel Smithson's page. Her profile photograph shows a vapid thing. She smiles widely and her cheeks are smooth and tight and her teeth are fake-looking and her hair is red, Viking-red, not blood-red. It's dusky. The sort of shade bruises sometimes turn, and I think for a moment what it'd feel like to mark her exposed flesh. She's short and she's young and she's far too obsessed with herself.

If I were given a contract to write the most banal statements imaginable, Hazel Smithson's profile would be my finished product.

Believe in yourself.

You can do anything if you put your mind to it.

You're beautiful.

Remember to breathe today.

You're worth the world.

On and on and on, incessantly, these vacuous statements flood her feed and people feed on them. They like them, comment about them, tell her she's wonderful and insightful and brave.

Brave? *Brave?*

There's nothing brave about typing out a few words and taking some over-sexualised photographs. Stalking the perverts of the night, doing what is necessary, eliminating future rapists and monsters... that's bravery.

I go to my bookmarks and click the post I saved a few days ago. The photograph was taken on Hazel and Jamie's wedding day. Jamie looks dapper and happy in his suit, as though there's not a devil lurking behind those frustratingly bright eyes of his. I despise how they shimmer, those eyes, how they stare into me.

I think he can see me. I think he knows what I am.

Hazel looks magnificent in her wedding dress. Her hair tumbles around her shoulders. Her smile seems genuine and, ashamedly, it makes me wonder what it would feel like to wear a ring instead of take one from a corpse. It makes me want to open that smile wider with a box cutter, slit from the corner of her lip right up to her ear, and then keep dragging until her carmine grin seeps into her too-perfect hair.

But Hazel doesn't know her husband, and I very much doubt Jamie is privy to his wife's deepest desires, her innermost secrets, the conclave of her unspoken wants and hates and uncertainties. There is a great lie in marriage: that one person can know another.

I scroll through the comments. Before I decided to act upon my long-withheld desire, I had avoided social media. I still have no accounts under my name – except on freelancing websites for work – but I have become somewhat obsessed with scrolling. I've made a dummy account so the website doesn't block me out. They're determined to get their hooks in. It *is* addictive, which is probably why so many morons wander the streets with their stupid eyes fixated on their palms.

Am I any better?

Yes, this is research. That's why it's not the same.

One comment reads, **Congratulations. Maybe there'll be a little Hazel or Jamie on the way soon?**

I want to reply and tell the commenter that, unfortunately, Jamie Smithson isn't going to live long enough to father any children. But of course I don't. Commenting is for cattle, and I am a wolf.

5

JAMIE

"I swear to God, kid, I'd go mental without you," Ray says on speakerphone. I'm sitting in traffic on the Severn Bridge, the day dim and depressing. Or maybe it's me. After two weeks with Hazel, I never enjoy leaving her. "Bunch of pussies, your generation. No offence."

I laugh. "None taken, boss."

"But you're the exception." I can tell he's eating by the way he grunts between words. "What are you, thirty?"

"Close enough."

I'm twenty-six, but Ray is an ex-alcoholic and he has problems with his memory. And, anyway, only an idiot corrects their boss. At least in my business. Kissing arse is the name of the game, and even if it pisses me off a little, it pays well enough that I can live with it.

"Exactly. Thirty, but you've got that old-school mentality. Fucking Barbara. Emailing me with this holiday shit. What am I supposed to do with that?"

"I'll sort it. You don't need to worry about it. It's out of your hands now."

"See!" Ray yells, as I inch the car forward and fight the urge to slam my fist down on the horn. Nobody knows how to drive these days, I swear. "That's what I wanted to hear." A pause. "You're coming to my birthday party when you get back, aren't you?"

"Wouldn't miss it for the world. I consider you a friend as well as my boss."

I lay it on thick in this last line, and Ray coughs out a laugh. "All right, all right, calm down. Just get this sorted."

"I will. You can count on me."

"I know I can. Speak later."

I hang up and let my head fall back. There's some trouble at the tollbooth that really isn't my problem. The business with Barbara won't be an issue. She wants the ground-level grunts to be allowed to swan off on holiday whenever they feel like it, but it's simply not in their contract. I'll explain it to her. If she gives me any problems, I'll lay it down flatly.

That's why Ray splits my time between the two offices. He knows I can put people in their place.

I try not to think about how I got here. A man should always keep moving forward. But I've got to give myself some credit. I left uni at twenty-two and I went straight to work for Sunny Skies Recruitment. Right away, I knew I was made of stronger stuff than my colleagues. They were always complaining, bitching about how they had to stay late, how their work phones never stopped ringing.

I made a point never to complain. I never took a sick day. I back-stabbed and I broke rules and I threw people under the bus, and now, in my mid-twenties, I own a three-bedroom house in Clifton, I drive a Range Rover. I'm married to the woman of my dreams. There's no way I'm going to let some lazy slackers ruin that.

Finally, the cars inch forward.

I relax my grip on the steering wheel, smiling as a memory hits me.

Are you trying to break it, tough guy? Hazel said on one of our earliest dates, when we were stuck in traffic. I didn't know what she meant, and then she reached over and touched my hand. *Relax. If we miss our reservation, take me to McDonald's. I don't care, as long as we're together.*

I grin like a jackass all the way through the tollbooth.

The workday is long, but I'm full of energy when I return to my hotel room... a swanky room, paid for by the company. I spend some time on Skype with Hazel, but afterward I'm left lying in bed at ten o'clock with nothing to do.

I've never enjoyed sitting around doing nothing. TV shows bore me. Books are even worse. I can't just *sit here*. I'd head down to the gym but I'm still sore from yesterday's workout. Or maybe that's an excuse. Maybe I knew what I was going to do the second I left the Sunny Skies offices.

I could call up some of the blokes from work to come out with me, but I don't trust them to keep their mouths shut if they see me chatting up a woman. It creates other problems too. It's not like I can pull them aside and say, *Listen, man, I might randomly leave the club to follow this woman home.*

That's why, once I've showered, sorted my hair, and changed into a fresh suit, I head out alone.

I take a taxi to a club in the city centre.

Even on a Monday night, there's a line out front. The women are dolled-up, university students and older women wishing they were university students. A lot of the men look cheap and soft and self-loathing. They stand like girls with their arms crossed against the slight cold. Or else the bigger ones stand puffed-up, as if they can't let their muscles speak for themselves.

I feel pretty satisfied as I walk to the front of the line. "Jonesy."

The bouncer nods. He's a boxer and a vending machine rolled into one. He knows I'll slip him fifty later if he lets me in. We don't exchange money now. That's the way poor people do it. After my childhood, I refuse to act like a poor person.

"Mr Smithson." With a nod, he steps aside. "Have a good night."

I walk up the stairs and to the bar, sitting at the end of it.

The club is built with the dance floor separated by a hallway from the bar section, so the music isn't as loud. There's a separate bar in the club area, which, combined with their policy of not allowing people to move drinks between the bar and the dance floor, keeps it quiet out here.

People will be heaving and sweating on the dance floor. I prefer to sit quietly and nurse a whisky. Sometimes – most times – I'll have a few drinks, make some small talk with whoever's around, and then head back to the room.

But then there are the times when my whole world will transform.

The fun part is I never know what night is going to be *the* night.

"Well, well, well, look who's back," the barmaid says, dancing over to me with a smirk.

Yasmin's probably around forty, a punky type, with one side of her head shaved and the rest of her hair flowing down to her shoulder. She's got tattoos all over her neck and hands and even one on her face. I can see how some people might be attracted to her, but I see her as a friend. She's been nice to me ever since I started working in Cardiff. "Still drinking whisky so you can pretend you're James Bond?"

I chuckle. "Pretty sure he drank Martinis, baby girl."

She shivers and throws me a look. I know she hates it when I call her *baby girl*. That's what makes it fun. "Go fuck yourself, Wall Street."

"Get yourself something."

"I was going to."

I laugh as she grabs the bottle, flipping me the bird with her other hand. I reach for my wallet, and then stop mid-movement when somebody bumps into my shoulder. I turn, ready to tell them to mind where they're going. It must be some drunk arsehole.

But when I see the woman standing there, staring at me, I can tell it wasn't an accident. She's tall and thin and her hair is black. She's got one of those hipster fringes, almost right down to her eyes. I reckon she's about ten years older than me. She's got that stylish older lady thing going on, and it really gets me fired up. There's something about her eyes. Confident, sassy.

I smile. "Excuse you."

"Excuse *me*? Do you think we're blind, prick face?"

"Prick face? Did you just call me prick face?"

"It's bloody freezing out there. And here comes Mr Important, cutting the line, acting like he shits gold. Just who do you think you are?"

Maybe I'm a little twisted, but she couldn't have made me more interested if she'd tried. She doesn't care about me. She's not trying to impress me. She's one hundred per cent herself.

"Well?" she snaps.

"I'm the bloke who wants to buy you a drink."

She rolls her eyes and walks to the other end of the bar. Her black dress hugs her lithe body and it has little jewels on, like stars in a night sky. It's captivating.

"Getting a good look?" Yasmin jokes, sliding my whisky over to me.

"You can't tell me she's not nice to look at."

"I wouldn't kick her out of bed. Are you gonna pay or what?"

I hand her my card. "Her next drink's on me."

"Sure, Romeo, whatever you say."

I pick up my whisky and take a small sip. It settles hotly in my belly and immediately I feel my body getting a warm buzz. I won't take another sip yet. I always pace myself. I've seen how pathetic men can be when they're shitfaced. My old man was a right booze hound before he got ill.

Yasmin walks over to the woman and they exchange a few words. A moment later, she returns to me, shaking her head. "She says she'd rather drink sewage water than let you buy her a drink."

"You're joking. She really said that?"

Yasmin smiles broadly, clearly enjoying herself. "I'm giving you the toned-down version."

I look over at the woman, raising my glass in a toast. She stares blankly at me for a few moments, and then places her handbag on the bar and roots around in it. She does this for a few seconds, and then brings her hand out, aiming her middle finger at me with an unapologetic smirk.

Flipped off by two women in the space of two minutes. It's got to be some sort of record.

I need to know her name. I need to know more about her. I need to know why she's nearly forty but she's at a bar alone, drinking alone, instead of in bed with her husband, instead of caring for her children.

I need to possess her, to stand over her as she sleeps, to make her mine. To take it back, the pain and the regret. I need to fuck her brains out.

It doesn't normally happen this soon. But I can't deny it.

The game has started.

6

BEFORE

There were nine of them, all adults, and they were standing in a circle in the small dim room. A bulb hung from the ceiling and it was a naked bulb. It threw its light, but only dimly, and in the centre of the room there was a chair and on the chair sat a woman. The woman was frail and thin. She looked forty, but that was life's cruelties working its dark magic on her; she was only twenty-seven. Her name was Constance.

The room was called the Rainbow Room because it could be any colour. To the untrained eye it was a dull stony grey, but that was only if the observer was unfamiliar with Charles Maidstone's conception of reality. Charles was a wealthy man, an academic, and the leader of this group.

Everything was nothing; nothing was everything. Language was unreliable, as were perceptions.

These were his tenets, and it never seemed to matter to Charles or his followers that they made no sense. The more confusing and indecipherable his babbling, the more they believed.

They were morons, right down to their leader: stupid fucking morons.

Charles was tired of academia so he had moved here, to this ignored part of England, to bring into reality what he had written extensively about. Nothing existed except for the narratives by which people lived. Religions, sciences, schooling, addictions, relationships, pleasure, pain, hope, work, sex... everything only existed within the constructs by which people lived. It was patently untrue, but honesty and dishonesty were tools of the system – or so he said – and thus evidence didn't matter.

Charles had inherited a great deal of money from his family. These means, combined with a near-spiritual conviction this was the right thing to do, had led him to this countryside cul-de-sac. He had paid over asking price for most of the properties, and if a homeowner didn't want to sell, he found ways to make them see reason.

Here they were, the original settlers, and they were welcoming a new devotee to their cause.

Constance wore no shoes. Her toenails were cracked and caked in mud. She looked around the room with a mixture of fascination and fear as the Comrades' humming got louder and louder, timed purposefully with Charles' footsteps across the room.

He loomed over her. "What is your name?"

His eyes peered from horn-rimmed glasses. He wore his beard wild and tangled. His hair fell in grey-brown sheets.

"Constance. But people call me Connie—"

Charles slapped her across the face with so much force she fell from the chair. The momentum caused the chair to collapse backward. As if by machine-driven reflex, one Comrade righted the chair and another righted the person. Constance wheezed and stared up at him, as if captivated by a flame, her eyes flickering with something reflected in this man, her master: this man who had found her on the street, fed her, fucked her, and brought her here.

"What is your name?" Charles' tone was unchanged.

She knew what she had to say. They had rehearsed this. It was part of the ceremony. "Constance. But people call me—"

He hit her. She fell. The chair fell.

Everything was returned to its rightful place, as the Comrades hummed, and their humming got louder, and the room was filled with their humming and the light danced in their eyes and none of them wore shoes.

Charles stepped back and held out his hand. Somebody tenderly laid the grip of the pistol against his palm. The world would've been a much better place if he'd put the barrel in his mouth and pulled the trigger.

Instead he let it sit there for a few seconds.

"The gun is loaded," he said.

"The gun is loaded," the chorus came.

"And?"

"And the gun is empty."

"And?"

"And the gun is loaded and it is empty. The gun is a cat in a box, both living and dead."

"Yes." Charles stepped forward and laid the barrel of the gun against Constance's head. It must've been cold, or she must've been scared despite her previous conviction, because she shivered. "Yes, yes, yes."

"Yes, yes, yes," Constance moaned.

"What do you wish me to do?" Charles said.

"There is no *do*," Constance whispered. "There is only *say*."

His beard twitched with the suggestion of a smile. "Fine. What do you want me to say?"

"I have wasted my life. I have no purpose. I am a whore but it's not my fault—"

The Comrades chanted, "It's not her fault, it's not her fault."

"Society made me this way. I am different but society doesn't care about differences, only narratives, and the narratives are bullshit anyway."

"Good," Charles said. "Now do it, my dear. Do it and die. Or become one of us."

The woman's hands trembled as she reached for the gun. She grabbed the barrel and opened her mouth and she put the barrel in her mouth.

"Do it." Her words were distorted around the metal of the gun. "Do it. Do it. Do it."

The humming reached a crescendo and then fell silent when he pulled the trigger.

Click.

Cheering exploded in the small grey multi-coloured room. It sounded like one voice. The Comrades had practised this moment for hours and hours to achieve the right sound.

"Good." Charles smiled, letting the gun drop to the floor.

"I'm... nothing?" Constance murmured.

"Silly girl. You're everything. Now, claim your prize."

He reached into his pocket and brought out the glass pipe, and he lit it, and he took a long inhale and handed it to her. Her hand snatched out eagerly, betraying her need. She took a large hit.

Oblivion fell. And, for a sweet moment, she really did believe the walls were a rainbow.

7

MILLICENT

This place is truly repulsive.

The bar was probably shiny proud silver once, glittering when it was freshly made. Now it is a patchwork of stains and stickiness. The façade remains – it is still, technically speaking, silver-coloured – but it doesn't glitter as it must have in the beginning. The music is far too loud, even from here. People constantly walk back and forth between the entrance and dance floor and the smoking area and the toilets.

What a pathetic waste of life, I try to tell myself, as I watch a group of young women flutter by, laughing, carefree, confident in the knowledge they have each other and always will – for tonight, at least, and that might as well be forever. Yes, how sad, what a useless mass of unspent energy. And yet there is, truthfully, a part of me that longs for such a connection.

I repress a sigh and offer a cattle smile to the barmaid. She smiles back, and then leans forward with a secretive glint in her eyes. I despise myself for being able to read her expression, but I've forced myself to pay very, very close attention to the quirks of people's faces.

If I am to imitate them, I must know them better than myself.

"He's still trying to come to terms with what you said," she says, and then makes an homicide-inducing little laughing noise. "That was top quality."

I toss my head. "Some men think they can do whatever they want. I think it's our duty to put them in their place, don't you?"

"Oh, *definitely*," the barmaid says, before wandering off to serve somebody else.

Definitely, really?

Perhaps she'd like to grip the blade next time I go hunting. She'd faint at the first sight of blood. Maybe I'll shove a rag of her own in her face and see how tough she is then.

Still, it's tumbling together as I knew it would. Jamie isn't the sort of man who deals with rejection well. I try not to let any nervousness erode this moment, but I can't deny there's an ember of it within, trying to spread and become something more.

He is, after all, the man I may die for.

When I put him in the dirt, I don't intend to do it in the dark. I've done too many of my important deeds without the aid of the light. When the police discover what I've done, they'll want to take me someplace murkier than a park at 1am. I'll do what is necessary, as I've done my entire life.

I would rather slit my wrists and hang myself than lie entombed within cold metal bars.

Another gaggle of women passes me, with the obligatory vulturine men trailing after them. "Come on," a woman caterwauls, waving her hands like she's having a fit. "I *love* this song."

"Taylor Swift," one man says, and I picture what it would be like to drive a screwdriver into his overly groomed beard. "Why's it always gotta be Taylor Swift?"

Shut up, you foolish nothing, you non-entity.

Sometimes I wish it was culturally acceptable to spit in people's faces. Fucking pathetic weasel, trailing after them like a dog for scraps.

I take a sip of my diet Coke. There's no alcohol in it, but one can drink Coke at a bar without looking conspicuous.

I envision smashing my glass across Jamie's clean-shaven cheek as he walks over to me. "I think we got off to a bad start." He takes the seat next to mine. "I'm Jamie."

"Okay, Jamie." I keep my voice mostly cold, but let in a little flirtatiousness, enough to let him hope. "Now I know your name. That really has made my day much better."

"Aren't you going to return the favour... your name?"

I look down as though I'm shy, which isn't entirely an act. Looking him in the face is difficult. He has something of his father in his eyes, even if they're not the same colour. There's something there: the intent.

I can tell he likes the shyness. He thinks he's making progress.

"Millicent." I sound like the most chaste choir girl in the village. "But everybody calls me Millie. Are you here to piss me off even more? I should warn you, I'm not in the mood for arseholes."

"Bad day?"

"Something like that."

"Maybe a drink'll help, eh?"

I gesture to my glass. "I have a drink."

"A *real* drink." He adjusts his shiny cufflink. I wonder if he's doing it on purpose, to draw my eye to this statement of wealth. Should I give him that much credit? "I've been watching you since you came in. There's no alcohol in that."

I giggle. "Okay, creep."

Oh, look at me, such a delicate little flower. Do come and pick me, kind sir.

"Hey, I'm just looking out for you. Sitting at a bar with a non-alcoholic beverage. That's, like, a crime."

Like-like-like. What is this modern fascination with saying the word *like*? A man shouldn't have to punctuate his sentences with that word, over and over and over. He should get a lash across his back every time he says it, to cure him of the habit. I'd happily wield the whip.

"Am I striking out here?" he says.

"I didn't realise we were playing a game."

Which is a lie. It's just not the game he thinks.

He chuckles, looking closely at me. It's unnerving and I wish he'd stop. I don't like the way it's making me feel, the things it's making me remember. His eyes are truly, unashamedly, unequivocally captivating. "I don't think I've ever met a woman like you, Millie."

I roll my eyes, oh-so-precious, even if he's right. He has no idea how special I am. But he will. "If I let you buy me a drink, will you promise not to use any more cheesy pickup lines?"

"What line? I meant it."

"*Jamie*," I say, and he flinches.

A cascade of emotion shivers across his face and then he settles down.

I've just done something extremely clever. Earlier today, I watched his wedding video on Instagram. He and Hazel were cutting the cake and, when he playfully dabbed her nose with some icing, she tossed her fiery hair and said, *Jamie*. I rehearsed it for an hour. I'm not even sure why. But it was worth it.

I've always loved playing with dolls.

"All right." He shrugs. "No lines. Just one drink, okay?"

"Fine. If you absolutely must—"

"Oh, I must." He's back to his cheeky-chappie routine.

"Then I'll take a vodka and Coke."

I don't intend to drink a single drop of alcohol tonight, or on any night. It never does good things to me. It's difficult enough to maintain this façade without chemicals interfering with it.

Jamie calls the barmaid over and she exchanges a look with him and then with me, as though she thinks we're involved in some kind of love triangle. She's trying to tell me something with her eyes, and for a mad moment I wonder if she knows about Jamie's night-time invasions. But I'm certain she doesn't. She's getting way too intimate way too soon because she can't control her drinking. Her eyes are glassy.

She's weak and unprofessional. She drinks on many of her shifts.

This isn't the first time I've been to this bar and observed these two together. This is just the first time I've done it up close.

It was much easier when I was skulking at the door to the dance floor, when I was behind Jamie in line for coffee, when I was sitting in his workplace lobby pantomiming a phone call and watching him pass by. It was much easier when I was invisible to him.

I've broken the seal now. There's no going back.

"Millie."

Jamie's hand is on my shoulder. His touch is too soft.

"Why are you touching me?"

Fuck. I've broken character.

Something in my voice must spook him, because he snaps his hand away at once. "I'm sorry. I didn't mean to... Shit, I'm sorry, all right?"

"No, it's fine." I make myself bright again, even as my fingers twitch with the desire to grip his throat, hard, dig my nails in until I puncture skin and get to the meaty grisly bits people are made of.

"Your drink is here and you're staring off into space like a..."

"Like a what?" I say, giggling again, a veritable party girl.

"I don't know. Like somebody who stares off into space, I guess?"

"Oh. Silly me."

Absolutely *not* silly me. I'm the cleverest person Jamie's ever met by far.

"So, what do you do for a living?" he asks.

Of course he'd want to know this. People like him, in well-paying jobs – jobs that devour all their time and require justification – love to validate their existence with questions like these. He wants me to tell him my job is worse than his and his job is incredible and, most offensive of all, he wants me to do it without simply coming out and saying it.

"I'm a freelance writer. It's very boring." Look – an honest statement. "What about you? Oh, I'm sorry."

This seems like the perfect time to fake a phone call, before he blabbers on about Sunny Skies Recruitment. I take my phone from my bra, intentionally, knowing he won't be able to resist looking. It makes me sick to do this, but I'd be a fool not to use my sexuality against him. I know how much little Jamie loves older women.

I glance at my locked phone screen, making sure I angle it so he can't see.

"I have to take this. And I've got work to do. I only stopped in for a quick drink. But apparently the world won't even let me have that."

"Somebody important?" He's doing an utterly terrible job of hiding his disappointment.

"A friend," I say. I invent. "She's going through a divorce at the moment. It's a whole thing. Anyway, it was nice to meet you. Do you want money for the drink, since I haven't touched it? Or will you drink it... or?"

I sound unforgivably ditzy. Put a bullet in my head, please.

"What? No. Don't worry about it. It was really nice meeting you, Millie. Have a good night."

Hopping off the barstool, I adjust the hem of my skirt. Again, bile swirls around my belly. But I know his eye will be drawn to the movement, to my bare thighs, and I didn't put in all the work at the house for nothing. Giving him the sort of wave an awkward, shy, interested woman would, I head toward the exit.

Perhaps I should end this here. I could wait in an alleyway that has a line of sight on the club's exit, bulrush him, fall upon him like a wild animal, with teeth and nails and spit and blood. But how can I be sure I'd feel it, feel anything, if I devoured my meal before it was warm?

I need Jamie to cook, to burn if he has to.

8

JAMIE

I'm going to follow her to her car or taxi or bus.

I need to see her and there's nothing wrong with that. She's a pretty lady, but there's something more about her. I could've been anybody to her. She didn't even look flattered when I offered to buy her a drink. I normally get *something* from women, especially the older ones I target for my game. They don't expect a – let's face it – handsome bastard like me to glance twice at them. Normally they melt, sometimes dragging me home the first chance they get.

I want to encourage her to come out of her shell a little.

I hand the doorman his fifty on the way out, annoyed I have to do it in the open.

But nothing's going to stop me from getting another look at Millicent – Millie.

Everybody calls me Millie, she said.

I want to know who everybody is: her friends, her family, her acquaintances, her hobbies and her hopes and her fears.

Who are you, Millicent-call-me-Millie? Let me put you together piece by piece.

I spot her at the end of the street, waiting to cross the road.

The light turns green and she walks on, moving awkwardly in her heels, making her seem drunker than she is. I don't want some sicko seeing her like this and taking advantage. Say what you want about me, but I've never touched a woman, never hurt a woman, never violated a woman like some men do.

I stick to the shadows as I trail her, hugging close to buildings. I used to play rugby when I was a teenager. I'm pretty athletic and I know how to move efficiently, without drawing attention to myself.

Thunder Thighs moves like a ballerina, my coach would say, and we'd both laugh.

I have no clue where Millie's going. I expect her to climb into a taxi or turn into a building any moment, but she keeps walking. Her phone call with her friend must've ended quickly. There was only about a minute between when she left and when I decided to go after her.

The traffic grows lighter and the streets become quiet. There are hardly any people about. We're heading toward residential streets. She's doing something completely mental. She's *walking home* from a club. Nobody walks home, especially in heels.

Millie, what a puzzle you are.

She's got a stunning lack of self-awareness. Most women glance behind them from time to time when they're walking alone in the dark. They have to be sure they're not being followed. And, when their too-quick search doesn't find me, they assume they're not. But Millie doesn't look behind her once.

She brings me to a quiet street about an hour after she left the club. My legs ache a little, my feet throbbing in my stiff shoes.

She walks to the end of the street and heads into the perfect house. It's detached. No security lights blink on. There's no sign of an alarm system out front. I don't spot any cameras, and people tend to put these in obvious places to deter burglars. The garden is long and the space between her house and her neighbour's is even longer. A tall hedge blocks the view to most of the ground floor and some of the upstairs. She doesn't switch on any lights.

The door closes, and the house remains still and dark and dead-looking.

I should leave it here. I have her address. I've done a decent recon of the place. But I'm hard and excited and everything about this is perfect. It's like this house was designed for my desires.

What sort of idiot would I be if I walked away now?

She's offering it on a platter. It's like she's doing it on purpose, the same way sweet Lacy stuck her arse out in her sleep a couple of weeks ago. Thinking about that makes me stiffer. The base of my cock is throbbing.

I glance up and down the street, waiting for a neighbour to come out, for a light to blink on. Something needs to stop me. I haven't done even a tenth of what's required to make this safe.

I should think of Hazel, of our life together. I should think of Ray and how he'd react. I should think of my parents. But Mum's gone and Dad has too, even if his body is still hanging around.

I walk carefully past her hedge and toward her front door. I'll make sure it's locked and then I'll leave. Of course she's locked her front door. Everybody locks their front door. It's not like Cardiff is some small village.

I turn the handle. There's no resistance. I push the door. Still no resistance. It opens with a slight whine, showing me a hallway that ends in the kitchen. There's a living room to the left, and then a staircase off to the right.

It's time to walk away. I've come too far already.

Stepping into the house and slipping off my shoes feels so natural. I won't let my footsteps give me away.

My throat gets tight with anticipation as I walk to the base of the stairs. The house smells clean, hospital-clean, and it has an empty feeling. I wonder if she's recently moved in. There are no photos on the walls.

I stare up at the stairs, almost lost in the darkness. There's a window at the top letting in a little moonlight, but the curtains are closed. Normally, I'd know by now which steps creak and which are safe. I lift my foot and then withdraw it straight away, moving to the side and pressing myself against the wall.

She's still awake. She only just got in. I can't hear her, but that doesn't mean she's not up there. She's a freelance writer and she said she had work tonight. I don't hear any keys tapping, but some people type quieter than others.

For hours and hours, I wait. It's an annoying part of this process, but it's necessary. Impatience helps me in my day job, but in these excursions, patience is the name of the game. The world is quiet this far from the city centre.

Finally, I glance at my phone and see it's 3am. Surely she's asleep by now. Not that it matters.

I have her address. I should leave.

I imagine Mum screaming at me, telling me I'm disgusting, broken. But it doesn't work. I've spent too long waiting down here to abandon Millie now. And Mum has no right popping into my head like this. She lost it a long fucking time ago.

Luckily, the stairs don't squeak. I walk on my tiptoes, my arms at my sides for balance, breathing as quietly as I can.

There are three rooms up here. Two bedrooms and a bathroom. The door to the bathroom is open, showing a recently-cleaned toilet and a plastic cup without a single toothbrush inside. One of the bedroom doors is open too, showing a well-made single bed. Empty.

I move to the third door. My excitement waned as I waited, but it's stoked again. My mouth is somehow dry and filled with saliva at the same time. My balls feel heavy.

I put my ear against the door, expecting to hear breathing, or something, anything. But there's silence. I can *smell* something. Rotting food.

There's a light coming from underneath the door, a yellow glow.

I should turn back. This is my last chance.

I grab the door handle and twist it slowly, making the movement last half a minute, not making a single sound. I push the door open and step silently into the room.

The stink washes over me, and there's blood, and guts, and there are pictures pinned on the walls lit by heavy lamps. For a second, I'm sure I must've fallen asleep down there. This must be a nightmare.

I focus and bring it into some sort of order.

Millie isn't here. There's no en suite and the room is small. Millie hasn't been here all night. I have no idea where she is. She must've gone out the back door before I worked up the courage to come inside.

A bunch of gore is piled on the bed, long bloody entrails and guts and mulch and a bunch of other twisted stuff. I can't tell what animal it came from. Or if it came from a person. I can't see a body or anything that would identify the mess. It stinks, making me gag and cover my mouth.

Animal or human, it doesn't matter. I shouldn't be here.

The photos are of dead men, their heads smashed in, their faces eviscerated brutally. Every one of them has been slaughtered in the most animalistic way imaginable. Next to the photos she's pinned newspaper articles, with headlines like, *Police Still Looking for Park Murderer*. All of the headlines she's selected, whoever the fuck this woman is, are about how the killer hasn't been caught.

There are more photos. Of me.

I'm walking out of the office.

I'm sitting at a café window on my phone.

Jesus, I'm chatting up a woman at a bar. I'm walking out of Lacy's bungalow. There are photos of the woman before. We're sitting together in the cinema, but thankfully I had the presence of mind not to hold her hand or touch her when we were in public. Still, it doesn't look good. The photos go on.

She's been following me for at least six months.

I step forward, hand raised to tear them down. But why? She has copies. Of course she has copies.

None of this makes any sense.

Did she kill these men? Why is she following me? What does she want?

I run down the stairs, my breath loud in my ears. I never should've come here. There's something wrong with her. I've never taken photos. I've never arranged a sick murder scene, with the blood and the guts and everything. It's plain wrong.

I yank the door open and run down the street.

It's only when I round the corner I realise I've forgotten my shoes. But it's not like I can go back for them.

I keep running.

9

HAZEL

"Jamie? Are you even listening to me?"

He's been staring down the garden, across our small-but-lovely swimming pool, to the sauna he had built when we returned from our honeymoon. I've given the garden a bit of a spruce up these past couple of weeks, clearing out the winter clutter. The grass is freshly-mown and the potted plants are in order. It looks great, ready for some springtime snapshots.

He keeps staring, his eyes glassy and weird. It's like he's looking at something that isn't there. I normally like his dreamy expression. But only when it's aimed at me. It makes me wonder if he's thinking about the unspoken things between us, the ignored things, and that makes me want to scream. Our time together is *our* time.

How are we supposed to pretend we're normal if he doesn't make the effort?

"*Jamieeeeee.*"

"Sorry, what?" He smiles, but that doesn't hide how tired his eyes look. "Sorry, H. I was miles away."

I gesture to his breakfast, which I make him every Saturday and Sunday if I haven't got other plans. In the week, he's

43

normally gone before I wake up. "Are you going to eat something or shall I throw it out?"

He glances at his scrambled eggs and bacon, and then does that classic Jamie thing of running his hand through his messy hair. "Sorry. Yeah. Course. What were you saying?"

I take a sip of my cucumber juice and try to pretend it's not horrible. We've all got to make sacrifices. "I was thinking we could go and see your Dad today."

"What? Why?" He picks up a piece of bread and tears a chunk away with his teeth.

"Because he's your dad. And he has Alzheimer's. It's the right thing to do."

"He was demented long before he got ill. Let him rot."

"Jamie! That's a terrible thing to say."

He shrugs and tears off another piece, hardly seeming to chew before he swallows.

"You've been acting weird ever since you got back last night. Did something happen in Cardiff you need to tell me about?"

He shakes his head, aiming those butter-wouldn't-melt-eyes at me. "Just work."

I sigh. I can tell I'm not going to get anywhere this morning. "What do you think about going to see him then?"

He groans and rubs his jaw, like he's trying to scratch away his light beard. "I've told you what I think. Why're you so set on it?" He pauses, looks closer at me. "Oh, I get it."

"What? What do you get?"

"No, it's good. I thought my wife had been replaced by an alien for a second."

"If you have something to say, why don't you come out and say it?" I lift my cucumber juice for another sip. But I don't want another sip. It's revolting, like this insinuation is revolting. I slam it down on the table, making a loud glass-on-glass noise. "Fine. Then I'll say something. I think you're acting weird because you did something bad in Cardiff. I think it involved another woman."

"What? Where is this coming from?"

He knows full well where it's coming from, but sometimes it's like we can believe the surface of our marriage is the real thing, that there are no sleazy depths.

He reaches across the table and takes my hand, smoothing his thumb over my knuckles. Tingles dance up my arm. Even after two years of marriage, he still does that to me. I can't deny how much I love him. I can't even try.

"You know I'd never cheat on you," he says passionately. "It's me and you, remember. Hazel and Jamie against the world. I'd die before I cheated on you."

"Good." I'm unable to fight the smile that lifts my lips. "Because if you did, you wouldn't have much problem dying."

He nods. "Right."

"Because I'd kill you."

"Yeah, I got that."

He sits back and picks up a piece of bacon, shoving it into his mouth and grinning over at me. I laugh, shaking my head at how dorky he looks. I know this silly side of him is just for me. Maybe I was reading too much into him staring across the garden. I know his job can be very stressful.

"We'll go and see him," he says. "And you can take as many photos as you want. The old prick might as well come in useful for something. That's why you want to go, right?"

I fold my napkin and dab at the corner of my mouth. "It isn't about the photos. But thank you. I will. It's about raising awareness. Lots of my followers are in the same position as us, with a sick family member, but they aren't fortunate enough to have my platform. They want to know I understand where they're coming from. It's about making a connection."

"I know, I know." He holds his hands up. "You know me. I'm an old man when it comes to this stuff."

"Yes, but you're *my* old man. In fact, I think I see a few grey hairs."

"Ha-ha-ha. Imagine if I said that to you. I'd be face down in the pool."

"Yeah, and that's if you're lucky."

We laugh together and go on eating, and I think about ways to frame the visit to Frederick on my Instagram. One of the big influencers – a real pro who goes by the name Zany Zora – recently posted about her grandfather dying from, or with, Alzheimer's. In any case, the hashtags all somehow related to the disease. The photos were intimate and real. Brutal. Transformative.

She gained fifteen thousand followers in three days and the post became her third-most liked.

I don't want to visit Frederick for the sole purpose of taking photographs though. That would be tacky and mean. Jamie doesn't make enough of an effort with his father. If I can bring awareness to the issue in the meantime, I think that's a win-win.

I study my husband's face, the way he smiles at me, sort of wolfish. I study his gleaming eyes and I wonder if there's more going on. But Jamie and I don't lie to each other. We never have. Our bond is too deep. Even about the nasty stuff – the evil stuff – we tell the truth.

I meant what I said. If he ever cheated on me, I'd do something drastic. I've given myself to him when many of my friends are single, jet-setting, partying. But we found each other. We chose each other.

Nothing matters but him and me. In a marriage a wife has to demand respect.

10

JAMIE

I hate visiting my old man. I hated it before he got ill and I hate it even more now.

He's *old*. He had me when he was sixty and he was always too old for my mum. She was around twenty-five. I'm not one to judge a man for having a younger girlfriend, but there's something sick when it's my own mother. He reminds me of my childhood, which I don't like thinking about.

He sits in his armchair next to the window, looking out at the poxy communal garden. He's wearing a brown shirt that hangs off his skinny frame. He used to be a meaty son of a bitch, scary-looking, but now he looks like a beanpole. I used to think it would bring me some relief, seeing him broken like this. But it doesn't. I don't want to be here.

I still have no clue what happened in Cardiff with the photos and Millicent and that whole mess. During the two weeks I was there, I kept expecting her to pop back into my life. I wanted to come back to Bristol for the weekend, but Ray needed me to work, so I worked. Then I'd return to my room or hit the gym. I steered clear of the club.

I can still smell the guts and the rest of it, the reek of all that gore. I can still see those photos.

"Jamie," Hazel whispers from beside me. "Say hello. Don't be rude."

She's got her phone clutched in her hand. Her eyes have got a hungry, determined look. Nobody could call my wife unmotivated.

I walk over to him and he turns, but not enough to see me. His eyes settle on his old brown shoes tucked neatly beside his bed, the same way I arrange my shoes when I go exploring. That was a real pain in the arse, walking the streets of Cardiff in my socks.

"Dad?" I sound like a child. I hate this *shit*. "Dad, it's me. It's Jamie."

"Umberto? Bertie? Eh?"

"Who's Umberto?" Hazel whispers.

She has her phone on silent, but I can hear the *tap-tap-tap* of her thumb against the screen as she takes photographs. She'll have at least five hundred by the time we leave.

"I don't know," I tell her, keeping my gaze on Dad. "He's never mentioned him before. Maybe a character from a TV show or something?"

"Bertie." A watery smile spreads across his face. Part of me is certain this is an act. Any second now he'll leap from the chair and smack me across the back of the head. "I knew you'd come back. Come on. Sit down."

"Sit down, Jamie," Hazel urges, walking off to the side to get a better angle.

She's not going to quit, so I take the seat next to Dad. "It's a nice day, isn't it?"

"Oh, aye. Lovely day. Nice and sunny. Can't complain when the weather's like this, can we?"

This is the worst part. He's smiling. His voice is friendly. He sounds like he loves me. He never sounded like this before he got ill. Every time I come here, I'm somebody else, names I don't recognise.

"No," I say. "I guess we can't."

He smiles and lets his head fall back, gazing at the sunny garden. Then the smile becomes a leer and he gets a look I *do* recognise. It's almost comforting to see the real Frederick come out to play. "She knows what she's doing, don't she? Walking around like that. Strutting her stuff. Oh, aye, she knows what she's doing, the sweet little thing."

I want to grab the loose skin around his neck and tear it until it peels away.

The *sweet little thing* he's talking about must be Mum. He has no right to talk about her like this, to degrade her with his perverted look.

"Nice day," he says a moment later, settling down.

"Nice day," I echo.

"Can't complain, can we, Bertie?"

"No, sir."

Sir. I don't even call Ray *sir*.

"Such a polite lad. Such a good lad. You're going places. I'm telling you. You're the best of the bunch. You're a real good boy, you are. You're like me."

"Sure."

I'm nothing like you, you pathetic old fuck. You lived in a two-bedroom flat with damp creeping over the walls. You spent half your waking hours complaining your benefits weren't enough to buy you the cigarettes and booze you wanted. You wouldn't survive a goddamn second in my world, so keep your mouth shut.

"Can't complain," Dad says.

"No. We can't complain."

I raise an eyebrow at Hazel. She peers at me over the top of her phone. My wife is good at reading me, even if I don't share every single thing with her. But I can tell she knows how much this is bothering me. She nods toward the door.

"All right, Dad. I only popped in to say hello."

His eyes flicker closed. "We had some fun, didn't we, Eli, old boy? Yeah, we had some damn good times. You're a good man, Elijah."

I'm barely listening as I rush for the door. When we're in the hallway, I pace as quickly as I can without worrying the staff. I head for the reception and sign out, muttering something to the receptionist when she asks about the visit. I think I tell her it went well. Whatever I say, it's a lie.

I stride across the car park, past the cheap-looking cars to my glittering Range Rover. It looks like a tank. It promises safety.

"Jamie, slow down." Hazel walks up next to me.

This is my life. My wife in her pink yoga leggings and pink hoodie, in her expensive trainers. Her red hair is tied back and without any make-up on, she looks so beautiful, so naturally gorgeous. Her freckles show in the spring sunlight.

This is what I am. Not that. Not *him*.

"I just want to go, H."

"I'm sorry. I shouldn't have made you come."

I've recently had my tinted windows cleaned and they're shiny, reflective.

That's how I see Millicent, standing on the other side of the street. She's leaning against the bus stop, arms crossed over her middle, looking right at us.

It *is* her, isn't it? She has the same fringe. She's the same height, the same build, the same everything.

"It's fine." I pull Hazel into a hug and stare into the window, wondering if I'm going mad. I kiss my wife on the cheek, squeezing her close to me. "Let's get out of here."

"Okay, whatever you want. I love you."

"I love you too. Come on."

I walk around to the driver's side and open the door, and then I peer over the roof at the bus stop. There's nobody there except a mother with a pushchair, one hand rocking it back and forth and the other idly scrolling on her phone. I keep staring for a few moments. Maybe Millicent will pop back into existence if I look hard enough.

"Jamie," Hazel says. "Is something wrong?"

I'm not going crazy. I'm not seeing things. I'm not being hunted.

"No." I climb into the car. "Everything's fine."

11

HAZEL

I link my arm through Jamie's as we walk toward the glittering entrance to the hotel function room. Ray has pulled out all the stops for his birthday, even laying down a red carpet and putting up barriers like we're celebrities. The champagne we drunk before the limo arrived – the *limo* – makes my whole body hot and bubbly.

I try not to let my imagination go wild, but I can't help but think this is what it'll be like when I'm Insta-famous. The only thing we're missing is the paparazzi. I pause to take a quick selfie.

"Who knew fifty-seventh birthdays were so special, eh?" Jamie says, tickling me in the side, as we keep walking.

I slap his arm. "Don't be a grumpy-kins tonight, Jamie."

"Grumpy-kins, me?"

I lean up and whisper in his ear as we near the door, the doorman holding it open for us. "Jamie, I need to tell you something." I know my breath must shiver across his neck. I feel his body get stiff and tense. I know the power I have over my husband, and I love using it. "I'm not wearing any underwear."

Jamie glances at me, and then at the doorman. He tries to say *thank you* but it comes out as a jumbled mess of words. I laugh and he smiles.

These are the nights that make it worth it, that prove – to the world and ourselves – Jamie and Hazel Smithson are going to be okay in the end.

"You're never going to stop driving me wild, are you, H?" His hand presses against the small of my back, burning through my dress, as we walk across the marble floor to the sign-in desk. Champagne is laid out on a long table, twinkling in the lights, glasses and glasses of it. It's so elegant.

"Nope," I say. "Even when I'm one eighty and you can hardly stand to look at me."

"Never gonna happen." He leans down and lays a soft kiss on my forehead.

"Hey." I shoo him away. "Don't ruin my make-up."

"Forehead make-up's that important, is it?"

Jamie turns to the man at the desk. My husband looks tall and handsome and dashing in his tuxedo. His time in the gym has paid off, his shoulders broad, filling the suit jacket sexily. He's shaved and it makes his jaw look square and strong.

"*No, no*," somebody shouts from beyond the desk, causing the guests to turn their heads. Some of them scowl, but when they see it's the birthday boy pushing his way through the crowd, their scowls become indulgent smiles and eye-rolls. "I will *not* have my best worker standing out here like some commoner. Jamie, mate. Come here."

Ray swaggers around the desk, tottering. His hair is grey and patchy, combed-over in an effort to hide the bald spot. His sweaty grin is genuine when he faces Jamie. I can tell it means a lot to Jamie for an older man to show him this sort of affection, even if he'd never put it in those terms. It's not like he ever got any from his dad.

"All right, boss."

Ray throws his arms around Jamie, hugging him in drunken good humour. He steps back and bows clumsily. "Gorgeous as always, Mrs Smithson."

"Thank you, Ray. This is really wonderful. A red carpet. You've gone all out."

"Fifty-seven, it's an important milestone." He leads us deeper into the room. We each pick up a glass of champagne as we pass. "You know why? Ask me why."

He walks slightly ahead of us. He doesn't see Jamie cock his eyebrow at me. There's a question in his glinting greens. *Reckon he's pissed?* I mask a laugh with a mouthful of champagne. I can tell Jamie doesn't find it entirely funny though. Ray was sober when Jamie first started working for him, but he's relapsed several times since then.

"Why, boss?"

"Because it's been seven years since I divorced that backstabbing whore!" He knocks back the entire glassful of champagne and then stares down at the glass, as though expecting it to refill itself. "But you two, you've got something else. You're a rare breed, Mr and Mrs Smithson. A happily married couple."

Jamie loops his arm over my shoulder, squeezing me close, kissing the top of my head. "I'm a lucky man."

I lean into him, and then step away so he doesn't mess up my hair. I swear he's on some sort of mission. At least he isn't in a mood like he was after visiting his dad. All day, he's been mopey, sitting around the house watching TV and eating salted nuts. Maybe he just needed a drink.

Ray leads us to the other end of the room, to the toilets. Even the sign for the toilets is fancy, inlaid with golden lettering.

"Any reason we're standing outside the loo, boss?"

"She shouldn't be much longer."

"Who shouldn't?" I ask.

"My new *squeeze*." He chuckles. "She's the most amazing thing that's happened to me in a long time. She's—For fuck's sake. Does it ever stop?"

He pulls out his phone and glares at the screen.

"Work?" I ask.

"Always, right, kid?"

"No comment."

Ray laughs. "No comment. Yeah, I like that. I won't be long."

He wanders off to the corner, barking into his phone. I take in the full majesty of the room. The ceilings are high and the chandeliers are bright. There's a stage at the far end, but the curtains are drawn. "Is there going to be a band?"

"Yeah," Jamie says. "Jazz, I think."

He brushes a strand of hair behind my ear. I tilt my head toward the movement. I love that he knows how much I like this. I love that he makes the effort to do it.

"I see you, Hazel Smithson."

"Are you trying to make me cry?"

"I see *all* of you."

"You're an evil man."

"You're never invisible with me."

"I've got half a mind to throw this champagne in your face. First the smooching and hair touching, now *this*? You really are trying to ruin my make-up."

"Everything you do, everything you are..."

Goosepimples prick my skin as his voice gets husky.

I remember how he stared into me at the altar, truly seeing me in a way I'd never felt before. Even if we had over a hundred guests, it felt like we were alone, floating above the world. I wish we could get married again. Wives should get a wedding a year with the stuff we have to put up with.

"I'll always be watching," we whisper at the same time, leaning close, our lips magnetised.

"Sorry about that," Ray says, interrupting the moment. "Ah, here she is." He waves a hand at the toilet. "My angel."

Jamie drops his glass and it smashes loudly on the floor, champagne spreading across the hardwood, the shards sparkling.

"Shit, sorry. I…"

"Butter fingers," the woman says. Her stylish black hair is cut into a fringe and she's wearing a dress with gemstones inlaid into it. She's thin, like ultra-thin, all sharp edges. And she's at least twenty years younger than Ray, but that's nothing new for him. "This must be the famous Jamie, darling. You didn't tell me he was so clumsy."

12

BEFORE

Constance – the woman who had lived a miserable life and had become homeless and had been saved by Charles Maidstone – lay on a pile of blankets in the middle of the candlelit living room. The room was empty of furniture and decoration, and this made the light swell with even more fervour, the expansion of the light colliding with and joining with the Comrades' voices.

She cried out and sweat glistened on her forehead and she was naked, utterly naked on the blankets, her belly shifting as she tried to push her child into the world. The faces of the Comrades were shiny with tears of joy, for this was the first colony-born child, the first who would be raised entirely in this brave new world.

"Ahhhhhhh," Constance wailed.

"Ahhhhhhh," everybody echoed, except for Charles who sat in the corner and smoked a tobacco pipe and stroked his beard contemplatively.

A man sat on one side of Constance and a woman on the other, for Charles had insisted both sexes participate fully in the birth. But it was clear the woman was doing most of the work.

She had been a nurse in her previous life, before she went to work at the factory where most of the Comrades were employed. Factory work was humble work. Nursing was part of the societal lie people had been born into, presuming to nudge the scales of life and death. Still, it was useful here, for she knew the necessary procedures that came along with the bloody business of birthing a child.

What harm could one more hypocrisy cause?

Charles rose to his feet and immediately all noise ceased, even that of the woman in labour. He paced up and down the room in his bare feet and his raggedy brown corduroys and his ill-fitting sullied shirt. To wear clean presentable clothes implied a person thought appearances reflected spirit, and that was another lie.

Charles inhaled and blew smoke and the smoke rose and the smoke danced in the candlelight.

"Who will raise the child?" he said.

"Each of us shall raise the child," the Comrades chanted.

He stared at the woman who was giving birth to his daughter. "Who does the child belong to?"

He needed her to know this more than anybody, for she had become silly in her pregnancy. Not being able to indulge in her beloved mind-altering chemicals had done bizarre things to her metaphysical make-up.

"The child belongs to nobody," they yelled. "A child cannot belong, for people are not meant to be cattle. And yet the child belongs to everybody, for a child must be raised to know it is not a servant."

Charles puffed on his pipe as he slipped a thumb through his belt loop. "It is the collective duty of everybody to eradicate the collective."

He returned to his corner and sat there smoking and fiddling with his pipe as Constance brought the child into the world. The louder she wailed, the louder became the wailing of the Comrades. This was because they were all birthing the child, not Constance alone. It was a fallacy to believe that, because she happened to live within the body that was the vessel for the child, she was solely responsible for its birthing.

After much screaming and chanting, and agony on Constance's part – there were no pain-reducing drugs, for they were part of a metanarrative which fooled people into believing life was painless – a baby's cry filled the room.

Charles rose and all was silent but for the wailing of the child.

He walked across the room with his pipe clutched between his teeth and he accepted the baby from the arms of the nurse.

"Let me hold her," Constance said, quietly at first. Then her voice rose. She kicked, despite her exhaustion. "Let me hold my baby. Let me hold her! Let me hold my baby! *Let me hold my fucking baby!*"

"Comrades," Charles said, looking at his child's mother with a lip-curling of repulsion. She needed to get a hold of herself. She'd promised to remember her place during the naming ceremony.

"Let me hold my—"

Somebody placed a hand over her ranting mouth, quieting her words. Interrupting the man who'd brought them here, the man who'd let them see the light, was not the right thing to do.

"We shall name this child Millicent," he went on. "And like the great activist Millicent Fawcett, she will go into the world and challenge the societal constructs the sheep accept without question. She will be the first of the true changers. She will grow and thrive in an environment without imprinting."

The Comrade with their hand over Constance's mouth cursed as the raging mother bit down, desperate to be allowed to touch her daughter. From the way the child wailed, an impartial observer would be forgiven for believing little Millicent felt the same.

"She will be the best of us," Charles said, blowing a cloud of smoke into the baby's face.

Did Constance really cry out for her child, begging to fulfil the role she would spend the rest of her life neglecting?

It's impossible to know, and yet surely she must have felt something, some ember of maternal instinct in those moments after the birth, with her consciousness clean of the drugs Charles pumped endlessly into her.

Surely she cared, if only once.

Or perhaps she shit that little girl into the world without a second thought, shoving her into the arms of the nearest Comrade without even glancing at her.

13

MILLICENT

"I'm sorry," Jamie says to the waiter, proving that no matter how much wealth he accumulates, he'll always be an impoverished self-conscious nobody at heart. He likes to parade around like a big shot, but he's not fooling me. A truly wealthy man would never apologise to the help. He's a scared little boy, shivering in the dark, desperate for Mummy to make everything okay.

Ray ignores the hotel employee and directs his overlarge sweaty smile at our circle of fakers. "Stop saying sorry. You didn't do it on purpose."

"Yeah, I know."

What a sad lost lamb. He has no idea what to do. Here I am, dressed exactly the same as when we met last, with my hair and my make-up and my clothes purposefully identical, as though I've slipped from that night directly into this one.

He stands there, fish-mouthing, as his wife places her hand on his arm and gives him a private look. I've never been looked at like that, with attention and care, with so much knowledge of the inner performance of my soul.

Hazel is enthralling in the flesh, which bothers me. I don't feel the itch to cut her as achingly as I did when she gleamed on my laptop screen. Now I feel a different urge, confusing and unwanted. She's worked her hair into a puzzling weave, criss-crossing, and inlaid the pattern with fire-coloured gemstones to enhance her natural hair colour. Her dress is red. Her heels are red.

It's almost like she knows tonight is truly about blood.

"Relax." She giggles. I wonder if something lurks beneath the laugh or if she's truly as facile as she seems. "See?" She gestures at the waiter, retreating with his dustpan and his champagne-soaked rag. "No harm done. I'll get you another glass."

Ray's hands make a wet meaty sound when he claps them together. He's such a revolting pig. "Anyway, allow me to *finally* introduce my queen, my angel, my Millie."

When he places his hand on the small of my back, it takes every ounce of self-control I have not to rake my fingernails down his cheek. I can almost feel his flesh peeling off. I can see, smell, taste the blood. "It's nice to meet you," I say airily, fluttering my eyelashes.

"Yeah." Jamie rallies and offers me his hand. "It's a pleasure."

I take his hand and feel the strength of him, and, perversely, I am relieved he's strong. I stamp down on the feeling. I shan't allow myself to think such thoughts again. I have to stay true to my course.

"The pleasure's mine." I hold on for a little longer than is necessary.

He pulls away as though I've caused him pain. Perhaps I have. I was squeezing quite hard.

"Tell him how we met." Ray nudges my shoulder in that annoying manner of his. Everything about him is simply too much. He reminds me of a man I slaughtered once, three or four kills back, a hobo pervert singing and swaggering along the waterside. He was begging to be pushed in. "You won't believe this, Jamie."

"You tell it, dear. You make it much more interesting than I ever could."

Ray grins, hearing precisely what he wanted. It's stunning how quickly men like Ray will accept what they see and hear. They never stop to dream that the army of kneelers circling them have agendas of their own. They live in a world where everybody wears a mask except them, and, because they are maskless, they assume we must be the same.

I am not the same as you, Raymond Evans-Leigh.

"Ah, here she comes," Ray says loudly when Hazel returns to our circle. The four of us move away from the toilets, toward the centre of the function hall. The band is assembling on the stage. The so-called fun will begin soon. "I was telling Jamie how Millie and me met. You'll wanna hear this, dear."

Not *dear*, you idiot. *Deer.*

"I was at a café, right. You know the trendy one on blah-blah-blah, and the blah-blah, and then she blah-blah and I said blah."

I can't stand listening to him prattle on. He laughs and smiles and I do the same, in all the right places, but mostly I watch Jamie.

It's like there are two realities. One is the surface of the water, where Ray and Hazel float, and the other is the deep dark underside. That's where Jamie and I dwell, stealing glances at each other as we say and do the conventional things.

Ray makes it sound wonderful and romantic.

All I did was order a coffee and purposefully spill it on him as I walked by, and then I glittered and fluttered and said I was oh-so-sorry, and before I could even get the apology out of my painted lips, he was calling me *sweetheart* and ogling my breasts.

"And we've been inseparable ever since!" Ray guffaws. "How's that for love at first sight?"

"Love, my Hercules?" I look at him with a devotee's smile. Father would be proud. Maybe he is proud, looking down... no, up, he'd be looking *up* at me. "Isn't it a little soon for that?"

"Hercules?" Hazel says, and then takes another sip of champagne. That's the fifth sip since we met. Her glass is almost empty.

I despise intemperance. When people drink and smoke and inject, they get the confidence to do things they'd never dream of sober. They can detach from themselves and perform all manner of cruelties, no matter how innocent the child is, no matter how desperate for love, for attention, for something real. Get anybody drunk enough and they'll paint depraved images on a little girl's naked body.

I haven't touched a single drop. I simply change glasses when Ray isn't looking.

"It's what I call him," I gush, placing my hand on his arm. "Because he's *so* strong. He's like Hercules. Except I think Ray might be a little stronger."

Ray cackles and Jamie forces laughter through clenched teeth, but Hazel only takes yet another sip. Her eyes remain on me the whole while.

She thinks she knows what's going on here. She sees me as yet another gold digger. I'm sure Ray has had his helping of those over the years, and it's only natural Hazel would brand me the same. It makes no difference to me. She doesn't know who, or what, I really am. And Ray is far too intoxicated, both on my words and his indulgences, to care about the opinion of his employee's wife.

"Jamie," I say. "I hear you're a real up-and-comer in the company. I think Ray even said you were his *heir*."

"I do my best." He stares at me with rage shimmering across

his clean-shaven jaws. The little lad really has made quite the effort this evening.

"You're being modest. Ray absolutely sings your praises."

You-bitch you-bitch you-bitch, his eyes roar, and inside I prance like a naïve child. This is the most fun I've had in years. I can't remember the last time I felt like this. I could kill every man in this room and walk out an innocent woman if I wanted to.

"I work hard." He grinds his teeth. I don't think he knows he's doing it.

"Don't be a dickhead." Ray chuckles. "You're much more than a hard worker. You're my right-hand man. You're my executioner. You're the only person at the company who doesn't skive off every chance they get."

Hazel gleams at this praise, as though it was directed at her and not her husband. I refuse to believe she's as happy as she seems. Doesn't she know what her husband truly is? What would she do if I showed her?

They exchange another look. They keep doing that, side-eyeing each other. If I didn't know better, I'd say they were in love.

"Darling," I say. "Do you think it'd be rude if I gave them a business card?"

Ray's eyes become vacant. He doesn't care about my freelance writing career. He doesn't care about anything I say or do if it doesn't involve flagellating myself at the altar of his ego. "Course not." He scans the hall for another glass of champagne. The sot.

I reach into my small clutch handbag and take out two cards. I look down to make sure I give the correct card to the correct person.

One reads: *Millicent Maidstone, Freelancer Writer: Quality Prose Every Time.* There's a phone number and an email.

The other bears my address – the address of my rented Bristol accommodation – with a couple of sentences written in neat calligraphy beneath: *Meet me here on Monday at 1PM. If you're late, I'll tell your wife how you like to rape women and sniff their hair.*

I hand Hazel's over first and, as she's busy reading it, I quickly give Jamie his.

His cheeks turn the colour of bone as he looks down. He glances up, his jaws pulsing, his temples pulsing. I know his insides are doing the same, throbbing and twisting and torturing. I know he's thinking about the violent things he'd like to do to me. But he can't, and that's what makes it so energising. The poor lost boy is forced to slip it into his inside pocket and plaster a pretender's smile to his face.

"I love your name," Hazel says. "Millicent Maidstone. Very Victorian."

"See, I thought Marvel." Ray snatches a glass of champagne from a passing server. "You know, how the names always start with the same letters. Like Peter Parker. Um, Bruce Banner? There's more, but you get the point."

Of course the drunkard can't remember. I don't care about him though. I care about Jamie. He can't stop looking at me. This is much, much better than I dreamed it.

14

JAMIE

I walk toward the electronics shop with Millicent's business card in my hand. I've never hit a woman, but this bitch is making it pretty damn tempting. *Rape women and sniff their hair.*

What a ridiculous thing to say. I've never hurt a woman in my life.

She completely ruined my weekend. After her little show at Ray's party, I was forced to smile and banter with her the whole night. I wanted to neck as much champagne as I could get down me, but then I might let my true feelings out.

She was kissy-kissy with Hazel as the jazz band played, the two of them dancing and laughing together. "I know she's with him for his money," Hazel said on the journey home, her head falling onto my shoulder. "But I like her. Gold diggers can be good people too, right?"

Maybe gold diggers can, but I'm not sure about lunatics with a fetish for blood.

I pause outside the shop. It sells DVD players, which is insane. I wonder if they sell steam engines too. I can't see an entrance to a flat. I wonder if this is another one of her tricks.

I'm wasting my lunch break in this grimy part of town. A

light rain falls and I can feel a bunch of kids across the street eyeing me up. One of them is pulling wheelies as another takes a massive drag on a joint.

A man pokes his head out the door. "You all right?"

"Looking for a flat, mate." Hazel tells me I sound more working class when I talk to people like this – beer belly, sleeve tattoo, cigarette tucked behind his ear. "I was given this address."

"Ah, yeah. I thought you meant *flatmate* for a second. It's round the side. Look."

He points to an alleyway. It reeks of piss.

"Millicent lives up there?"

"Yeah, moved in a couple of weeks ago. I don't use the flat anymore. Moved in with my missus. Nice little earner, actually."

"All right, cheers."

I walk past an overflowing bin and find a metal staircase. The door's paint is cracking. I knock and immediately she calls out to me.

"Come in, Jamie," she sings, as though we're best pals.

I walk through the small bare flat. It's clean but there are no personal touches. It reminds me of my first year uni accommodation.

I find her in the living room, sat on a tatty armchair in a black suit, looking weirdly sleek and stylish contrasted with the cheap surroundings. She crosses her legs and smiles at me. "It was so nice of you to come."

"What do you want?" I bark. "Who are you? Why are you doing this to me? You were at my dad's care home, weren't you? I saw you."

She tilts her head, looking at me like I'm mental. I throw her crumpled-up business card at her. It lands in her lap, but she stays completely still, staring.

"*Talk*, for fuck's sake."

"I know what you like to do, Jamie Smithson. I know you like to sneak into women's houses at night. I know you've done it at least twice, and I know deviant behaviour of that sort is addictive, and a man like you, a poor lost little lamb like you, you wouldn't be able to resist doing it again and again. So, in summation, I know you've done it far more than twice."

"I don't know what you're talking about."

She giggles. It's eerie, such a girlish sound coming from her sharp face. "How many of them have you raped? How many of them have you hurt? How many have you tied to the bed and forced to call you *Daddy*?"

"None," I snap.

"Oh, that's right, you'd prefer for them to call you *son*, right?"

Pacing over to her, I clench my fists and glare, but she doesn't move. If I wanted to, I could dismantle her in two seconds flat. Doesn't she know that? "People have hobbies. I like to ski. This isn't any different. I don't hurt women. I..." I trail off, shaking my head. "I don't have to explain myself to you."

"Oh, but you do. I've got photos of you meeting with women who don't look very much like your wife. I've got videos of you sneaking into Lacy Emberson's bungalow, and out. I've got you, Jamie Smithson, by the short and curlies, as the saying goes."

"Listen, you psycho. If you even think about showing those photos to anybody, I'll kill you. Do you understand? I will *execute* you. I've got stuff to lose right now, but if you took my wife, my job, my house away from me... just know that, all right? Know who you're messing with."

She stares as though I haven't spoken. There's nothing behind her eyes. She's like a shark or a lizard. She doesn't look human. "Do you think your fascination with home invasion has something to do with your mother abandoning you when you were ten?"

I take a step back. There's something uncomfortable about being so close to her. "How do you know about that?"

"That sounds like a question. I'd prefer an answer."

"What do you want? Money? Do you want money?"

"It would make sense." She drums her fingernails against the arm of the chair. They're painted the same black as her hair, and her eyes are framed in dark make-up. It annoys me how attractive I find her. "Mummy walks out, and poor ickle Jamie is oh-so-upset he doesn't get to suckle on her ripe tits anymore—"

"I'm warning you—"

"So he sneaks into women's houses and he looks down and he imagines Mummy didn't run away after all—"

"You have no right to talk about my mother—"

"And if it makes him excited, if he touches himself, he's not *really* thinking about his sweet mummy, is he? No, because that would be *disgusting*."

I roar and kick blindly, not even sure what I'm doing. My foot smashes into the TV stand and the cheap material caves inward. I turn back to her, panting, everything in me aching with the need to make her hurt for these lies. What a twisted way to frame things.

She hasn't moved an inch. "Feel better?"

"You're a killer. Do you think I'm stupid? All those photos, all those dead men. Those weren't the sort of photos the police release to the public."

"I'm a *serial* killer, thank you very much. I have killed ten men. You will be my eleventh. But you'll never get me to say that again. I'd be foolish to risk it."

The corner of her lip twitches.

Fuck. "You're recording this conversation."

She shrugs. "Oh, I don't know. Perhaps I have a recording of you talking about how sneaking into women's houses and watching them sleep is the same as skiing. Or perhaps I don't. You'll have to live with the possibility. But don't stress, my little lamb. If something is possible, it is also impossible. Reality is a mere collection of words."

"What the fuck are you talking about?"

She flashes her teeth. "I would explain it to you, but I fear you'll be dead long before you get the point."

"You admitted you're a serial killer. Your recording doesn't mean shit."

"Silly me. If only there was a way to selectively cherry-pick quotes from a recording. Perhaps some enterprising inventor will develop such an esoteric form of audio manipulation one day in the future."

"An edited clip? It'll come across as fake. It'll be choppy. Nobody will believe it. You heard of deep fakes? You can make people say anything these days."

She shrugs with an airy sigh. "I suppose you'll have to take the chance."

I groan and pace up and down in front of her armchair, opening and closing my hands.

What am I supposed to do here?

If I hurt her like I want to, I'll go to prison. The shop owner saw me come up here. Those kids saw me come up here. It's not like I've dressed down for the occasion. I'm wearing a suit and a Rolex and cufflinks. They'll remember me.

"Getting a little light exercise?" She tracks my movements the same way an animal would. Even smiling, her eyes are alert and ready. She must have a weapon on her. It's the only way this confidence makes sense when I'm so much stronger than she is.

I stop in front of her. "Who are you? Have I done something to you in the past?"

"Hiding a lot of skeletons in your closet, are you?"

"No. It's just... what do you *want*?"

She tosses her head, sitting up straighter. "I want the light. I want to feel the sunlit rays and I want people to know I'm not like them. I am not a person, because people are weak. *Men* are weak. Women are the same. Women can be worse, but there is a specific kind of weakness in your breed that truly repulses me. I seek it out and I destroy it. I am an avenging angel."

I throw my head back and laugh, howling, gripping my sides. It's not as funny as I'm making it seem, but I know this'll piss her off. She's full of herself, talking like she's on a stage.

"Stop laughing. Stop *laughing at me*."

She jumps to her feet. She's wearing block heels and she's tall for a woman. We stare at each other eye to eye. A siren blares by outside.

"Why?" I chuckle right into her arrogant face. "It's funny. The light? An avenging angel? Sorry to break it to you, sweetheart. But you're just a sad little bitch living above an electronics shop."

She steps away from me, smoothing her hands down her suit jacket. "Congratulations, Jamie. Few people can make me snap. You might want to be more careful in the future, however. I may not be so forgiving next time." She drops into the chair with a yawn. "You can leave now."

I feel lost. Surely this can't be it. "But you haven't told me what you want."

"Yes, I have."

"From me. What do you want from *me*?"

"Weren't you listening? I want the light, and you're going to give it to me. Please collect your shoes on the way out. I've left them next to the door. That's normally where you keep them, isn't it?"

"But—"

"Leave now," she says with an edge to her voice, "or I scream *rape*."

I clench my hand into a fist. I lift it. I glare at her.

But there's nothing I can do, not now at least.

I stride down the hallway. My shoes sit beside the welcome mat. I think about picking one of them up, charging back in there, beating her to death with it. But I've never killed anyone. I'm not a violent person.

Even if I want to hurt her – and I do – there's no way I'd get away with it.

I pick up my shoes and carry them down the stairs.

15

HAZEL

I stand in front of the mirror at the gym, turning to the side so the shape of my leg catches the light. I make my smile airy and carefree, even if that's not how I feel. It's Jamie. He's been acting weird since the party on Saturday. I thought a new week might be a new start. But it's Tuesday and he's still mopey. I don't like it.

I didn't marry a sulky little kid. I feel like he's not holding up his end of our relationship.

The gym is quiet, the yoga-mat section empty apart from a woman I vaguely recognise from my other visits. She sees me taking a photo and grins. I smile and roll my eyes, as if to say, *I know, but I can't help it*. And I can't. I'm not ashamed. I look really, really hot.

I want to take a photo. Sue me.

I take a few more and then wander over to the inner-thigh cruncher. I don't know the official name. Jamie and I come to the gym together sometimes, and he calls it the *pussy pounder*. That always makes me laugh, but I'd never dream of using it on my Insta. Some of my followers are like twelve.

Exercise is so good for the soul. Now it's time to bake in the sauna. #blessed #livingmybestlife

I add some more hashtags with my app, post it, and then finish up my last few sets.

My legs burn, but I don't feel as floaty and happy as I usually do after a workout. Maybe it's because I know what I've got to sit through later, with Mum and Dad.

Or maybe it's because, this morning when I told Jamie I loved him, he didn't hear me. *Eh?* he grumbled, walking out of the en suite. I told him again. He said it back, but not with the same passion he usually does. It bothered me.

I want our marriage to stay perfect for the rest of our lives. Or, if it can't *actually* be perfect, I at least want him to *act* like it is. That's the agreement we made when we said our vows.

"Ooph, you're really working it, aren't you?"

I look up to find a man standing near my machine. His brown hair is in a bun and he's wearing a tank top to show off his sleeved tattoos.

"I'm just finishing up, if you want to use it," I tell him.

He smirks like a weirdo. "There are a few things I'd like to use."

"What? I'm confused."

"I'm talking about you, hot stuff. I'd like to use that tight body of yours."

I stare and stare, waiting for him to disappear. I've heard about douche-lords like this on social media, but I've never actually met one. "Are you joking?"

"Ah, come on. You're attractive. I'm attractive. Let's smash our bodies together."

He can't be serious. There's no way he just said, *Let's smash our bodies together.* It's too ridiculous.

He moves forward. "You like it rough, don't you? I can tell—"

"What is it with men like you?" a woman says, standing up from the machine next to me. I didn't even see she was there. I was focused on my phone. "You can clearly tell she's not interested. She's tried to be polite, and you still feel the need to act like a pig."

I feel like I'm the sole audience member in a flash mob. I'm frozen.

And is... yes, it is. It's the woman with the Victorian-sounding name, from the party. Millicent Maidstone. Millie. She walks over to us and stares at the man. "Well?"

"I was trying to—"

"You were trying to find a woman who'd want to fuck you after you accosted her in a gym. Let me break it to you, dickhead. *They don't exist.* And if they did, they certainly wouldn't be interested in a loser like you. Why don't you do us a favour and fuck off?"

The man bows his head and skulks away.

"Sorry," Millie says. She's wearing black yoga leggings and a black tank top, with a black sports bra beneath. It seems to be her colour. "I felt like I had to... Wait a second. Do I know you?"

"Um," I murmur, still trying to wrap my head around what just happened. Maybe in a club guys speak like that, but not stone-cold sober in a gym. Maybe he was drunk or high or something. "From the party on Saturday? I'm Jamie's wife."

"Oh, that's right. Jeez, what are the chances, huh? It's nice to see you again."

"I can't believe you did that." I laugh. "I was completely frozen. I didn't know what to do!"

"Putting arseholes in their place is my specialty. What are the chances I'd be here to save you?"

"Oh, you *saved* me? That might be pushing it a bit. No, but seriously, thank you. I don't know why people think they can be so rude."

She waves a hand. "It's nothing. You're hitting the sauna now, right? Mind if I join you?"

I stand up. "Yeah, I am. How did you know?"

She pats her chest, smiling. "Because I'm watching you, Hazel Smithson."

Everything you do, everything you are... I'll always be watching. The words come to me as they so often do, with the tiniest of nudges.

I laugh a little uncomfortably. "Um, okay?"

"Sorry." She reaches into her bra and pulls out her phone. "I meant I follow you on Instagram. I saw your post. I was literally scrolling through your feed just now. And then I see you sitting there, and I'm like: no way, it's her. Seriously, one in a million chance. I have to say, I absolutely *love* your content. It's what inspired me to start coming to the gym."

"That's lovely. In that case, I *insist* you join me in the sauna."

"Wonderful!" She dances over and loops her arm through mine. "Come on, before more vultures start circling."

We leave the gym and walk into the changing rooms together. There's something about Millie I really like, and it's not just how she swooped to my defence. It's the way she feels comfortable linking arms with me when we hardly know each other.

I think we could become friends very quickly.

Millie laughs as we walk over to our lockers, which happen to be in the same corner of the room. "I forgot my champagne heels today."

"Champagne heels?" I take out my swimsuit and place it on the hook.

"Remember?" She pulls her tank top over her head. "From the party? We said champagne is so good they should make clothes out of it. And then we said we'd want champagne heels, and... It doesn't matter."

"I'm sorry. That night's a little hazy for me."

"You said it was the funniest thing you'd ever heard. But I understand how alcohol can make people forgetful. *Hazy Hazel*, huh?"

Do I sense some judgment there? If so, it's not fair. She was as drunk as me.

I change into my one-piece and Millie changes into a black bikini. I notice she has a tattoo on her hip bone, a date: *13/03/95*. She's also wearing a simple rope necklace with a plain rectangular pendant attached.

She sees me looking and smiles.

Moving with a dramatic flair that makes me laugh, she points at the tattoo. "This, my inquisitive new bestie, is the date my life changed forever. And this—" She points to the pendant. "Is a custom waterproof USB memory stick I had made when I started my novel. You see, I'm a teensy bit paranoid. I don't want anybody stealing my ideas, so I take it everywhere."

I want to ask what she means. *My life changed forever*. How? What happened? But I can leave it for another day. I don't want to pry.

"I can honestly say I've never heard of anybody doing that before. You're an enigma, Millicent Maidstone."

"Is that a bad thing?" she asks, as we carry our towels and water bottles to the sauna's entrance.

"No. All my favourite people are a little strange."

We reserve two recliner chairs with our towels and then take our water bottles into the sauna. There are a few people in the Jacuzzi at the far end, but we've got the sauna to ourselves. Millie climbs to the top and sprawls out, letting her head fall back. I sit on the lower shelf and rest my head against the opposite wall, so we're looking at each other. It's a decent warm temperature, not boiling like it gets when people pour too much water on the stones.

I want to say something to her, but I don't want to come across as rude.

"What?" she says.

"What?" I echo, and we both smile.

"You're looking at me funny."

"Okay, fine. But promise you won't take it the wrong way?"

She makes an *X* over her chest with her forefinger.

"I can't imagine you and Ray together."

"Why not?"

"I don't know. You seem so... Hmm, I don't know. Forget it."

"Come on, H."

Only Jamie calls me *H*. Strangely, I don't feel the need to correct her.

"I don't seem like his other girlfriends, right?" Millie says. I nod. "I know how it looks. But the truth is, I like Ray. I think there's more to him than meets the eye. Men like Ray think they want a piece of arm candy, subservient and silent. But they're wrong. He needs a woman who knows how to put him in his place."

I nod again, but I'm not sure she's right. I think Ray really does want an airhead. Or a new model every few months. I hope he doesn't break Millie's heart.

"You and Jamie seem like a fantastic couple," she says a few moments later. Both of us are coated in a fine layer of sweat. My mouth is getting dry. "You really seem to gel."

"That's nice of you to say. Yeah, we work great together. We make a good team."

And like a good team we cover up for each other's mistakes and imperfections. But I can't tell Millie that part.

"How did you meet?"

"University." I won't give her the full version. That belongs to me and Jamie, nobody else. "I was doing media studies and he was doing business. I was a fresher and he was in his last year. I knew from the start he was different. He really seemed to *see* me, you know?"

"I think so." She's looking at me closely, really listening. I love being looked at like that.

"I never had that growing up," I go on. "I never felt like I was seen. My dad was away a lot for work. He was a captain on a cruise ship. And Mum was... I don't know. Maybe she never wanted to be a mother." I shake my head. My cheeks are burning, and not from the heat. "I'm sorry. I don't usually overshare."

"I don't mind. I know exactly what you mean. Nobody has ever seen me – the real me – either."

"How so?"

She taps her pendant. "A writer is only as real as their work, and I'm too scared to show mine to anybody."

"Maybe I can take a look one day?"

She smiles. There's something vulnerable about it, the same way girls used to smile at school when they thought a cruel joke was coming. "Yeah, maybe. Do you see your parents much?"

I groan. "Funny you should mention that. I'm having dinner with them tonight."

"I take it you're not excited?"

"*So* not excited. But Mummy needs to be able to tell herself she's made an effort."

Millie puffs her chest up, grimacing in the most hilariously OTT way. "It sounds like you need your knightess in shining armour there to protect you."

"I'd love that. But it's such late notice."

"I'm not doing anything tonight."

"Wait. Are you serious?"

"I wasn't serious. But I am now. I'd love to have dinner with you and your parents."

I know this should feel weird. I've only met this woman twice. But there's no harm in getting to know Ray's girlfriend. And there's something refreshing about Millie. She doesn't seem fake and self-obsessed like so many people I know.

"Last chance to tell me you're joking. Or I'm one hundred per cent forcing you to eat my lasagne tonight."

"That bad, is it?"

"The worst."

"Now I *have* to try it," she says. "As long as you don't mind?"

"Not at all."

We meet eyes and she smiles. It's been so long since I made a new friend, a *real* friend, who sees me for who I really am.

16

MILLICENT

My mobile phone refuses to stop vibrating against the desk. It's the most annoying sound I've been subjected to in a long time, and that includes Ray's wheezing after we kiss.

I glance at it. I know who it is. I know what he wants.

He can wait. I'm busy.

I turn back to the laptop screen, scrolling, endlessly scrolling through Hazel's feed. Meeting her today wasn't chance, of course. I didn't expect to get an invite to the family dinner so easily. But that's the way with plans sometimes. When they go awry, it isn't always in a bad way.

A good predator knows how to use the terrain to her advantage.

I knew she was having dinner with her parents this evening because Hazel is a creature of the internet. Her personal Facebook is set to public. I cannot fathom the insanity of such a decision, but she isn't anomalous in that regard.

The phone ceases buzzing, there's a pause, and then it buzzes twice, telling me he's left another voicemail.

I pause on the photo Hazel took today, studying the shape of her mouth, the glint in her eyes. She smiled at me earlier, and when I smiled in return, it didn't feel as feigned as it ordinarily does. There was something there, a breed of humanity.

This is an unforeseen development. The woman on the screen is silly-looking: futile, facile, redundant. I hate to say it, but in the flesh, she is different. Twice now I have felt this conviction: at the party and the gym. She reminds me of myself. I can see how insecure she is beneath the glamour, the same way I was as a younger woman.

I have to remind myself why I'm here. It has nothing to do with Hazel Smithson or her sparkling unreality. Hers is a life filled with friends and holidays and laughter and art and feelings. It's the sort of life I was denied, and which I accepted long ago would never be mine.

I don't *want* that sort of life, do I?

Opening the desk drawer, I take out the lockbox and remove the key from the slot I keep in my memory-stick pendant.

I open it and retrieve the engagement ring, placing it on the desk and letting it sparkle in the late-day light. It looks no less cheap than it did when the corpse gifted it to me, but somehow my perception of it has changed. It's a curious metamorphosis. I can more easily imagine bearing such an item now. I don't quite know what to make of it.

I take out my dolls. There are two women and a man, and each of them is burned and broken and half-ruined. I place them in a circle and move Millicent over to Jamie, and raise her hand and bring the hand down on his chest. He groans and falls, and then Millicent and Hazel hold hands and skip off together.

Tears rise unexpectedly into my eyes. This happens sometimes: this capricious appearance of emotion.

There is a problem with this pantomime, however. I have learned enough about people to know Hazel won't be my friend if I kill her husband. Or perhaps I'm allowing myself to be too easily defeated. Perhaps I simply have to think harder. The right words – the right construct – and the greatest of edifices implode, and marriage is not an especially sturdy structure.

My phone vibrates again, the bothersome thing. Hazel was right when she called me Victorian. I wish I'd been born into a letter-writing culture.

"What?" I hiss, putting it on loudspeaker.

"Finally," the man says. "I've been trying to call you all afternoon."

The impertinence in his tone rankles. I think about feeding him strips of his own skin, piece by piece. I've never toyed with my victims like that before, but it might make a nice change. And if I'm going to end this with my death, why not cause a little mayhem beforehand? Maybe I should hunt this failed abortion down and teach him some fucking manners.

I pick up Jamie and move him over to Hazel. She collapses backward and he collapses atop her. He slaps her and spits on her and hates her. Is that the way of their marriage? Does he beat her? Or does he abuse her in more creative ways?

"Hello?" the man says.

"Yes, hello. What do you want?"

"My money. We agreed half before and half after."

"We agreed you'd make your performance believable. *Let's smash our bodies together.* You sounded like an idiot."

"You said I should come across like a sexist asshole. Isn't that something a sexist asshole would say?"

It amuses me that he cares enough to defend his acting. I found him on an online message board, yet another theatre student with too many bills and too few opportunities. He would've crawled around on the floor and snorted like a pig if I'd told him to. He has no self-respect. He's pathetic.

"You didn't come across as human in the least." I should know. I've spent my life imitating them. "You were—"

"I was trying—"

"Quiet," I snap, letting Jamie and Hazel drop. "I wasn't done talking, you fucking rapist *cunt*."

"Woah. Jesus, all right. Christ."

"You were a caricature," I tell him flatly. "If you want to make it as an actor, you can't despise the person you're portraying. To become somebody, you have to *be* them, both inside and out. People don't hate themselves, not deep down where it matters."

I wonder if any of those Comrades hated themselves after what they did to me, marking my flesh dozens of times in dozens of different ways, with more tools than I can remember. I wonder if any of the men ever stared at themselves in the mirror, begging their reflections for some explanation...

How could they do this to a child? How could they find pleasure in a little girl's inferno?

"You failed," I snap, pushing away the past. "You don't deserve the second half of your payment. I should ask for a refund, truthfully."

"That's hardly fair," he whines. "I did everything you asked. Your friend was impressed, wasn't she?"

"You were amateurish. But, because I've decided to take pity on you, I'll pay you what you mistakenly believe you're owed. But first you have to do something for me."

"What?"

I sit up straighter and brush down my hair. I shouldn't have to stoop to this, but it's what I need. At the very least, I have to make the effort.

"I'm going to send you a text. You will recite the words to me, passionately, with heart. Make it *humane*. Make it *real*."

The man sighs. "Then you'll transfer the money?"

I followed this man home after we met, just in case I needed to put a fright into him. He has no idea how close he is to waking up with me standing over his bed, a rag of chloroform in one hand and a blade in the other.

"Yes. But fix your tone, or we're going to have a problem."

He swallows audibly, unsure of how to reply, the same way most people are when I show them my true self. "Okay, sure. I'm sorry. Send the text. I'll do whatever you need me to."

"Good boy."

I copy and paste the text from the note where I saved it – transcribed from an Instagram video – and send it to him. A few moments later, he says, "Right, I've got it. Let me put you on speakerphone."

He clears his throat and I take the engagement ring and hold it against the tip of my finger. I close my eyes and try to imagine the face of a man I could love. He has kind eyes and a clever smile and he would never deride me. He would never hurt me. He loves me and he is not rainbow-coloured.

He is an impossible man, but that doesn't matter.

"I see you, Millicent Maidstone. I see all of you. You're never invisible with me." With each word, I slip the ring further and further up my finger, the cold metal kissing my skin. "Everything you do, everything you are, I'll always be watching."

A pause, a breath – and nothing. I feel nothing.

I open my eyes and aim my finger downward. I'm too skinny for the ring anyway. It slides and clatters against the desk. "Very well. I'll send the money."

I'd rather send him an envelope of anthrax, but I have to keep him docile. Otherwise, he may inform Hazel she was an actor in a play without ever suspecting it.

17

BEFORE

"You must understand what we're trying to achieve here, little lamb." Comrade Charles paced up and down the Rainbow Room and waved his pipe, and his pipe smoke danced and his daughter watched with eyes that never stopped tracking his movements. "Have you noticed how the men and women share the labour in all things? Cooking and cleaning is not solely a feminine pursuit, as has been mistakenly promulgated in this patriarchal society."

Millicent could have said the labour was not shared equally, because her father didn't contribute. He spent most of his time in his office, bashing at a typewriter. He never finished a single piece of work. He'd tear the paper to pieces, roaring that language was insufficient to capture what he was trying to say. In the evenings, he'd sit in one of the Comrades' living rooms as they detailed the innumerable ways they'd failed the cause that day. She'd never seen him scrubbing a floor or dusting a curtain rail.

"Yes, Father—"

"Charles," he snapped. "My name is Charles, and even that is a mere representation. My real name would be a list of all the things I have ever done. But you see how that might become cumbersome, don't you?"

What a load of incomprehensible shit this man spewed. He deserved what happened to him in the end.

"Yes, Charles."

"So you understand."

Millicent nodded. "Yes, I understand."

"What do you understand?"

"Everything in society is a construct. All the things people do, they only do because it's learned behaviour."

"And you accept that?"

"Yes, Charles."

"Hmm." He tapped his pipe against his teeth, *click-click-click*. "Are you telling me the truth?"

The thought passed through her precocious mind: *What truth, Father? There are only words.* She was very clever for her age, already far smarter than most of the grown-ups in her life, even if she was still too confused and naïve to act upon her genius. "Yes."

He reached into the back pocket of his tatty mud-brown corduroys. The girl knew better than to react when she saw what he'd done to her precious dolls. There were three of them, two women and one man. She'd stolen them from a supermarket, one at a time, over the course of a month. She was clever at stealing things and, even when some nosy Nelly tried to stop her, she knew she could make them go away by saying she'd tell the police they tried to touch her. She was constantly fascinated by how people let her get away with things.

But not Comrade Charles.

He'd burnt off most of the women's hair, and their skin was charred and crumpled in places now. The man's face was hardly a face. He'd ruined them and it wasn't fair.

"What are these?" She stared defiantly. "Hello? Am I audible? Little lamb, you better start explaining yourself."

She knew better than to let any emotion into her voice. "They are my dolls."

"Your dolls." He shook his head. "Surely you can see how this is a problem. With this one act, you have undone much of what we're trying to accomplish here. Who taught you to want to play with these?"

The question confused her. She'd taken to sneaking away from their cul-de-sac and exploring the wider world, and sometimes these wanderings took her to the supermarket. She'd pick up packets of crisps and eat a few and then put them back. She'd move things from people's baskets and trolleys without them looking, and then follow them and giggle to herself when they doubted their sanity at the checkout. She'd seen the dolls and she'd wanted the dolls and she didn't understand what he meant.

"Do you think I enjoy this?" He dropped them and grabbed his belt, freeing it from its loops. "I don't know why you refuse to understand."

"Father."

"My name is *Charles*."

"Please don't hit me, Father. I don't want to be hit. I don't think I deserve to be hit."

"No? Did you play with these? Because I have it on very good authority you were down by the rocks, playing with these like a stupid little girl."

Somebody had ratted on her. It was unacceptable.

"Please, Father. I was pretending they were us, me and you and Mummy, and we were going on holiday and—"

"*Shut up, you little fucking whore.*" He wasn't Father or even Charles anymore. He was Master, as some of the Comrades sometimes called him. He was God. He was going to make it very difficult for her to sit down for a while. "Turn around and take what you deserve."

The door burst open and Constance flew in. "Charley!" she shouted. She was wearing a long dirty dress and her hair was wild and her cheeks were sunken and haggard, and she looked half-alive, but she was Mummy and she was here. "You won't touch her. I won't allow it."

Millicent let out a cry and buried her face in her mother's belly. "Please, please," she moaned, as a sob made her voice quake and shiver. "Mummy, I wanted us to be happy. And now he's going to hurt me."

"He is not. Unless he wants me to go to the police and tell them about the things that go on here."

"Connie—"

"Fuck off, Charley."

Comrade Charles rolled his eyes, and then leered viciously at Millicent. "Do you truly think this woman loves you, little lamb? She's using you. She's trying to get her ration sooner than she's earned it. Fine. I'll show you what she really cares about."

Comrade Charles left and Millicent rushed over to her dolls. She held them up to her mother. "Look. It's me and you and—"

"Did you see his face?" Constance stared at the open doorway.

"Mummy, I think we should go. I think me and you should go and then we'll be happy."

"Hush. We're not going anywhere."

Millicent cradled the dolls to her chest and Comrade Charles returned and he handed Comrade Constance the glass pipe and she smiled and she kissed Charles on the cheek and she fluttered from the room without pausing to look at her daughter. Charles remained in the doorway, shrouded in pipe smoke. Millicent often thought about the pipe smoke going *poof* and making him disappear.

"See, little lamb. It's a show. She doesn't love you. Do you know why? Because she's not your mother. You have no mother. You have no father."

"I'm keeping these dolls," Millicent said.

He chuckled grimly. "Oh, is that so?"

"Yes. Because if you try to take them from me, I am going to sneak away and go to the police station and tell them Charles Maidstone has drugs here, and he hits children, and he's a sad pathetic cult leader who can't even finish a single page of a book."

Her father's face became red with rage. He glared at her. He needed her to shrink before him, she knew, the same way the Comrades shrank. But Millicent stood up straighter and she stared at him and it was the scariest thing she'd ever done, but she did it.

"You're pathetic." He turned away. "You're a joke, little lamb."

He left and she slumped on the floor, and she curled into a ball with her dolls cradled to her face and she wept. She would later come to learn this was the wrong response: this, in fact, made her pathetic. This made her deserving of his punishment. But it would be years before she'd realise this, and in the meantime her only option was to succumb to her anguish.

18

JAMIE

I groan when I see Richard's Rolls Royce in the driveway. I forgot we had dinner plans. I wanted to crash when I got in.

Today has been a pain in the arse. Ray won't shut up about how *Millie is different*, about how he's *never felt like this before*, about how they *could really be something*. Sometimes I find myself looking up to Ray. In the business world he's a smooth operator. But other times I pity him.

I sigh and climb out, practising smiles the same way I do before an important meeting. I'm not a fan of Richard and Amelia. I called him *Rich* once and he corrected me like I was his servant.

I still don't know what to do about Millicent. I've been chewing it over ever since I met with her yesterday. I want to throttle the bitch and dump her in the River Avon, but I'd get caught. And really, do I have it in me to strangle a woman to death? I don't think so.

I open the door and glance at the security alarm keypad, checking it's disabled. It's a habit I can't break after so many years spent hunting. I smell lasagne and I hear raised voices. I dump my briefcase in the hallway and head to the kitchen.

This is going to be torture.

I expect to see my wife standing at the obsidian kitchen island. What I don't expect is Millicent fucking Maidstone with blotches of blood and gore covering her shirt and neck.

She freezes and stares at me, and then the bitch smiles.

I clench my fists and move toward her. This is it. She's made my decision for me.

"Where's Hazel—"

"I'm *so* sorry." Hazel emerges from the pantry with a kitchen towel clutched in her manicured hand. She dresses like a businesswoman when her parents come to visit: suit trousers and shirt and block heels. The same type of outfit Millicent was wearing yesterday. "I can't believe I did that."

Millicent holds my gaze as she takes the towel. "It's no bother. Accidents happen."

"You always were such a clumsy thing," Amelia says from the back patio, her posh voice grating.

Hazel rolls her eyes. "I only went and spilled sauce on our guest, didn't I?"

She faces Millicent, moving the way she does when she's anxious. Everything is quick and jerky. I'm not surprised she spilled the sauce. I hate how nervous her parents make her. I hate that Amelia insists on having these dinners, when she doesn't give a damn the rest of the time. At least my old man never pretended.

Most of all, I hate the way Millicent is grinning at me.

"I'll get you a change of shirt. I'm really sorry, Millie."

"You didn't do it on purpose, H."

H? Fucking *H?*

I wait for Hazel to correct her, but Hazel smiles. It's the sort of smile she reserves for her actual friends, not people she barely knows. There's me, there's Trish who she's known since

93

she was a child. A couple of others, people she's known for years. But Millicent Maidstone?

"Go and sit with Mum and Dad." Hazel brushes her hand along my side as she passes. Her touch is delicate, innocent. She doesn't deserve this. "I'll bring you out a drink in a sec."

I grab her hand and lean close, lowering my voice. "You good?"

She nods. She thinks I'm talking about her parents. "You know how it is. Go on. I need you for backup."

I give Millicent a wide berth as I walk around the kitchen island.

She rests her elbow against it and grins, as if daring me to do something. "It's nice to see you again, Jamie. Thank you for inviting me into your wonderful home."

Yeah, like a vampire. Of course she has to be invited in.

My head pulses. I'm getting a tension headache. "No problem."

"Hazel is such a doll." She glances over to the patio. "I've always loved playing with dolls."

"If you hurt her," I growl. "If you even *try* to hurt her, I'm going to—"

She throws her head back and laughs. Even if I know it's fake, it sounds so real I almost want to ask what the joke is. This woman could win an Oscar.

I hate her. She needs to go. She's poisoning my home.

"Oh, Jamie," she says in a ditzy voice. She talks loud enough for Richard and Amelia to hear. "You are *sooooooooo* funny."

I head out to the patio. Richard stands and offers me his hand, like this is a business meeting, like I'm here to impress him. He's wearing a suit that makes me feel cheap. He's a smart-looking man, with rigid posture, always in control. Amelia has pearls in her ears and pearls at her throat and her make-up makes her look like she's at a funeral, in the coffin. I bloody wish that was the case. At least it'd give Hazel some peace.

I shake hands with Richard and we exchange pleasantries, and then I go through the rigmarole of telling Amelia she looks wonderful. She hasn't aged a day. What a load of horseshit. I'd rather hack off my nuts than spend one night with her.

Some women get more beautiful as they age, but there are others who fight it, who cake their faces in pale white make-up and drape themselves in jewellery like it'll rewind time. She even smells wrong, sickly sweet, and I repress the urge to gag.

If I was in a bad mood before, I'm livid now.

They're *laughing* in there, my wife and the psycho.

How can I tell Hazel what's going on without Millicent releasing the photos and the recording? I could explain the photos, maybe, but that's only assuming she hasn't got more incriminating stuff stowed away. She said she's got a video of me sneaking into a woman's house at night. And the recording, where I basically admit to what I do? She could be lying. Maybe she wasn't recording the conversation. But she could also be telling the truth.

Hazel appears at the door. Millicent stands at her elbow in one of Hazel's tie-dye T-shirts. "Since Miss Clumsy ruined the lasagne, why don't we order a takeaway?"

"Fine," Amelia says, in that Margaret Thatcher voice. I want to scream in her face, *Just speak normally, you pretentious bitch.* "Whatever is easiest for you, dear."

The evening wears on and I pound as many ciders as I can get down me.

Old Richie boy sips from a glass of whisky. I know for a fact nobody prefers whisky to cider. They drink it to seem sophisticated, the same way I do when I'm hunting. It's the perfect prop for his perfect image. Every now and then Amelia calls him *Captain* and I have to stop myself from laughing or flipping the table.

Captain? She makes it sound like he was in the Navy. The prick worked on a cruise ship.

I say as little as I can get away with. Richard tries to talk to me about car engines or some shit, but I don't care. He barely looks at his daughter. Amelia is worse. It's like Hazel is an *inconvenience* to her.

Millicent does the right things in the right places. She titters along with Amelia and she tells Richard he *must* work out, oh, he *must*, he looks so strong. She talks about her freelance writing career and Richard and Amelia *actually care*. They take an interest. Amelia even asks follow-up questions and Millicent starts banging on about a shower gel job she had a couple of weeks ago, and isn't that the funniest thing, isn't that hilarious and we should sit here ignoring our daughter and laugh with this stranger instead.

"Hazel's got a contract with a make-up company." I sound more pissed than I realised. I haven't stood up in a while. My plate looks like a bomb's gone off. I've probably eaten two-thirds of everything we ordered.

Hazel flashes her eyes at me. I know what she's trying to tell me. She wants me to be quiet and let them keep walking all over her.

"I'm just saying." I cover my mouth with my hand. I thought I was going to puke for a second there. Close call. "She gets paid to show off their products on her Instagram page. She's almost at a hundred thousand followers. Do you have any idea how many people'd kill for that?"

"I suppose so," Amelia says, but she's not getting it.

What is her fucking problem?

Why is she determined to put her daughter down all the time?

The whole table pauses and everybody stares at me. Hazel glares. Richard's doing his wannabe-Navy routine, making his upper lip stiff. Amelia's mouth falls open like somebody crushed a baby's skull and poured the contents onto her plate.

Millicent is doing a poor job of hiding her hungry smile.

Oh... *fuck-fuck-fuck.*

I said that out loud.

"Excuse me?" Amelia snaps, stuck-up as hell.

Screw it. It's out there now. "I've never seen you give Hazel any credit. She works hard to build her following. She's read so many books about marketing. She's learned the software. She takes pride in her appearance. She inspires people. But you care more about this stranger than your own daughter."

"Jamie," Hazel says stiffly.

She's at my side, her hand on my arm. She's looking down at me and there are tears in her eyes.

What have I done? Oh, God, I didn't want to make her cry.

"Can I talk to you for a second?" I can tell she wants to let out a sob. But she doesn't. She's stronger than me.

I stumble as I head toward the kitchen. Hazel leads me over to the sink. I lean against the counter as she pours me a tall glass of water.

"Drink it," she snaps.

I take it and knock it back in one, the same way we used to pound beers and ciders at uni.

We like to drink with Jamie, 'cause Jamie is our mate...

She pours another glass and slams it against my chest. Water swills over the edge.

"Drink it."

I drink, and she pours a third. My belly is starting to ache.

"Drink. It."

I groan and place the empty glass down. The room is spinning.

"You're going to apologise to my parents. You're going to blame it on the alcohol. You're going to say you don't know what came over you."

"But it's true. H, you deserve credit. You're amazing. You're so *good*, right down to your... to your soul."

She moves close, smiling up at me. At least she's not angry. Or maybe she is. Maybe she's angry and she's smiling. "I love that you want to stand up for me. But that's not the way to do it."

I sigh and pull her closer. I wish I could just hold her for the rest of the night. "I think I've had too much to drink."

"You *think*?" She brushes something off my shirt, probably a noodle or another Chow Mein ingredient that somehow missed my mouth. "Come on. Get your game face on."

She's right. My wife's always right.

Which just makes this even more painful. I know how much she fears humiliation in any form, a hand-me-down from Amelia, who'd rather lop off an ear than face any kind of shame, public or otherwise. It means I have to go out there and play nice, even when there's a killer at the table, a psycho bitch who could bring my whole life tumbling down.

And I don't even know why.

19

HAZEL

I sit on the bathroom floor, staring with teary eyes at the rejection email.

While we enjoyed your art, it begins.

That's such a horrible lie to tell. If they enjoyed it they would've accepted it.

My head aches from last night, from the wine and from the way Jamie went weird with Mum and Dad. But he was drunk and thankfully my parents accepted his apology, even if I could tell Mum still felt uppity about it.

We don't think it's quite right for this display, it goes on. We wish you the best of luck and encourage you to submit again in the future.

I've read the email like ten times. I first opened it after I used the toilet, heading for the bathroom door, and then I leaned against the wall and slid down and now here I am.

It's not fair. None of my art, not a single piece of work, has ever been accepted. I understand I'm not some super-skilled portrait artist or whatever. I know my stuff is more abstract. But it was a call for *anybody* to have their art exhibited.

I've got eighty thousand Instagram followers. I could publicise the heck out of the event. I mentioned that in my submission email. I fail to see how it counts for nothing.

I look at the window and the sunlight, and it makes me think how another artist, some pro who went to art school, would be having a bunch of deep thoughts. They'd be thinking about what *type* of yellow the sunlight is, and what it represents, but I don't.

I'm useless. I have nothing to offer.

Jamie went about it in the wrong way last night, but he was right about Mum. She showed way more interest in Millie's work than she's ever shown in anything I've done.

She resents me. She never wanted me.

Oh, great, and now I can't breathe. Everything's getting loud in my ears and my heart hurts and my chest is getting tight and I know what this is. I know it's a panic attack. But knowing it and accepting it are two different things.

Maybe I'll pass out on the bathroom floor and Jamie won't find me until this evening.

"Stop it," I murmur, bringing my knees to my chest. I want to be as small as possible. "Stop, stop, *stop*—"

The pain makes it so I don't have to think about anything else.

All that exists is the feeling of my teeth against my skin, sinking deep, deeper, until I'm sure I'm going to hit something important. I keep biting, squeezing, pushing my arm up against my mouth so I can clamp onto my bicep.

My mind is empty. It doesn't feel like pain. It feels good.

Maybe I'm not meant to be a social-media star. Maybe I'll never crack one hundred thousand. I gained two followers yesterday, *two*.

I'm doing everything right, aren't I?

I stop, letting out a shaky breath. I stare at my teeth marks.

"Shit." I stand up. "Fuck's sake."

I haven't done that in years. The last time was before I started university. I had a problem in my teens, but I thought I had it under control.

I throw the bathroom door open and run through the house. I walk into our bedroom and over to the vanity unit, throw the drawer open, and take out some concealer. The bite mark twinges and aches as I apply the make-up. I wince each time I touch the tender spot. But, eventually, it disappears. It's like it never happened. I can always brush it away in photos if the make-up isn't enough.

I need to *do* something. I can't sit around the house, feeling helpless. I'm not helpless. I didn't get eighty thousand followers by being pathetic.

I change into my sexiest lingerie, the red set I wore on mine and Jamie's wedding anniversary. It's lacy and frilly and stylish.

It makes you look like a Christmas present, Jamie said when he saw it, his stunning bright greens flooding with hunger.

Then open me, husband.

I take my phone into the en suite and put my foot up on the marble-effect sink counter, sticking my ass out, arching my back to draw attention to my breasts. I aim the phone at the mirror. I smile, and I study the smile. I need to make it more realistic. I laugh and then let the laughter go silent, holding the pose.

I take dozens of photos and then return to the bedroom, dropping onto the unmade bed. My plan was to get my chores done after yoga and breakfast, but the rejection letter has derailed things.

Absolutely LOVE my husband for splashing the cash on this new lingerie. #confident #livingmybestlife

I add more hashtags, and then stare down at the photo. I've

never posted anything this revealing before. I know it would get me a ton of new followers. The big stars post photographs like this. Why shouldn't I?

I add **#ifyouvegotitflauntit** to my hashtag list. But I don't believe it. Maybe I do have it. Maybe I don't. Either way, I don't want to flaunt it for anybody except my husband. If that makes me old-fashioned, I'm old-fashioned.

If I was single, I'd post this in a heartbeat. But I know Jamie would freak if he saw this online. I'd *want* him to be angry. He owns me as much as I own him. That's what marriage is. I wouldn't like it if he started posting shirtless photos.

Jamie and I value loyalty above everything. It's in the DNA of our relationship. Honesty in all things, even if we're both a little twisted.

I delete the post, falling backward onto the bed and staring up at the mini chandelier on the ceiling. It's not as shiny as when we first had it installed. I need to dust it, but I don't have the energy.

My phone vibrates. Not a text. A phone call.

I glance at the screen. It's Greta. We met on a social media course last year. She has one hundred and fifty thousand followers.

"Hey, bitch," I answer, sassy. My voice doesn't sound like my own.

But faking it is one of my specialties: faking enthusiasm in the bedroom, faking smiles and laughter and optimism, and most of all showing the whole world a fake face so they can never, not even for a moment, see the real me. It's better that way, for everybody.

"Hey," Greta says. "Are we still on for drinks later? Please, please, *please* say yes! I've spent *all night* listening to this absolute douchebag drone on about his family issues. It's like: listen, friend, if you didn't have a ten-incher we wouldn't even be having this conversation. Know what I mean? Like it's my problem your mum's sick or whatever."

She laughs and I laugh, even if it isn't funny.

"Yeah, I'm super psyched for it," I say. "Shots, shots, shots."

"*Yaaaaaas*, queen." Greta laughs. "Wear some pink, all right? I want us to match for the pics."

20

MILLICENT

A couple of days after the hilarious dinner with the Smithsons – oh God were those front-row seats worth the price of admission – I walk by the pond, sighting the old man out of my peripheral vision. I stride over to the woman, hate scorching my insides, burning me until I'm convinced my bones are going to melt.

There he is: the sad old lecher, no memories to assuage or abuse him. He stares at the ducks and his hand sits limp in the bag of breadcrumbs. His face is slack and stupid, utterly vacant, and glee whelms up inside of me at the sight.

If they gave me two minutes with him and a piece of wire, I could make their jobs much easier.

I approach his carer and barely resist the desire to do her serious damage. She should be ashamed of herself. Caring for demons makes you a devil. She's empty-eyed and she wears simple sad clothes and she sucks on a cigarette, blowing the smoke away from her charge and glancing over at him every few moments.

"Afternoon," I say.

"Um, afternoon?"

"Can I be cheeky and bum a ciggie?"

Her eyes light up. There's nothing people love more than thinking everybody is as weak as they are. "Yeah, all right." She takes one from the packet and hands it to me. "I'm quitting tomorrow, anyways."

Of course you are, you broken thing.

She's been *quitting tomorrow* every day since she began this habit, I'd wager.

I take the cigarette and hold it as naturally as I'm able, and then I tilt my head at her, and she laughs. I laugh. What great friends we are. She hands me a lighter and I bring the cigarette to my mouth, lighting it. I suck enough to make it spark orange-red, but I don't inhale. The taste is detestable.

Handing her the lighter, I say, "So you're the sad bitch who's taking care of this waste of skin then?"

She takes a step back, staring as though she's awoken from a long sleep to find herself caged with a wildcat. "What?"

I approach her. She backs away. I keep walking forward and she keeps backing away. She has never been so scared. I can see it in her eyes, in the way her half-smoked cigarette trembles and ash falls like rainbow dust.

"You're pathetic," I tell her. "Is this really the best you can do with your life, taking care of this excreta while filling your lungs with poison? There's something wrong with you."

She puffs herself up, her defence mechanisms flaring. "Who the fuck do you think you're talking to..."

She trails off when I stare, and stare, and keep staring. "Weren't you going to make a threat?"

"What do you want?" she whispers, withering under my brilliance.

"I want to do this." I stick my tongue out and place the end of the cigarette against it. There's a tiny *hiss* and a tinier pulse of pain, but it's worth it to see her cattle lips quiver. I spit and toss it to the ground. "Wait here. If you interfere, I'll drown you in the pond."

I walk over to the old man.

"Wait, what are you doing?" the woman bleats, but she stays where she is, looking around the empty park as if the trees are going to help her.

I walk in front of the bench and lean down, staring into the man's eyes, set within a landscape of folded skin. I grin like a wolf, right in his face. He reeks of care homes and sweat and shaving foam and shit. He reeks of hate.

"Hello."

"Kitty." He nods to his lap, and for a second I think he means *that*. I reach for my inside jacket pocket where I keep my blade. But no, he's indicating the breadcrumbs. "Kitty, help me. The ducks. I'd like to feed them."

"Who the fuck is Kitty?"

"That's me," the woman calls, gravitating toward us cautiously, as though she knows I could leap over the bench and dig my thumbs into her eye sockets any moment. "I'm Kitty. He gets confused. He's ill."

"He was always ill, just not in the way you think. You know me, old man. You know what you did. You know what your *son* did, don't you? *Don't you?*"

His smile falters and he lets out a wailing noise.

The woman inches closer. "Please. Whatever it is, he doesn't remember. He's a sick old man."

My fingers twitch for the knife. I could do it. Physically speaking, it wouldn't pose any serious challenge.

With one fluid movement, I could reach into my pocket and lash the knife out, severing his papery throat, and then, as the cow fled, I'd chase her down and fall upon her and that would be that. But it would surely mean my capture. It's daylight. I haven't checked if there's CCTV.

I'm not here to kill an old man whose soul has left his body, if he ever had a soul to begin with.

"Get a new job," I tell the woman, as the husk continues to wail. "These people you care for, you moronic bitch, you have no idea who they are, what they are, what they've done. Just because somebody lives long enough to lose their mind, it doesn't make them good."

Kitty whimpers. "Please go."

"Get a new name too, while you're at it. Kitty? I should throw you off a cliff for having such a pitiful name."

"Please."

"You're pathetic." I stride away from the carer and the wailer and the ducks. "You're a joke, little lamb."

21

BEFORE

C louds moved across the sky and a flock of birds cut a line across them, and the cliffs were like a series of jagged broken faces below. The sheer cliffs were half a mile from the Comrades' cul-de-sac, separated by fields and pockets of trees, and the fields were verdant and beautiful in the flowering of summer. As the cul-de-sac became closer, the nature became civilisation and there were houses and roads and cars and clothes drying on wires between the Comrades' houses.

Before Comrade Charles had bought the property, the Rainbow Room had been the workshop of an amateur carpenter. Charles ordered the Comrades to gut it and make it as empty and nondescript as possible – this so he could flood their minds with its kaleidoscopic potential.

It sat at the end of the garden and the grass was long and thick and when it was windy the grass blew and waved like countless tiny green arms. The door was made of simple wood but it was scarred with the onslaught of many winters, with wind and rain and hail, and perhaps soon it would need replacing, but for the time being it was an effective seal against what happened within.

Comrade Philip and Millicent were in there and they were the only ones in there and nobody else was in there with them.

"Anything is possible." His voice splintered like weathered wood. "In the Rainbow Room, my angel, *every*thing is possible."

The girl said nothing, but she was in there. She was in there and she said nothing. Nobody can blame her, can they, for being silent?

Nobody can say it's her fault. She was a child. She was a fucking child.

"How can something be wrong if nothing is right? You don't have an answer. Because you know it makes sense. No wrong, no right. It doesn't take a rocket scientist to figure that out."

The talking ceased and something else took its place, and above them, far above them, the clouds continued to drift and drift.

The grass shivered as a Comrade walked down the side passage of Charles' home, moving through the shin-high grass. He was a thin man and he was a tall man and he had a pale purple birthmark on one side of his face, from the top of his cheek to the corner of his lip, almost forming a crescent, like a moon, and some of the Comrades called him Purple Moon because of this.

He placed his ear against the door and his purple moon twitched as he smiled. He smiled and the girl was in there and she said nothing. She would always think about that, for years to come, even after she'd left most of this pain behind: her silence, her complicity.

He knocked in a very specific way, using his knuckles and his fingernails: *rap-a-tat-rap-rap.*

Comrade Philip knew it was Purple Moon and the door opened and, for a brief moment, Millicent could see her house and some of the grass and even a portion of the sky. But then Purple Moon hurried inside and closed the door and the little girl closed her eyes so she wouldn't have to see him reach for the buckle of his belt.

~

Things happened to her young mind which she didn't understand, causing her to become curious in ways she had never imagined, to become overly bold with boys: both of the group and of the greater world. She didn't understand it was wrong, because it happened in the Rainbow Room and there was no wrong or right in there. And yet there was a feeling inside of her, this twisted thing, screaming she was broken, she was rotten.

She was tied to a chair in the middle of the Rainbow Room, the night cold and the darkness full around her, deep pitch; it was the same if she kept her eyes open, or closed them. She had woken with hands over her body, binding wrists, binding ankles: a strong grip around the zip-ties and they carried her like cattle down the stairs.

This was Father, she knew, and she knew it was going to be bad. She let out a small whimpering cry and hated herself for it. She was a brave girl and she knew what she had to do: what she had to endure. She wouldn't let herself crumble, even when she heard footsteps approaching and a man letting out a gruff sigh.

The door flew open and there were torches in her face, dozens of them, undulating meteors of light smashing into her. She slammed her eyes shut, certain they'd blinded her. All she could do for several seconds was pray she could still see, even if it meant gazing at what they were going to do to her.

Father's voice boomed. "Open. Your. Fucking. Eyes."

She forced her eyes open and took in the scene, even as her head ached under the glare of the torches. There were a dozen Comrades, more of them filing into the room each second.

Millicent cringed away from her father's brown corduroys and the knife he held in front of him, his hands crossed calmly.

Mother stood at his side, gripping onto his shoulder, hardly able to keep herself upright with how much she'd smoked and drank.

"Tell us what happened, Comrade Philip," Father said, tapping the knife against his belt buckle, *click-click-click*.

Comrade Philip stepped forward, looking old and disgusting and like Satan, like the fucking Devil as he stood there with his old face and his fake frown. His eyes were wolfish and bright and evil. How did nobody see that? Or perhaps they saw, and they didn't care; Millicent belonged to all of them, and thus to none of them. She was alone and perhaps one day she'd learn how to weaponise her isolation.

But for now all she could do was cry and stare and wait.

"She touched my son inappropriately," Comrade Philip said. "He didn't know what she was doing. When he explained it to me, I was absolutely disgusted."

"He isn't your son if I'm not Charles' daughter."

The words came by themselves, flung from her precocious lips. She was much smarter than him: than everybody in this room. Grown-ups pretended they knew what was going on, but really they just said whatever they needed to. As soon as they got what they wanted, they flipped, becoming evil, like Mother, like Father, like every single person she knew.

Comrade Philip's face filled with rage, the real him coming out.

"Enough," Father snapped, holding his hand up, the one not clutching the knife. "Is this true, Millicent?"

She floundered. She couldn't lie to her father, the Master, whatever he wanted to be called. She couldn't lie, because he could always tell. Some of the Comrades whispered he had magical powers.

What could she say? She'd only been repeating what she and Comrade Philip did in the Rainbow Room. The poor girl didn't yet understand the crime of what he was doing; she only had a vague feeling of the wrongness of it. She would hate herself for that in the years to come, how she didn't rage and scream and fight.

But childhood is a prison of the mind.

"Yes," she murmured.

"Fucking whore," Comrade Philip snarled.

Mother sneered. "My daughter, the ugly slut."

"You disgusting wicked girl," an elderly Comrade hissed, holding up a wrinkled fist and shaking it at Millicent.

The comrades crowded her with their torches—"You dirty fucking bitch"—and they leaned close and they spit on her —"Let's rape her"—as they waved weapons in her face, knives and screwdrivers and box cutters—"Act like a slut, get treated like a slut"—and Father stood back with his arms folded and smiled, and sucked on his pipe—"Let me cut this bitch"—and Mother draped her arm across him and laid her cheek against his shoulder—"fuck her up, fucking hurt her, fucking hurt her"—and Mother closed her eyes and smiled.

The little girl was being beaten, she realised, as though she'd fallen into her body from a distant watching place. She jolted into the physicality of the torture: of the weapons pressed against her flesh, of the pain of their assault, and most of all of their words, their evil fucking words. They tore at her, making her question if she truly was what they were claiming.

She coughed and she tasted blood. Somebody grabbed her hair in a tangled fist and tugged her head back, snarling in her ear. "You deserve this. You *know* you deserve this."

And then some of them left and some of them stayed, and the ones who stayed did things to the girl: things that made her float up and through the ceiling, up into the sky, which was dark and laden with stars which glittered and sparkled and danced mystically, as if purposefully putting on a show to distance the girl from what was happening beneath them.

There was a room and there was a rainbow and there was a slice of the sky, and finally the girl found her voice. She begged no, *no*, over and over – she screamed *no*. But they never listened.

22

JAMIE

I spin in my office chair, looking out the window. It's raining and the sound of it, *tap-tap-bloody-tap*, is starting to piss me off. I spin again and look around my office, across my large desk to my cream sofa in the corner, to my plant, a plant I don't even know the name of. I don't water it. One of the grunts does that.

I pick up the photo of me and Hazel on our honeymoon. We're standing in the shallows on the Maltese beach, the water screensaver-blue. We look happy, my arm around her, a big goofy grin on my face and a sweet-as-sugar smile on hers. This wasn't one she posted online, which might be why it's my favourite. She looks so *Hazel* without her usual Photoshop touch-ups.

It's Friday, which means it's been almost a week since Millicent Maidstone popped into my Bristol life. And three weeks since she set me up in Cardiff.

And what have I done? Fuck all. Because what *can* I do?

I go over the problem in my head, trying to puzzle it out. Normally, in work and life, I don't give myself much time to think.

You go, go, go, Hazel said to me once. *That's why I love you. You never hesitate.* She was right. I've always acted on instinct, but my instincts aren't giving me any answers.

It's not like I can ring the police. Maybe she's lying about having video footage of me sneaking into Lacy's bungalow. Maybe she's lying about recording my confession in her flat. But I can't take the chance.

All I can think about is bashing her skull in. I dream about it. I woke up last night hugging Hazel so tightly she laughed and stroked her hand along my forehead. *Did my sweet baby have a bad dream?* she teased, kissing the sweat from my cheek.

She knows something's wrong. She probably thinks it's work. I can't bear to think how she'd react if she knew the truth, the whole truth.

Suddenly, my office door bursts open and Ray walks in. He slams it behind him and strides over to the desk. He looks like shit. His cheeks are proper beetroot-red and he's sweating. "Why haven't you sent the Quinlan report?"

"What?" I sit up, shaking my head. "I did. I sent it first thing. You think I'd let that slip?"

Oliver Quinlan is one of our biggest clients. I always triple-check everything I do when he's involved. But did I... no, I didn't. I didn't triple-check the email. We've been having connection problems lately, something to do with the line, the IT bloke said, as if that's my goddamn problem.

I turn to my laptop and bring up the email. "Shit. It didn't leave the outbox. I'm sending it now. I'm sorry, boss. I don't know what happened."

Ray drops into the seat opposite, waving a hand. "All right, relax. Simple mistake, kid. I was worried you hadn't done it, that's all. You need to get your head screwed on. We can't be having slip-ups like this. Understand?"

"Yes."

"You're good, right, Jamie?"

"Yeah. Why do you ask?"

He shrugs. "You seem a little distracted. You know you can talk to me, right? I might be able to help."

Sure, Ray, let me tell you how your new girlfriend is a serial killer who's set her sights on me for some reason. Let me tell you how I check if I'm being followed any time I step from my car and how this psycho bitch killer – your girlfriend – is becoming friends with my wife. And there's nothing I can do about it.

But Ray *might* be able to help, I realise.

Why didn't I think of this sooner?

I feel like a jackass. I could've asked him on Monday. Hell, I could've asked at the party.

"Actually, there is something," I say, getting excited. It feels good to have a vague plan of attack. "Remember last year, when you had... you know, those problems with your ex?"

Ray grimaces. "She left a dead rat in my sink. She was nuts."

"And you hired that bloke, the private investigator, to look into her."

"Private investigator?" Ray chuckles. "That's not what Tom Brown is. He's... he's no one, Jamie. He's a creepy bastard. Ex-military is my best bet."

"You met him through your brother," I say, remembering. Ray's brother was in the Marines.

"Yeah. You want me to arrange a meeting?"

"Could you?" I can't hide how eager I am. I should've thought of this on *Monday*, for fuck's sake. My head isn't working properly lately. It's her, Millicent, messing with my mojo.

"He doesn't work cheap."

"I know. But I need this. I don't know what else to do."

Ray leans forward, placing his elbows on my desk. His hand comes to rest near the photo of me and Hazel. I want to tell him to get his sweaty hand away from her, but I don't. "What is this?

You fuck the wrong woman? You owe the wrong people money? What?"

"It involves a woman." Which is true. If you can call that shark-eyed freak a woman.

"Oh, Jamie." He nods matter-of-factly. I know what he's thinking. *We're the same. We can't help ourselves.* Maybe he's right. "Of course I'll set it up. It'd be such a shame for you and Hazel to break-up. You two are a rare breed. A happily married couple."

We are, aren't we, happily married? We have our problems, like any couple – or maybe our problems are unique – but when you get past that crap, that noise, we're genuinely happy. I believe that. I think Hazel does too.

"Thanks, boss." I smile. Maybe this is my way of fighting back.

Ray claps his hands together and then reaches into his suit jacket pocket. "Little tipple is in order, I'd say, to take the edge off."

He brings out his leather-bound flask. I haven't seen it since I first started working here. I was the one who supported him while he quit. He cried in my arms one night, begging me to help him. It was one of the ways we became so close so fast.

I glance at my laptop, at the clock. It's just gone midday. "I thought you weren't drinking before three o'clock?"

He scowls. "Rationing. It's not the way to live your life. Some men like a drink and that's the end of it. What's next, rationing our love, our kindness, our souls?"

This is her. This is Millicent.

I've known Ray for half a decade, and he has never once used the word *soul* with me. I'd be hard-pressed to think of a time he's said *love* or *kindness*. She's pushing him to drink, because... well, because she's mental. She's deranged. She likes to make people suffer.

"Go on." Ray offers me the flask, a challenge in his eyes. I know that look. He's deciding if he can still trust me. "Unless you're going to make me drink alone?"

"Of course not." I slug a nasty mouthful of whisky, fighting the urge to gag as I hand it back to him. "When do you reckon I can meet this bloke, this Tom Brown?"

Ray takes a long sip and wipes his mouth. "Don't know. Shouldn't take too long. Maybe early next week. Maybe tomorrow. And kid, I should warn you. He can be a little intense."

Intense is good. Intense is what I need to fight back against this bitch.

23

MILLICENT

Lots of things happened to me when I was a child, but I cannot lament them.

Much of it led me to find solace in words; there is simplicity in language reality doesn't possess. With words I can distance myself from what happened when I was a girl, when those greasy men took their pound of flesh.

I remember the healing that came after the worst of it: weeks in bed, unable to move, Mother reluctantly bringing me a metal bucket to piss and shit in, and every now and then some food...

But only if Father allowed it.

Sometimes he let me go hungry so I could process what I had done wrong. *Processing*, he called it, as though I was a computer. He thought he could program the right codes and make me in his image, but his image was sloppy and amateurish. Instead I used his suffering to make my *own* image, the predator in the dark, the huntress with the knife or the rock or the piece of wire.

I sit in a café, near the back, my fingers poised over the keyboard. I've got a flat white next to my laptop, and for a second it looks like a photograph, like something Hazel would post online. I feel my fingers twitching for my phone, something I've never experienced before. I push the impulse down, but it's curious, this need I feel to fit in with her.

We haven't met since the dinner, but we've been texting, bantering like we're going to become best friends. It's a novel experience.

Sometimes I don't feel like I'm faking it. Sometimes it feels real.

I stare at the Word document, at the words I've just brought into reality. I can't stand to look at it for long. I close the laptop and take a sip of my coffee.

A mother sits on the other side of the café, a swollen specimen with five rats screaming and making a fuss over every little thing. She looks up and sees me staring as she's cleaning a chin with one hand and wrestling a boy with the other. She smiles, because she sees the façade. She sees my suit jacket and my kind eyes and my professional demeanour.

I return her smile, even as I imagine tackling her through the window and leaping on her. I'd take a shard of glass and drag it up from her slit to her neck, slicing her middle right open, screaming madly in her face as blood pissed from her useless body.

Still, those children will probably have it better than me, even with a wreck for a mother, with her sports-shop jacket and her gaudy faux-gold chain. We called people *cattle* in our... religion, cult, what? Whatever it was, we called them cattle, and none have fit the description more than this troll.

Yet part of me glows when she brushes hair from her son's face. She must love her boys to worry over them so much, to bring them to a café, to do it all by herself.

Rare shame touches me. She doesn't deserve to die. It's the fucking *men*.

They were always the worst, the ones who found unique

ways to punish me. Some of them told me I enjoyed it, insisted upon it, as they committed their monstrous acts. They would plead even as they did it... even as they did things that made it impossible for me to reply. They would ask, beg for deliverance.

You like it. Look. She likes it. Listen to that moan. A bitch don't moan like that if she's not having fun, does she? Do you? Answer me.

I close my eyes and take a breath. Exploring these avenues is dangerous. But lately I can't seem to avoid them.

It's the writing.

Or it's being close to Jamie, to the life he's made: to his wife, Hazel, who tugs at parts of me I'd rather leave untouched. She makes me wonder what it would've been like to have a sister, a true comrade instead of the liars in the Rainbow Room.

Every single one of them could smile when they were in public, could clap other men on the back, could tend to their sick children. They wore masks – nowhere near as effective as mine, but good enough for most – and only let their true selves out when they had a child tied to a table.

That's why I refuse to feel guilty about what I do, because they earned it, either in the past or in the future. They all do something unforgivable somewhere along the way. They all steal what lust they can, whenever they can, ignoring the feelings of their lovers, partners, victims.

If I were to take the most upstanding man in the country and put him in a hotel room with a scared girl and complete assurance nobody would ever find out, he'd take her the same way all men do.

Scratch a little beneath the flesh and they reveal themselves to be monsters.

They stole any chance I had to be normal, and somewhere along the way I stopped trying. But a possible new path is opening before me. I may still execute Jamie and end my own life before the police can apprehend me, but what if Hazel is offering me something I was always denied? Perhaps she's my chance at beautiful mundanity. It's worth a try, at the very least.

That's why I've chosen to nudge reality into my favour, to move Hazel's limbs the same way I moved my dolls when I was a girl, contorting them into whatever shape I needed them.

Finally my phone buzzes. The number is *Unknown*, like he said it'd be.

"Hello." I use my professional voice. The woman across from me probably thinks I'm taking a business call, but this is very personal. "Thank you for ringing."

"So polite." He laughs gruffly, sounding like a teenager. Maybe he is. "Bit weird you wanted to talk on the phone."

"I've been messed around in the past. I don't want it to happen this time. If I pay you to do something, you have to deliver."

"And talking helps with that how?"

"Because I will know if you're lying to me. If you're just trying to take my money. And I will make it my mission to find you."

He snorts laughter. My temples pulse. If this little bastard had any idea who I am, he wouldn't dare disrespect me. At least, he *sounds* little, little and pathetic. "Jesus Christ, lady. It's only a grand. Relax. I'll do what you want. How fast do you want it to start?"

I drum my fingers on the table. The Dark Web is a useful place: for drugs, for services impossible to find on the regular internet. I've had fun using it in the past for a variety of projects, all of them used as predator's tools, the same way less imaginative hunters use knives and tapes.

This man calls himself a hacker. I don't like the term. It sounds too science fiction, too ridiculous. But if he can make Hazel desperate, that's all that matters. When she's desperate, she'll be more inclined to seek solace in her new friend.

And then what?

I'm not sure exactly.

But I can't stop thinking about her perfect life, her perfect hair and teeth and her shiny smile, a smile that makes me think nothing truly bad has ever happened to her. Perhaps being a part of it will help me believe nothing bad has ever happened to me. Or perhaps it will fail, and I'll be forced to revert to blood.

"Hello? Are you there?"

"Yes." I clear my throat: too much thinking. "I want it to start slow, and then get progressively worse."

"Easy. There's lots of potential here. What did she do to you, anyway?"

"That's none of your business. Just do your job."

"Fair enough." The sound of tapping keys in the background. "From what I've seen, this is going to drive her really crazy."

That we can agree on. I wonder if I should feel guilty, but there is no wrong; there is no right. There are only words. And when this is over, perhaps I'll be there to speak the right words to Hazel, in the right combination to make her love me.

Yes, maybe that's how this will end: in hope instead of blood.

24

HAZEL

Jamie groans, dropping into the poolside chair. "Can't we just have our drinks?"

It's a warm Friday night and we've decided to have a few cocktails in the garden. The lights around the pool make the water shiny. The sky is clear and lovely-looking. I've gone through the effort of doing a full face of make-up and fixing my hair, and Jamie's still in his work clothes, looking handsome in a rugged way.

"I don't see the problem with taking a few photos."

He rubs his jaws. He hasn't shaved since the party. He's got a prickly black beard, with a few white hairs dotted here and there. He's going to be a real silver fox one day. "There's not a problem. I'm just not in the mood for a photoshoot."

"It will take two minutes, if that." I try to keep my tone level, but the fact he's arguing with me is annoying. He knows social media is part of the deal with me. He knew it before we got married and he should know it now. I put up with a lot from him. He should do the same for me. That's what a marriage is supposed to be. "Please don't make me fight you on this."

He makes to pick up his drink and I shake my head quickly. "I can't even have a *sip*?"

I gesture at the cocktail glass, with the stick positioned perfectly, the lime wedge angled perfectly, with everything just so. "After we've taken the photos, you can neck ten glasses if you want."

"H, we don't even know who's looking at that stuff."

I clutch my phone harder. "What do you mean?" My shoulder throbs from the bite. "My followers are looking at it."

"And who are they? They could be anybody. Bunch of fucking weirdos online. If you had any sense, you'd delete that stuff and find something worthwhile to do – H, Hazel, *wait*."

But I refuse to wait if he's going to speak to me like this.

I march through the house and up the stairs, picking up speed when I hear Jamie hurrying after me. Tears prick my eyes, but I don't want to cry. I don't want to be weak. I understand if work is stressing him out, fine, but that's no reason to be cruel.

I haven't done anything wrong. I wanted to capture how wonderful our lives are: or at least how wonderful they *seem* from the outside.

I march over to the wardrobe and pull out my suitcase, throwing it onto the bed. Jamie paces over to me and, grabbing it, he tosses it to the floor.

"I'm sorry. I didn't mean that."

"You promised you wouldn't say things like that anymore." I fold my arms and face the window. The garden is even prettier from up here, the lights seeming brighter. "You said I could make this my career. You said you were *proud* of me."

"I am." He wraps his arms around me and tries to make me soften against him, but I keep myself rigid and cold. "I'm sorry. That wasn't about you. It's work. I made a mistake today."

There's pain in his voice, a side of himself he rarely lets out.

He hates when he doesn't do every little thing right. "What mistake?"

"It was stupid. I sent an email. I thought I did anyway. But it didn't leave the outbox."

"Jamie, that's silly."

"You know what I'm like. I can't stop thinking about it. What if I make more mistakes? What if it all comes crashing down?"

I turn to him with a laugh. He always does this to me, somehow, finds a way to rip me out of whatever bad mood I'm in, even if he's the cause of it. Especially when he's the cause of it. Maybe that makes us both a little messed up. "Over an email? Come on, that's melodramatic."

He shrugs, looking lost and boyish. "Maybe. But the point is, H, I'm sorry. All right? Let's go outside. We'll take a million photos. A *billion*. I don't care."

"It's not the same now."

He brings his face close to mine, smiling like he did the first time I saw him. I never expected him to be there. I never expected to care so quickly, so violently, with so much certainty. I just wish it had stayed like that; I wish he hadn't added the extra parts, the parts that fill me with resentment. "I see you, Hazel Smithson—"

"I'm not in the mood."

"What can I do to make this right?"

I shrug, looking out on the garden again. Is there an itsy bitsy part of me that likes it when we're like this, when he knows he's done wrong and he'll do anything to prove how much he loves me? Yes, maybe there is, and I won't feel guilty about it.

Little moments of disrespect can stack up if a wife lets them.

"I've got an idea," he says, a quirk in his voice. My smile twitches, but I don't face him. "H, switch your phone on. Start recording me."

Now I'm interested. I turn. "Why?"

He grins. "Just do it. Trust me."

I open the camera app and start the video, aiming it at him. The lighting is really good in here.

"All right, ladies and gents, boys and girls." He offers his endearing smile, the one that lets him get away with so much. "It's Friday night and I've been a real arsehole to my lovely wife, the woman of my dreams. It's nothing serious, but to show her how sorry I am, how dedicated I am, I'm going to jump off our balcony into the swimming pool."

I gasp and his grin gets wider, and then he starts moving toward the balcony door behind me. I want to tell him no, don't do it. It's too dangerous. But another part of me is captivated. I move backward, holding him in frame the entire time.

He's not really going to do this, is he?

He's waiting for me to call out, to stop him.

The automatic light switches on and Jamie approaches the balcony railing. I've seen photographs from when he used to play rugby, and he has the same look in his eyes now, a couldn't-give-a-fuck look. It's like he's accepted he might get injured, but he won't let himself worry about it.

I move to the edge of the railing and look down. The pool must be more than five feet away, maybe more. There's no way he can do it without a running start.

But I keep watching, keep recording, as he grips the railing. He kicks one foot over and then starts to move the other.

"Jamie." I place my phone on the table and move toward him. The fear flurrying through me tells me he's worth it, even if he's far from perfect, maybe even *very* far. I can't stand the idea of him getting hurt. If that's not love, what is? "That's enough. You've proved your point."

He straddles the rail. "I can do it."

"I believe you. But please come down. You're a madman, Jamie Smithson."

He climbs onto the balcony and I grab his face in my hands and stand on my tiptoes, and I kiss him passionately. He groans and kisses me back, lifting me and placing me on the table. I can feel my phone digging into my bum.

I want the heat of his body. I want to feel how much he needs me. I want to belong and, with Jamie, I do. I always will.

"I love you," I gasp between kisses.

"I love you, H." He moans. "You'll never know how much."

We kiss again, melting into each other. I drag my hands along his neck and his shoulders and then down his back, feeling his taut muscles beneath the fabric of his suit. He tastes of Jamie. He smells of Jamie.

"Where were you going to go?" he says, our noses tickling each other as we remain close.

What's he talking about? Oh, the suitcase.

"I don't know. Anywhere. I just needed to get away from my mean grumpy husband."

"I'm sorry."

I place my hand on his chest, feeling the hammering of his heart. "I know. It's okay."

"It's not okay. You deserve respect. I'll work harder. Sometimes I forget... Just because I was raised like an animal, it doesn't mean I have to be one, you know?"

"I think that's a very mature thing to say."

"Would you?"

"Would I what?"

"Leave with me? Start a new life, go to Europe or America or wherever else?"

I prod him. "Nah, you're too much of a bully."

"I'm serious."

"Why? We have such a lovely life here."

"I know. But we could have an even better life somewhere else. Humour me."

"Your job..."

"I could make money anywhere," he says, his emerald eyes gleaming with confidence. I love that about him. He's always so sure he'll land on his feet.

"Hypothetically speaking, yes, of course I would. It's me and you against the world. I'd follow you to Hell."

Sometimes when Jamie and I talk like this, I feel like we're putting on a show for an invisible audience: saying and doing the things a madly in love couple would say and do. It makes me wonder if he feels the same: that we're constantly hovering on the surface of our marriage, never delving deep to where it matters, to real issues... But we're not a couple of *real issues*. We're a couple of big dramatic gestures and exaggerated statements.

"Are you okay?" he whispers, his eyes flitting with worry, reminding me of my reflection for so many years. It's the need not to be alone, to never be alone.

"Yes." I push the unhelpful thoughts from my mind. "I'm sorry. I was a million miles away. Come here."

I pull him into a kiss, stifling that little voice inside that tells me something is wrong, that something has been wrong since the beginning.

25

JAMIE

People can say what they want about Ray, but the man can deliver. I woke up this morning to a text telling me he'd made the connection with Tom Brown. He sent an address and told me to be there by eleven.

Don't be late.

I drive through the industrial estate, scanning the units.

My head's a little groggy from last night. After the madness on the balcony, after the mind-blowing sex, Hazel and I returned to the pool and had our cocktails. I smiled extra hard for her in the photos. I felt like a jackass for taking out my anger on her. She doesn't know any of this is going on, and it's definitely not her fault.

If I have my way, she'll never find out.

Pulling up in front of the unit at the end, I glance at my phone, making sure this is the right one. There's scaffolding all over it and it looks like they're stripping the paint or something.

I jump out of my damn skin when he knocks on the car window.

A man around Ray's age stands there, real skinny-looking, bald. He's wearing a leather jacket and gloves. He looks like he'd kill me and dispose of my body without any hesitation.

I roll down the window. "Are you Tom Brown?"

"You're late," he says. I glance at the dash. This guy's going to chew me out over two minutes? "Did you bring the money?"

Five grand. The bastard better be worth it. Luckily, Hazel had a brunch date booked with Trish, so she wasn't around to see me raid the safe.

"Yeah."

He nods. "Wait a minute and then follow me."

I'd laugh at how MI5 this is getting if there wasn't a psycho killer on my case.

I drum my fingers on the steering wheel, letting my mind wander back to an idea I had last night.

What if Millicent isn't a killer? What if she got those photos on the internet and she's trying to freak me out? Just because she *said* she was a killer, just because she sounded convincing, it doesn't mean she is. She's clearly a good actress.

But I don't believe it. There's something about her. She's not like the rest of us. Maybe I break a few rules with what I do, but I'm not feral. I'm not like her. She didn't even flinch when I got angry with her in her dingy flat. A normal woman – a skinny-as-fuck woman like her, with no way to defend herself if I attacked her – would've reacted, would've looked scared, anxious, something.

She only stared... like a freak, like a *killer*.

I climb from the car and head after Tom Brown, ducking under a scaffolding beam. The insides have been cleared out. It's all brick dust and needles and beer bottles. It's dark except for shafts of sunlight coming through broken bits of the wall.

Tom Brown walks up behind me. "I need to frisk you, Mr Smithson."

I spin on him. I really wish this prick would stop sneaking up on me. "You're joking."

"I can assure you I am in no way joking." It's difficult to place his accent. It's almost posh, but it's also rough. If nowhere had an accent, it'd be Tom Brown. "Up against the wall."

"Fuck me." I walk over to the wall and place my hands against it.

He pats me down efficiently, slipping his hand into the pocket of my shorts and taking out my mobile. With the same movement, he takes the envelope full of cash from my other pocket. He's quick for an older man.

He opens the envelope and glances at the notes, and then slips it into his jacket pocket.

"Don't you want to count it?" I ask.

I'm sure he almost smiles. "I did."

He pulls my phone case open and takes out the battery, and then slides the SIM out. He does it quickly and smoothly. I don't even have time to react. By the time I've thought to ask what he's doing, it's over, and he's handing it back to me.

"Has anyone ever told you you're a little paranoid?"

"How can I help you, Mr Smithson?"

"How much has Ray told you?"

"Let me hear it from you."

This is the difficult part. Ideally, I'd tell him about Millicent's murder shrine and how she's been following me for at least six months. I'd tell him about the stand-off in her flat where she told me she's a serial killer. But then I'd have to mention Lacy and the other women.

"It involves Ray. It involves his girlfriend, I mean."

He stares. "Okay."

"Basically, she's been threatening me. She's saying she's got some dirt from my past. I don't know what she's talking about, but now she's started hanging around my wife too. I want her out of my life."

"I don't do that," Tom Brown says. "If you're implying what I think you are."

"I don't want you to *kill* her." I do want him to kill her, but it seems that's off the table. "I want you to look into her. I need something on her so she can't use whatever she has against me. I want to know who she is, where she came from, why she's doing this. Anything I can use, basically."

He nods. "A deep dive into her personal history. That won't be a problem. Do you have any idea what she has on you?"

"Nothing. She has nothing."

There it is again, that almost-smile. "You would be a special man if there were no skeletons in your closet. What could she have? Who have you wronged in the past?"

This is another problem. The most reasonable conclusion is Millicent is somehow connected to one of the women. But it's not like I can tell him that.

And, anyway, I'm certain none of them ever woke up – well, almost none.

"I don't bloody know," I grumble.

"It will be helpful if you draw up a list of people who may have a grievance against you. It could be something that seems small to you. Please think hard. This woman may be connected to them in some way."

"I'll get right on it."

Tom Brown reaches into his pocket and takes out a small notepad and pen, the sort I've seen police use in TV shows. "I'll need that now. I also need to ask you an ethical question."

I take the notepad and flip it open. I'm going to have to bullshit my way through this. I had a couple of dramatic break-ups when I was in my late teens and there are plenty of people who have gripes against me in work. But there's no way I can give him a proper list.

"Ask away."

"Do you have any objection to me breaking laws in pursuit of this information? If you do, you need to make it known now."

I grin. Now we're getting somewhere. "No, Mr Brown. I'd be pissed off if you *didn't*."

Right there. I'm sure of it. The motherfucker just smiled.

26

MILLICENT

"Say it," he breathes, his face somehow becoming even redder. "Say it, baby. Call—me—Hercules."

Sometimes I'm convinced dear Raymond is playing a game with me, the same way I play games with everybody else. *Call me Hercules*. It's simply too absurd and obscene to be true. He sprawls out on the sofa, his belt buckle rattling around his ankles as I pump my hand up and down his grotesque worm.

But no, this is he: this is Ray, in all his unremarkable ignobility.

This is rather degrading, truthfully, but I'm sure a jaguar or a lioness or an eagle doesn't relish every part of her hunt.

"Oh, my Hercules."

Pump-pump-pump.

There's nothing sexual about this, but Raymond is utterly lost to the moment. His breath gets hollow and he wheezes, the belt buckle rattling like fingernails against a weathered wooden door. Tap, tap, tap, and now my mind is brimming with blood, blood-red, not cheek-red, and I'm cradling a vignette of Raymond lying gutted on the floor with his worm softening and sinking into tangled grey pubes.

"Again, again," he croaks.

"Hercules."

Pump-pump-pump.

I refuse to believe there is any woman who enjoys this. Perhaps if Ray was somebody else, somebody who smiled at me and ran his kind fingers through my hair: perhaps if he valued me as a human being and not just as lips and tits and a slit. But even then, I doubt I'd be able to find any solace in this act.

"Argh!" he grunts, doing his business over his wobbly belly. He has stretch marks, the indulgent pig, like a pregnant woman. He sickens me. I force myself to smile sexily as his eyes blink open. "That was really something, Millie. Goddamn."

I titter and turn away, playing up my shy role. The only way to remain somewhat chaste with a man like Ray is to cultivate a virginal aura. I cannot simply say to him, *I am not ready to let you invade my body, and I may never be ready.* That wouldn't be acceptable to a man of his hunger.

I have to play the English Rose, oh-so-delicate. There are no thorns on me, kind sir.

He leans forward as if to kiss me, and I turn my face even more. His lips squelch against my cheek: slobbery, *moist.* I've heard cattle complain they hate the word *moist,* but the feeling is worse. By the time he leans away, my cheek is drenched.

"I need to use the ladies' room."

He grunts and waves a hand. His eyes have taken on an impatient quality. *A man can't live off hand jobs, darling,* he said to me a couple of nights ago after one too many sips from his leather-bound flask.

I played it demure, but he should be careful. There is only so much a woman can take.

I walk across Ray's large gaudy apartment. It's a penthouse and it's five times the size of my rented accommodation. He thinks it's sophisticated, with its fur rugs and mounted moose heads and oversized sofas, but it comes across as desperate.

Into the bathroom I glide, shutting the door behind me.

I lock it and spin to the window. What a way to spend a Saturday, locked in this tower-top cell with an ogre, like a heroine from a fairy tale. But I don't need my hair to escape this creature.

I pick up a nail file. The handle is pink and has some inane writing on the grip. *Hot Stuff.* I wonder who it belongs to, and then I remember. It belongs to me: to Millie, rather. Not to Millicent.

I could shred him to hundreds of tattered pieces with this nail file.

The window in here is a stylised porthole, and it lets in a soft yellow glow of late-afternoon sunlight, and the light twinkles like the sun is trying to become stars. It glitters and wishes it could blind, and I smile, holding my face in the light.

Moments like these almost make me feel human.

Ray knocks heavily on the door.

Oh, fuck off, you inexcusable parasite.

"Fancy a Chinese for dinner, love?"

Of course, Ray. Let's shove more calories down your fat repulsive neck.

Also, love, *love*? This man loves his prick and his flask and nothing else.

"Sounds great," I say, starry-voiced, sun-voiced.

"What do you want?"

"I'll have a little of whatever you order."

"Yeah, if there's anything left." He cackles.

I stare at myself in the mirror and draw the nail file across my throat, and as I hold my gaze, I let fly with a hyperbolic giggle.

~

Ray eats like a man recently released from prison. He slurps noodles and crushes spring rolls and speaks as he eats. Flakes of spring roll spit across the table and hang in the air before floating out of sight. He chokes himself on massive mouthfuls of Coca-Cola and then resumes his gorging before he's swallowed.

He grins across at me, widely, fully persuaded I find him – find this – attractive. How can he be so blind?

That is the way with people: they see but they are also blind, they hear but they are deaf, and on and on, until their perceptions are so shrouded in duality they can only tether themselves to private invented realities.

"How's work, my love?" I ask.

"I don't want to talk about that place. It's driving me nuts."

I reach across the table and stroke my hand along his cheek, down to his jowls. This spot, right here, where I tenderly caress – it would make the perfect point for the blade.

I'd start the motion low down at my hip so he wouldn't see it coming, and then I'd drive up with all the power in my body, swivelling my hips to help with the momentum. I can hear it sinking into the soft fleshy spot. I can see his eyes brimming with betrayal, and I smile. "Is it Jamie? Hazel mentioned he was a little stressed out."

I haven't spoken to Hazel about the little lad, but this is hardly a leap of faith. Of course Jamie is going to be stressed. He's being hunted by a professional.

"Yeah." Ray dabs at his cheek. He misses most of the sauce and then lays the napkin down. "He seems a little distracted. It's a pain in the arse, but more than anything, I'm worried about the kid. I've never seen him like this before."

Tell me more, oh, tell me more.

"Have you tried talking to him about it?"

"Yeah, we talked a bit. I even had to link him up with one of my underworld pals."

I sit up straighter, maintaining my smile. But inside I am grimacing and baring my teeth and getting ready for war. "Oh?"

"You can't tell anybody. You can't tell Hazel."

"He's cheated on her."

Of course Jamie wouldn't give Ray the whole truth.

"I don't know." What a loyal sweat sac he is. "All I can say is this bloke I've hooked him up with, he'll make it go away. He knows how to get things done, dig up dirt, that sort of thing. Jamie'll be back to his usual self before long."

Jamie's *usual self* is a freak who lurks over women as they sleep, unaware, violated. I'm not certain what he does when he's in there, but I know men, and I'd be astounded if he didn't touch himself at the very least.

Nobody can tell me Jamie doesn't deserve what's coming to him.

27

BEFORE

The Comrades were frolicking and dancing in the middle of the cul-de-sac and Millicent was standing at the window. She was looking especially at Comrade Philip and his young wife as they clasped hands and danced together, swaying to the drumbeat a Comrade pounded out with his fist, a repetitive and non-melodic drumbeat.

Comrade Philip was grotesque and Millicent hated him and she wished he was dead, and she also hated his son who was called *the little sprite* by many of the Comrades. He was a skinny boy of five years who danced and pranced and made everybody smile at him, and it wasn't fair he should be happy when Comrade Philip took Millicent to the Rainbow Room and Comrade Philip was the little sprite's father. Purple Moon was there also and he was also dancing and laughing.

Millicent stared at the little sprite and the kitten he held in his hands. It was a small kitten and it was an orange kitten and the little sprite smiled like an idiot and he danced with it and Millicent stared and stared.

"I want to go away, Mummy."

There was a *hiss*, and the *hiss* was Comrade Constance

lighting and sucking her pipe as she melted into the sofa like candle wax, and her features were slack, and she was not really a person when she sucked on that pipe.

"Please," Millicent said. "I hate it here."

"Hush. And don't... call me... *Mummy*."

She was fading and Millicent scowled and curled her hand into a fist, and she kept staring at the little sprite and the kitten. Father was out there, swaying strangely as he curled one hand around a woman's waist and his other hand was around another woman's waist. He was touching them lower than their waist and he was grinning, and Millicent wondered what his grin would look like if he had no lips or skin or human qualities.

She focused on the little sprite and his kitten, and she hated him, hated him because his father told her there was no wrong in the Rainbow Room: hated him because his father was Comrade Philip, and Comrade Philip was friends with Purple Moon, and Purple Moon and Comrade Philip knocked secretly on weathered wood, and Millicent was trapped in there and somebody had to pay. Somebody had to pay.

There *was* right and wrong, and she was right, she was right: she was right.

Millicent went to her mother and slid onto the sofa and lay against her, and even if Mother did not hug her, or acknowledge her, she was warm and she was close.

A few days became a week and then it was time for the Comrades to dance and frolic and beat their drums again, and pretend they were both beating and not beating their drums, and the sky was red and yellow and blue and green and whatever colour Father said it was.

Millicent stood at the window and stared, and she smiled as

she stared, at the little sprite who was no longer cradling his kitten. He stood at the edge of the circle and he tried not to cry. He missed his kitten very much. He did not know what had happened to his kitten. His little bird of a mother – Comrade Diana – tried to comfort him. She rubbed his back and she said some silent words, but the little sprite was too busy remembering his precious orange kitty to respond.

Millicent stared and she smiled and the drums beat louder.

She was proud of herself for a long time: for weeks and weeks, she luxuriated in this pride. She'd done it... *she* had taken control. There was a problem – that snivelling rat who was her torturer's son – and she hadn't needed to ask the grown-ups how to solve it. They could never be trusted anyway. They always did what they wanted, when they wanted, *how* they wanted.

She went to bed one night and closed her eyes, bringing a stark vivid wonderful image to her mind's eye. She saw the little boy with his chest open, with gore smeared across his neck, with his eyes wide and bulging with crimson pressure. She saw him on the verge of taking his last breath.

A knock came at the door.

It happened again, louder this time. Nobody ever knocked on her door. It was late and the street was dead-quiet.

"Millie." It was her mother's voice, pitched low, secretive. "Come on. We haven't got much time."

Millicent's heart flurried with something new. She'd never heard such conviction in her mother's voice. She was always fading in and out of their life, eyes as glassy as her pipe.

"I'm taking you away from here."

"Mother," she said, her voice a croak, the poor naïve girl. "Really?"

"Yes. Can I come in?"

"Yes."

Her mother never *asked* to come in. She rarely entered at all, but on those rare occasions she visited, she barged into the room and right out again. Once she had stormed in with an iron in her hand, waving it around as her dressing gown opened in the middle, flashing her offensive nakedness at Millie. Millie had cringed away as she held the still-hot iron close to her face, baring her teeth. "Am I a fucking slave? Is that my lot, you little slut? I'm slave to a rapist and a monster, and I'm supposed to *love* you?"

Millie had forgiven her when she broke down, dropping the iron and wrapping her arms around her. It was easy for Millie to close her eyes and sink into that safety. Mother wasn't bad; she was just scared. That was a very stupid thing for the child to think, but a girl must have something to keep her sane, or at least to stop her from free-falling into madness.

And Mother's voice was good now, not low, not mean.

Millie wasn't scared as she sat up in bed, peering through the semi-darkness. The hallway light was on, silhouetting Constance. She wore a long coat and thick boots, her hair tied in an efficient bun. She dropped a backpack on the floor, the sort of thing Father would never let her wear: pink, with pins on the strap, girly.

"Is that mine?" Millicent asked, with too much hope in her voice. The girl should've kept her joy hidden, secret, buried deep in her belly with her desire for blood. But she was still unschooled in the ways of predators.

Mother flowed into the room, her eyes bright, her smile filling the girl with confidence. This was it: the escape. This was the moment Mother realised how stupid and pointless men were, all of them, and especially Father. "Of course it is. Come on. Pack some clothes. Not too much. We need to be quick."

"Where are we going?" Millicent slid from the bed and ran over to her chest of drawers. She had been waiting for this for a long time.

"Somewhere safe. Somewhere happy. Doesn't that sound nice?"

"Yes. It really does, Mummy."

"Good girl." Her mum's hand was on her shoulder. She was squeezing her supportively, and Millicent's smile glimmered across her face. It felt wonderful. She forgot about the kitty and Comrade Philip's son. Mother had even let her call her *Mummy*. "Hurry up now."

Millicent packed swiftly. She didn't want to annoy her mother in any way, to change whatever had triggered in her. They hurried down the stairs together.

Millicent's mind flooded with brighter vignettes, with she and her mother walking through a sunlit park together, hand in hand, and laughing when a dog cocked its leg and peed on a plant... or something, anything mothers and daughters do, the stuff she'd read about in storybooks.

"That's it," Mother whispered, leading her toward the door. "Just a little further."

In the years following, Millicent would relive these moments viscerally several times, and each time would snap something inside of her. She'd remember how her mother had gone werewolf, how her kind smile had turned mocking, and most of all how her father had appeared from the hallway closet like a killer. He'd held a hammer in his hand and his lips were twisted somewhere between a smile and a grimace.

His eyes were shining in a way Millicent knew well, the way they gleamed when he'd smoked the glass pipe too much. "I know what you did."

"What, Father?" Millicent murmured, but they were far past that. "I didn't do anything."

He'd called her *liar* and leapt at her, and he'd used the hammer; it had done devastating things to her body, and then *he'd* done devastating things to her body. He didn't invade her the same way Philip and Purple Moon did, but he used other means. Mother was there for all of it, sitting in the corner, lips puckered around her pipe as her eyes lit up blue with the gas lighter.

It lasted a long time.

When it was over, Millicent was barely able to stand. Only the ropes stopped her from falling.

Her hands were tied above her head and her tiptoes just barely reached the floor, and the sun was bleeding yellow-red through the window, or maybe that was the blood seeping down her forehead. He'd hit her so many times. He hated her. Mother hated her. She couldn't trust anybody: not even herself, and now the rage came, the white-hot rage, as she stared at her father pacing up and down with the carmine hammer in his fist.

He smacked the weighted end against his hand.

"Something's wrong with you." *Smack-smack-smack.* "You captured and tortured an innocent defenceless animal. You're broken."

He had broken her body, but he didn't mean in that sense, she knew. He'd bruised several ribs and fractured her pinkie finger and left burns up and down her left thigh. He'd caused her toes to swell and the joints in her shoulders to burn with agony. He meant her soul was broken.

Millicent stared hard at him.

"What?" He darted at her, squaring his shoulders. "Don't fucking look at me like that."

She stared and stared, because he wasn't real; none of this was real. Everything that existed was only a projection of her mind. She saw it now, as pain made her body weak; she could withdraw from it all. She never had to *be* there. It was the same as in the Rainbow Room, so she floated, up and away and she stared at herself from the ceiling.

There was a small girl: blood down her nightie, petals of it on her bare thighs, staining her feet like spilt wine. Her hair was tangled and her eyes were animal.

"I'm warning you."

She stared and stared and stared.

"Fine." He lifted the hammer and stepped forward. "You godawful fucking mistake."

The blow fell and her whole world trembled, and she floated away, away... she found herself back in her fantasy, only now Father stood next to the little sprite. His wrists were slit and he was swinging back and forth on a sturdy piece of rope, his mouth open in a rictus as though his final word had been *sorry*.

28

JAMIE

"Another, sir?" the barman asks, as I stare down at my empty whisky glass.

I don't even know what I'm doing here. I told Hazel I had to schmooze a client and she accepted it, because she's trusting and incredible and perfect. I've had client meetings before on Saturday nights. She didn't think to question it.

I don't deserve her. I don't deserve anything.

Hazel would leave me if she had any sense. She knows how broken I am. Dad fucked me up. Mum left, walked out on her own kid. What sort of a woman does that?

I can't pretend anymore. I deserve better than this. I deserve a life worth living.

Okay, Mum, that's bloody great. You swan off to Italy then, leaving me behind with Dad. That makes perfect sense.

I look up at the barman. He's older than me by at least ten years, maybe more. He's got grey in his hair and his moustache is brown-grey.

"What did you want to be when you were little?"

"Astronaut," he says, with a slight smile.

"What happened?"

He shrugs. "What always happens, sir? Life gets in the way."

I move my finger around the rim of the glass. It's Saturday night and I'm sitting in a hotel bar, the sort of place where men decades older than me call me *sir*.

I want to ask him how many I've had already, but I don't want him to cut me off. I must be coming across as more sober than I feel.

"I'll take another. Make it a double."

"Of course."

I glance at the clock above the bar. It's almost midnight. The place is still pretty busy, filled with elegant women and men in suits. Soft music plays. I should be here with my wife, but why? Why? She's going to leave me when that bitch makes it public.

I've got no word from Tom Brown yet. I have no way to contact him. After giving him the list this morning, he left, back to his not-smiling routine.

The barman brings my whisky. Knocking it back, I slide the glass over to him. "Another."

He frowns for a moment, but then he pours me a fresh glass.

I knock it back, coughing away the taste, the acidic bite of it. I don't like whisky. I only drink it when I'm on the lookout for my next obsession. But even then, I never pound it like this.

Whisky is a prop.

Right now though, I'm starting to like it. Life doesn't seem as sharp as it did half an hour ago.

"Another."

There's that frown again, but he pours it and then hands it to me. He uses a fresh glass every time. My old man would lose his mind. Freddie Smithson was always a stickler for the water bill, the cheap piece of shit.

I force myself to sip this one. I need to piss, but I don't trust myself not to stumble when I stand. It's hard enough to balance as it is.

A woman slips onto the stool next to me. I think maybe I'm staring at her, but for some reason I don't give a damn. It's hard *not* to stare. She's curvy and sensual-looking. She's got big expressive brown eyes and she aims this cheeky smile at me when she sees me staring. "Do I know you?"

"I wish you did." I think I'm slurring. *Come on, Jamie. Get your game face on.* A man could forget his problems with a woman like that. "I'm J—Justin."

"I'm Julia."

"The two *J*s."

She laughs. It's such a sweet sound, such an innocent sound. She's not the sort of woman who'd walk out when things got tough. Her cleavage is on display in the sparkling golden low-cut dress. The base of my cock aches.

She's not a woman I'd select when I'm on the prowl, but this isn't about that. This is just... what? It's pointless; it's an escape. I don't even know. I should drink some water and think this through, but I won't. Goddamn, there's something wrong with me.

"Can I buy you a drink?" I ask.

Deep inside, a voice yells at me to stop. I'm in Bristol. This is home turf. This is a mistake. But what am I doing that's so bad, really? I'm just talking. It's not my fault she's beautiful.

"Really?" she says, with a cute quirk of a smile, unsure, as if she doesn't know how downright smoking-hot she is.

"It'd be my pleasure. What's your poison?"

She gives me the name of a cocktail. Pretty girls always drink cocktails, expensive shiny things that work as props as much as my whiskies do. I watch her as the barman prepares it, seeing the way she looks at me, appraising, her eyes moving over my body and my suit and my Rolex and my wealth.

She loves it. She's hungry for it. I could do this. I ache for it.

"Where's your date?"

She purses her lips, sucking on her straw. "Who says I had one?"

"You come to a lot of bars alone dressed like this, do you? You look like you're going to a ball."

She flutters her eyelashes. She's spent a lot of time on them, I can tell. She hasn't got those globules women sometimes get. "I was here with my boyfriend, actually. But he... Let's say if there was a prize for breaking up with somebody in the worst possible way, he'd get first, second, and third."

"He broke up with you *tonight*?"

"It's our one-year anniversary. We booked this hotel ages ago. We were having dinner and that's when he dropped the news. I thought he was going to propose."

"Jesus Christ. Some men are animals, Julia. You can't blame yourself."

I refuse to believe what I do is worse than what her boyfriend did. Maybe I break a few trespassing laws, but I'd never shatter a woman's heart like that. It's deranged.

She places her hand on mine and looks at me in the way women sometimes do. It's a wild look, like they're ready to let themselves go. Women need to forget as much as men. What better way is there than hot, hungry, passionate fucking?

"That means so much," she says after a long pause. "It's awful. Now I'm up there on my own. I guess I'll spend the night crying and thinking about all the things I've done wrong. Why would he abandon me?"

I place my hand on her back, rubbing softly, feeling the way her skin burns through the fabric. "It's not your fault. It's his. He's an idiot."

"That feels good."

"So you're up there alone, eh?"

She purses her lips again. She knows what she's doing. I know what she's doing. But she's waiting for me to make it explicit. She needs her dignity, after all. There's a difference between being seduced and throwing herself at a stranger.

"Sounds like you could do with some company."

She keeps sucking on her straw, going *hmm-mm* as she nods, draining her cocktail. She's getting herself ready.

It's happening. I can already taste her, every inch of her. I can already imagine the way her face will get sassy and confident as I drive up inside of her. I can feel her fingernails on my back.

"What room are you staying in, Julia?"

"Fifty-four. That's where I'll be... by myself, crying myself to sleep. Unless a knight in shining armour comes to save me."

She hops from the stool and walks away, swishing her hips, glancing at me over her shoulder before she walks around the corner.

I stare down at my whisky. I don't have to do this. My balls are bluer than ice. I don't have to do this. I love my wife. But this woman needs a little release. Hazel will never find out. I don't have to do this. But Julia's up there, getting ready for me, probably peeling her golden dress off and arranging herself on the bed. I don't have to do this. Does she shave completely, or does she have one of those stylish Brazilian thingies women sometimes get? I don't have to do this.

I need to make her scream.

I don't have to do this, do I? Do I?

My phone vibrates. A text. It's Hazel.

Heading to bed. Try not to party too hard. There's some pizza in the fridge if you're drangry when you get home. Love you xxxx

I grin when I read *drangry*. We came up with it in uni, combining drunk, hungry, and angry. We've used it ever since.

I text her back, telling her thank you, telling her I love her. And then I stand and drain the last of my whisky and I walk the same way Julia went.

29

HAZEL

"This place is even prettier in the daylight," Millie says, smiling as she drops into the patio chair.

Pride fills me up. I worked really hard on the garden. It's nice to hear somebody praise it. It's not like Jamie has expressed much appreciation over it. But then again, he *did* offer to jump into the swimming pool in his suit. Maybe that counts for something.

"It's a lovely place to sit on a sunny Sunday morning." I nod. "Would you like a coffee?"

"That would be lovely."

I go into the kitchen and fix the coffees, watching Millie through the glass doors as the machine hums and whirs. She sits completely still with her hands in her lap, like a statue.

She's a puzzle to me. She's interesting and interest*ed*. She's stylish, with her black fringe and her dark suits. But there's something else there. She reminds me of myself when I was a teenager, vulnerable but hiding it, even though she's older than me.

She toys with her pendant as I lay the flat whites on the table.

"Getting any good ideas?" I ask.

"One or two."

"Can I ask what the novel is about, or would that violate your code of secrecy?"

"It's a little macabre. I don't want to put you off your coffee."

"I've got a stronger stomach than you might think."

She looks at me, properly looks at me, in the way I love. She sees me and it makes me want to clap my hands like a little kid. *Look, Mummy, I made a new friend.* I know I'm being silly, but I don't care. "I believe you. Okay, fine. It's about a serial killer, a woman, but she only kills bad men. She only kills men who would go on to hurt women."

"They haven't hurt women already?"

She turns to the garden and sighs. It seems like she's getting touchy. "There's this theme in the book. It's like, ah, things can be real... and fake. Alive and dead. I don't know. It makes more sense in my head, I guess."

"Hey, Millie." I stare at her until she faces me.

"Yeah?"

"It sounds like a great idea. Really badass. Like an avenging angel."

"Yes!" She giggles without a hint of self-consciousness. It's infectious. "That's *exactly* what it's about. An avenging angel."

"I look forward to reading some of it. I hope you don't mind, but I had a look at your copywriting profile. Your reviews are impressive. I read a few of your samples too. You're a great writer. Not that I'm much of a judge."

She glows at the praise. I get the feeling she needs to be seen as much as I do. "I've always loved reading and writing. When I was a little girl, there was this room, this office, at the end of the garden. It was—It had lots of uses, but sometimes my parents would send me back there. You know how parents are."

"A seen-and-not-heard sort of deal?"

"Yes, exactly. My father was a little strange. He thought books, stories—*narratives*, he called them. He thought they would have a negative effect on me. He only wanted me to read certain things, to think certain things."

"Woah, that's heavy." I pick up my flat white and blow on it. "Was he religious or something?"

"Yeah, I guess so. Anyway, I'd sneak books from the library and hide them behind the rain—the office."

I chuckle. "The rain?"

She picks up her coffee, mirroring my laughter. "I haven't got any caffeine in me yet. Give me a break."

"Did you start writing around the same time?"

She takes a sip, shaking her head as she lowers the mug. She doesn't react to the heat. "In my early twenties. I tried working a few different jobs, but I found it difficult getting bossed around. At least with freelance work, I don't have anybody breathing down my neck."

I want to ask about her tattoo. I don't remember the exact date, but she called it the day her *life changed forever*. That's what she said in the gym. But this is only the third time we've met. Maybe in a few weeks, when we've become closer, I'll ask her.

I raise my mug. "Cheers, Millie. I know you've got it in you to write an incredible story."

She beams and raises her mug. "To avenging angels."

"To avenging angels," I echo.

"His lordship has finally graced us with his presence," I say, still laughing from the story Millie just told me. *He asks me to call him Hercules*, she said, both of us in hysterics. *And when he cums, he shouts, "I am Hercules!"*

Jamie stands at the door in his dressing gown, his bright

greens flitting from Millie and back to me. He seems angry for some reason, which is hardly fair when he's the one who dragged himself to bed at half past three last night. "Morning," he grunts.

"Morning, grumpy-kins."

"Afternoon," Millie says, "if you want to be technical about it."

"Hmm," Jamie mumbles, striding into the kitchen.

"Will you give me a sec, Millie?"

"Of course. I don't want to get in the way of your marriage."

"What? No, that's not it at all."

She shrugs and leans back, placing her hands in her lap, staring down the garden with an enigmatic smile on her face.

I follow Jamie into the kitchen. He stands at the coffee machine, cursing under his breath as he tries to remove the pod drawer. I walk over and flip the lid open. "You have to flip it first, remember, you silly man?"

"Hmm." He grabs a pod and jams it into the slot. He flicks the switch way harder than he needs to, and then he glares as it thrums and his mug starts to fill.

"Jamie, is there any reason you're not speaking in complete sentences? Just so I know."

He sighs. "Why is she here, H?"

"She texted me and asked if she could come over for a chat. Why do you care?"

He runs a hand through his hair. "I don't—I... You know better than to make friends with Ray's girlfriends. He's going to drop her in a few weeks, and then it'll be awkward when she's still hanging around."

"Maybe. But that's not my problem. I like her. She's my friend."

"Your *friend*? You've known her for a week."

"So what? I'd only known you for a few minutes before I knew you were the one for me."

He smiles, his eyes getting hazy. For a mad moment I think he's going to cry. "Oh, H." He pulls me into a hug and kisses the top of my head, squeezing me tightly. "I love you."

"I love you too." I close my eyes and sink into him. "But please stop being silly."

"I'll try."

Millie clears her throat from the patio door. I turn to find her with her hands clasped in front of her. She's holding two envelopes. My name is written on one, and I see Jamie's on the other.

"I wanted to give you these before I left. It's a little something to say thank you for being so kind and inviting me into your home."

"That's lovely." I glance at Jamie. He's gritting his teeth, like it's Millie's fault Ray is an absolute pig toward women. "*Isn't* it, Jamie?"

"Oh, yeah." He forces a smile. "Really kind, Millie. Thank you."

She places them on the counter. "Could you please open them after I leave? I get a little self-conscious."

"Sure." Jamie strides across the room and grabs his card, slipping it into his dressing gown pocket. I hope he's wearing boxers under there. "I wouldn't want to make you uncomfortable."

"Thank you, Jamie. Ray's right about you. You really are such a great bloke. Anyway, I'll be off."

"Wait a sec." I reach into my pocket. "Let's have Jamie take our picture. It'd be a shame not to."

"Really? To put online, on your page?"

"Sure. Why not?"

She brushes down her suit jacket. "I'm underdressed."

I laugh. "No, Millie, you're really not. Come on."

I hand Jamie my phone and skip over to Millie, looping my arm around her shoulder. Jamie has his grumpy face on again. He always hates it when I put him on photo duty. He taps his thumb quickly, moving around a little, taking dozens of photos – I've trained him well – before handing it back to me.

He grabs his coffee. "I'm taking this to bed. This hangover's lethal. See you again, Millie."

Millie smiles. "Soon, I hope."

I walk her to the door and we share a quick hug. She walks down the driveway toward her car. It's a rundown Fiesta. Black, of course. And when I see it, I mutter a silent prayer that her novel takes off and she can afford something magnificent one day.

"Don't be a stranger," I call after her.

"I wouldn't dream of it," she calls back.

I return to the kitchen and open the envelope. It's a thank-you card, in big colourful letters. *I've never been very good at making friends*, she's written inside. *But thank you for giving me a chance, Hazel. It means a lot. With love, Millicent.*

30

JAMIE

It's Monday lunchtime, and instead of having some sushi with a client or talking shit with Ray over a burger, I'm standing in an abandoned industrial unit with a psycho's letter in my hand. This place is becoming my regular hangout spot. Maybe I should bring a foldout chair next time. Goddamn.

I almost shat myself when she took those envelopes out. I knew she was pulling the same stunt she pulled at the party. And I was right. Hazel's card was a fake little message about how Millie wants to be friends.

Mine read, *Enough games. You asked me what I wanted. What does anybody want, little lamb? Ten grand and you never see me again.*

She put a time and an address below: a park close to the city centre. I'm supposed to meet her tonight. But I'd prefer if Tom Brown gave me something I could use against her, something to make her stop.

Our savings aren't infinite. I've got six grand cash in the safe... well, one grand after Mr Brown took his cut. And I've got seventeen thousand in the bank. That's a lot for a twenty-six-year-old bloke, if I do say so myself. If I have to give her ten to make her vanish, fine. I'll do it. I can make more money. But I don't *want* to.

I was relieved when Ray came swaggering into my office this morning. *Got another meeting. Same place. One o'clock. I don't have to tell you not to be late. He's probably already got your grave picked out.*

I laughed.

Ray grinned, but it was a little shaky, a little forced. It's the booze. It's messing him up. It's Millicent. She's encouraging his worst habits.

I need her gone.

Tom Brown finally arrives, the hypocrite. The attitude he gave me last time when I was two minutes late, and he swaggers in like he's got all the time in the world.

"Afternoon."

The skeletal bastard frowns. "You know the drill."

"Yeah, yeah."

I put my hands against the wall and let him frisk me. He chuckles when he finds I've already taken my phone apart, leaving the separate pieces in my pocket.

"You catch on quick, Mr Smithson."

"Call me Jamie, mate. This is starting to get ridiculous."

"Okay, Jamie. I need to show you something."

I can't stop myself from smiling. Now we're getting somewhere. He needs to show me something. Surely that means he's got some dirt on this lunatic, something I can use to make her disappear.

"You've been digging into her past? What've you got? Please tell me it's something that'll make her think twice before she—"

"It's not good news. I'm still looking into her past, but this isn't about that."

He stares blankly at me, his expression impossible to read.

I make a *get on with it* gesture. "Okay..."

"How would your wife react if she discovered you'd slept with another woman?"

"What? Who the fuck do you think you are? I love Hazel. I'd die before I hurt her."

I remember the way Julia moaned for me, the way she bounced, twitched. I remember the way she looked up at me, with her wide eager eyes, and I hate myself. I hate myself, but I did it anyway.

"I broke into her flat," Tom Brown says.

"Right. And what did you find?"

"Most people express some shock when I tell them I've broken into somebody's home."

I'm not most people, Mr Brown.

"What did you find?" I snap.

He reaches into his leather jacket and takes out his phone. "A memory stick. Nothing else... nothing else of importance, anyway. Some clothes, stuff like that. But this is all that matters. I copied the video."

There's a lump in my throat. Whatever this is, it isn't good. He seems even more serious than usual.

He presses play and shows me his phone.

There I am, and there's Julia. The camera must've been hidden on the dresser drawers, but she purposefully left all the lights off except for the lamps above the bed. The video shows everything. It shows me. It shows her. She's moaning in pleasure.

I fuck her hard, passionately. I fuck her like she's my wife. I fuck her like I love her.

"Jesus Christ. That's enough. This was all you found?"

"Yes."

"Did you take the memory stick at least?"

"She's most likely made copies. And it would've aroused her suspicion."

I breathe heavily, running a hand through my hair. "She set me up."

"It looks that way, yes."

I wish she was here so I could wrap my hands around her throat, and squeeze, and *squeeze* until her eyes bulged out of her skull. She was following me Saturday night, the same way she's been following me for six months.

She's got me by the balls. She's a goddamn devil.

I'm going to have to pay her. What else am I supposed to do now?

Ten grand. I can live with that. Ten grand and Hazel never sees this. Ten grand and I get to keep my marriage. Why did I have to sleep with that woman? What the hell is wrong with me?

"Keep digging," I tell him. "This is fucked. This is beyond fucked. But keep digging, please."

"I will. In the meantime, you should be more careful."

I glare at him. If this is his idea of a joke, it's not even remotely funny. "Yeah, no shit."

31

MILLICENT

I stand at the edge of the river, the moon-silver water lolling at my feet, subjugating itself before me. It knows what I'm going to gift it: my dolls, the ring, my memories.

It was foolish to leave the lockbox in my rented accommodation, prey to Jamie's hired goon. If it were not for the *pump-pump-pump* with dear old Raymond, I wouldn't have known the hunted boy was striking back. I wouldn't have elegantly danced through the streets for his goon, never letting him know – as I hadn't let Jamie know in Cardiff – I was in charge.

I wouldn't have needed to hire the escort, to set up the hotel room. It was easy: telling Ray I was oh-so-sorry but I had to work tonight, and then driving to Jamie's home, and watching, grinning.

Where are you going, sweet Jamie?

When I saw it was a hotel, I had to clasp my hands over my mouth, fitfully laughing in my parked car.

It was as though he was a doll and I was fiddling his limbs into the right position.

A simple phone call, and there she was, my Julia. *Give me five to fix the hotel room*, I told her. And she said, *All right, but recording's extra.*

Fine, yes, you poor thing, you can have your paltry payment. What a sad existence she lives, peeling her lips apart and letting strangers splurge into her hole for a few hundred pounds.

Not that *I* had to pay. I took the money from Ray's wallet and, if he noticed, he never thought to ask darling Millie. He's also extremely negligent with his banking app. He types in the password right in front of me. He doesn't even check his statements.

Yes, I did all of that very well, but it's led me here, to this.

I hold my dolls in a tight fist, blinking back tears.

"I'm sorry," I tell my burnt lady, dropping her. She falls and she splashes. "I'm sorry. I'm sorry."

I let fly the men, and they go the same way as their old friend. Tossing the engagement ring costs me very little. It's a trinket, nothing more. It was never meant for me. It was meant for a woman who'd kiss my feet if I explained why I did what I did: who'd sing my name and beg me to teach her my craft.

Lastly, I run my fingers over my custom memory stick. I remember when I had this made in a computer shop in London, how I skipped through Hyde Park like a fresh-made thing. I wanted to scream at the passers-by, *Look what I have, look what I've done. Kneel at my legacy.*

I should not allow sentimentality to stop me, and yet I find I can't pull the memory stick from my heart. I've become too accustomed to its pressure against my skin: the coolness of it, the familiarity of my achievements.

I have abandoned my dolls. Surely that's enough.

I turn away from the water. I have a meeting with Jamie. The little lamb thinks it's going to be over soon.

We will see, Jamie Smithson. We will see.

~

I think of Hazel as I walk.

I told her truths about myself yesterday: about the Rainbow Room, about secreting away to sink into the world of books. I told her about the pain that festers ceaselessly beneath the surface of my livestock smile, and even if she didn't comprehend the true magnitude of my words, she cared. She empathised. She said *avenging angel* without my prompting, as though she could hear my thoughts shimmering in the air.

I need to stop this. I can't allow myself to care about this woman, this facile thing with her phoney smiles and her spurious beauty. I have studied the photograph she forced Jamie to take of us yesterday, and it's clear she used some kind of image-enhancement software to render us smoother, shinier, faker.

She changed me without my permission. I should hate her for that.

But I don't. She makes me *feel*. Not the light, but something. I told myself I was writing what was necessary when I filled up her card, but that's a lie. I meant it. She's giving me a chance at friendship.

I pause outside Tesco Express, staring through the glass windows at the brightness within.

The mother is wearing far too much make-up, with her hair far too effortfully styled. I can tell right away she's the sort of woman who cares more about herself than her child: her child who lifts two bottles of wine from her basket and places them on the shelf. The boy's eyes glisten with the onset of tears. The eyes are Jamie-green.

The woman scowls at him and returns the bottles to the basket.

My breathing comes far too frantically, clamorous in my

ears. Mothers should be there for their children, physically and mentally.

Self-medication is unacceptable.

I am in the shop, somehow. I don't remember marching through the entrance, but the air is cooler in here, the lights stark and abrasive.

The woman is at the self-service checkout.

"Mum." The boy's voice tremors. "Please."

I walk over to her and smile widely, so the security cameras will see a smiling woman and not the beast trying to erupt out of me. She looks up, her reflected smile shaky, her eyes cattle-curious as she decides if I know her or if she knows me.

"You're a pathetic alcoholic bitch," I tell her pleasantly.

"Excuse me?"

"I said you are a pathetic alcoholic bitch. Your son only wants the best for you. He doesn't want you to destroy yourself with liquor. Do you have any idea how difficult it was for him to stand up to you, to put those bottles back on the shelf? Do you have any idea how *shameful* it is for your own child to have to do that?"

She looks at me like my victims do, her eyes swelling with the certainty of her demise. She understands – I can see she understands – I am not like her. I am made of sabre teeth and fire-charred bone and I could slam her face into the self-service screen until she had no nose left, and she understands this as she gazes at me.

"I don't—What are you—You have no—"

I move closer, letting her see the restrained rage behind my eyes. Nobody tries to intervene. Outside the private closeness of this conversation, we must appear as friends. "If you ever subject your child to the shame of a substance-dependant mother again, I am going to find you, and I am going to slit your throat. Nod if you understand. I said *nod*."

"I'm having a party," she murmurs, nodding nonetheless, reacting to my command because she has no inner will. "The wine isn't for me, not just for me. He wants to buy some V-Bucks. It's this online currency. This Fortnite thing. That's why he doesn't want me to buy the wine. We can't afford both." She pauses. She hardens. "Do I know you? This must be a misunderstanding."

"I..." I shake my head, and then I glance at the boy. He's gazing at me as though I'm the problem. "Is this true? *Is this true?*"

He nods and buries his face against his mother's hip.

The woman begins to react, as the brain-dead will: slowly, always too late. "You have no right to..."

I stumble through the shop, clawing at my throat. Tightening and torturing, it closes. The air is suddenly too thin. Even outside, I can't breathe.

What is happening to me?

I find myself in an alleyway. I drop onto the stone and I shiver, and I keep shivering.

This isn't what feeling is supposed to be.

This is Hazel's fault. I can't be her friend. I'm not capable of friendship.

And yet I can't suppress the voice, not completely. It screams in a little girl's tenor, locked away in a grim stone cell, cracking as she begs the earless for some reprieve. I shudder, and the trapped girl screams, *Hold me, Hazel, hold me and tell me I'm a person just like you.*

32

JAMIE

I can feel the envelope against my chest, easily slotted into my inside pocket. There's something wrong with that. My old man spent weeks complaining about a tenner here, twenty quid there, and here I am with ten grand and it hardly weighs a thing.

The evening is rainy and the park is miserable-looking. I don't want to be here. But I don't have a choice.

A homeless man sits at the entrance, head bowed. He looks up as I walk by. He's got blond hair, with streaks of brown dirt in it. He doesn't say anything. He holds his hand out, giving it a little shake, cupped like he's ready to catch any pennies I throw at him.

I grit my teeth and walk on. I'd rather he tried to steal the money from me. Begging is degrading. Sometimes I have nightmares where I'm homeless.

The park is empty apart from a few kids on the far end. Millicent waits for me under a tree, looking like a horror villain in her black coat, black boots, black umbrella. She stares at me, not moving an inch.

I hate this woman.

Ten grand. I can stomach it. I need her gone.

She inclines her head as I approach. My shoes stick in the muddy ground.

"Millicent. I've got your—"

She reaches into her jacket pocket and pulls out a business card. She flashes it to me. *Turn out your pockets and show me your phone.*

"Are you joking?"

Her smile spreads slowly as she flips the card around. *Or I'll tell Hazel what you are.*

My jaws ache like crazy. I haven't grinded my teeth this much in years. I might have to start wearing the gumshield thing at night again. I don't have a choice. That's what I keep telling myself. As I take out my phone, all I can think is, *The fuck else am I going to do?*

Millicent switches off the recording app on my phone and shakes her head. "That wasn't very polite, was it, little lamb? I don't recall giving you permission to record me."

"Why are you doing this?"

"We're the same, Jamie."

"For fuck's sake. Are we really going to do this? *We're the same, you and I.* No, you psycho bitch, we're not the same. You're a serial killer."

"What a silly conclusion to arrive at." She tosses her head airily. She's confident. She's beautiful. Why can't she be wrinkled and scarred and ugly? "You saw some photographs and you immediately assumed I'd killed those poor men myself. Does that seem reasonable to you?"

"Who are you, then?" I clench my fists.

"Do you remember Sadie?"

"You know I do." Sadie was the woman I chose before Lacy. "You were following me, so why don't we cut the bullshit?"

"Did she never mention she had a sister?"

"No." I watch her closely. At least this would make some sort of sense.

"I'm her older sister. We were estranged when you preyed on her. Otherwise, it never would've happened. Silly Sadie, gullible Sadie... Do you have any idea how devastated she was when you ghosted her? Do you have any idea how insane it drove her? I couldn't let that stand. But I'm tiring of you now, of your little unimportant life. Hand over the money and you'll never see me again."

"But you were already following me. That doesn't make sense if you only learned about me afterward. Nice try."

She spreads her hands. "The money, Jamie."

"I'm right though, aren't I? That was one hundred per cent certifiable bullshit."

"It was both the truth and a lie. Now, the money. Please don't make me ask again."

"I've been thinking about that. I really don't feel like paying you."

She grins. It's all teeth. "That's because I haven't shown you the video yet."

"What video?"

I get ready to act surprised. Of course I know what damn video she's going to show me. The bitch set me up and now she's going to lord it over me. But I can't let her know I've already seen it, because then she'll know I've broken into her flat. Tom Brown is my best shot at fighting back. I can't mess this up.

She produces her phone with a flourish. And there it is. There's me and there's a woman who isn't Hazel, who isn't even in Hazel's universe. The moaning and the messy clash of our bodies is even sicker the second time.

"Okay," I growl, waving a hand. "I'll pay. And then you're gone, right?"

"Oh, Jamie. My meanie boyfriend broke up with me. Will you be my saviour? Will you fuck the break-up out of me?"

I take the envelope from my pocket. "I've got the damn money."

"I've only spoken to you for five minutes." She pouts and flutters her eyelashes. "But I'm already oh-so-desperate for your cock. Oh, what an absolute *man* you are."

"Do you want it or not?"

I won't explode like I did in her flat. I think she likes it. I think she gets off on it.

"Yes, yes." She sighs. "Ten grand and I go *poof*. Give it here."

"How do I know you'll really leave?"

"Because I have other, more important, pursuits."

"Killing people, you mean."

"I printed those photos from the internet to frighten you. I bought some offal from the butchers and spread it over the bed. Are you really so woefully impressionable?"

"Just speak normal. Fuck me. This isn't a Jane Eyre novel, sweetheart."

"Austen – Jane Eyre was a character. But I see your point. I'll speak your language. *Oh, you silky whore, you silky fucking slut.* What did you mean, by the way? Why were you calling her *silky*?"

"I was..." I laugh without humour, shaking my head. "I'm not playing this game. Take the money and fuck off before I lose my patience."

"It makes no sense. *Silky.*"

"She was wearing silk. She was soft. I don't bloody know." I wave the envelope in her face. "Take it."

"I've never known a man so desperate to part with such a large sum. But fine, if you insist."

She takes it and walks toward the path, heels clicking as she leaves me. And leaves my life, hopefully. Maybe this can work out. Ten grand is a lot of money to somebody who lives above an electronics shop. She can kill people or play with Ouija boards or whatever the hell she does for fun, as long as she does it someplace else.

Wait, what the fuck?

I rub rainwater from my eyes.

No, I'm not seeing things.

She's handed my ten grand to the homeless bloke, and the homeless bloke is running from the park.

By the time I reach the gate, he's disappeared from the park and the surrounding streets.

I run up and down, looking along alleyways, bumping into people and yelling at them to get out of my way.

He's gone. The bastard's disappeared.

I end up back at the park, panting, my chest tight from the running. I'm soaked with rain and sweat.

Millicent leans against the stone pillar by the gate, tapping her shoe against the ground. "No luck?"

I move toward her. "You fucking *bitch*."

Her free hand darts to her inside jacket pocket and pauses there. She narrows her eyes at me, flinty, focused. I don't like that look. She weighs half as much as me. I could snap her like a twig.

But I don't like that look.

"Did you really think this was about money? Could you honestly be so naïve?"

"What then?" I slam my fist against my chest. "What, Millicent? What the fuck do you want?"

"Perhaps I'll tell you before this ends. Or perhaps you'll bleed out before I get the chance. In any case, my purpose will be served. I will stand in the light."

"The light, okay," I say. "Let me help you. How can I help you get the light?"

These words are rubbish. But maybe I need to speak her language.

"If you truly want to help me..." She pushes away from the wall. I cringe back despite myself. Her hand is shifting in her pocket. "Take a very sharp razor blade and slit vertically up your wrist. Write the word *sorry* on the wall as many times as you can in your blood. And then, to ensure your worthless life is effectively extinguished, hang yourself as you bleed out."

She pulls her hand from her pocket.

I leap back, raising my hands. I'll smash her head in if she tries to stab me.

She pops a chewing gum into her mouth. "Want one? No? Okay. See you soon, little lamb."

She strides away, leaving me breathless. I feel lost. I don't know what to do.

33

MILLICENT

I used to believe in fairy tales. When I was a little girl I'd bury my head in these magical books, believing everything would work out in the end: the knight would charge and tip his lance, and all my life's difficulties would be unhorsed. I'd imagine I was a princess, bewitching and calm, and out there a prince was waiting for me.

I gave Jamie a good fright earlier this evening in the park. I'd arranged the dance beforehand: the homeless man would flee to a nearby church, skulking in the graveyard, and I would meet him and take my cut.

Seven thousand for me and three for him.

I think that's fair, especially because all he'll do is buy heroin and hookers and whatever else sad fucks like him indulge in.

Laughter gripped me when he actually showed up, my stack of notes ready. The only smart thing he did was hide his share. The idea of slaughtering him and searching his corpse occurred to me, but that would interfere with my plans.

Instead I got close and grinned in his pathetic face. *You should've run and kept it for yourself, moron.*

Now that playtime with Jamie is over, it's time to toy with his wife. But not in a cruel way, not in a selfish way.

Whatever I do to Hazel, it will be for her own good.

The more I think about it, the more convinced I become she can be my escape. She can bond with me and be my friend and share jokes with me. She can be the sister I never had. There will be blood and there will be pain, but after the violence I'll support her, become her closest friend.

But she might not realise how special I am unless I nudge her a little. It sounds like such a crazy thing: a hacker, the Dark Web. But the man came through.

I hit *refresh* and a smile peels across my face, like my skin is stripping from my cheeks. I giggle at the thought, taking a very small sip of whisky. It's rough and it burns my insides. I'll have to take a smaller sip next time; I feel far too woozy.

I take a breath, fighting down the thought that I'm like Mother. Here I am, seeking solace in oblivion the same way she did – the same way she'd humiliate herself and prostrate herself and even prostitute herself if it led to her fix. She didn't care she had a daughter to take care of, a life to be lived. She watched, she condoned, no, no... She *participated* in the torture, and all because of this.

I knock back the rest of the glass and hit *refresh*.

With each click I am taking something from Hazel, as though she's hanging from meat hooks in a windowless room and I'm wielding a whip. I imagine slashing the hot leather down her naked body, fine red lines appearing on her sumptuous skin. I imagine getting closer, nibbling the inside of her thigh, dragging my tongue close to her.

What the fuck am I doing?

My hand is wedged between my legs, the same way it would when I was a girl. There I was: the fucking *freak*, acting in inappropriate ways because it was all I knew. I can't touch myself as I fantasise about her. I can't ruin what we have, the same way the Comrades ruined what I had.

What Hazel and I have is going to be pure, platonic, honest.

I grip the edge of the table, my hands shaking, my whole body shaking with the need to do something.

It's those old memories, linked to the rare arousal, the rare longing for something, a hot human body pressed against mine. It's tossing my mind back to tangled pained recollections, the good inexorable from the bad. Vignettes attack me, schoolboys crowded round, one of them laughing and another chewing gum, standing over me...

I rise to my feet and pace up and down the room.

The only light comes from the laptop screen and the street outside. Music plays in one of the adjacent properties. It pumps and I wish they'd turn it up louder, so the whole building wobbled and I wouldn't have to think about this: about a note left outside my bedroom on Mother's Day.

Make sure to get your mother something nice.

I'd cradled that letter for a long time, trying to work it out, wondering why Father cared enough.

He didn't. It was a lie, a trick: one of his twisted games.

When I presented Mother with the bow I'd bought her – using money I'd cleverly acquired while roaming – she laughed in my face. Everybody laughed, pointing their fingers at me, as Mother danced around the room and rubbed the bow against her bare breasts and her bare vagina and everything else. Everybody was naked, all of us standing there naked, and I didn't think to question it...

What is wrong with me?

"No, no, *no*," I hiss. "They were evil. They twisted you. You were a child. You were a good person. Those motherfuckers changed you; they made you. And look what you fucking did. You ruined them. We gut that piece of meat real easy, didn't we, when we were old enough. Remember the eyes in the night-dark. Remember the way they flinch when they turn, if they turn, and the crunching sound their skulls make when they don't. Remember the bottle plunged effortlessly into their soft throats, the groan he made as he collapsed onto his knees and begged for his mother."

I cut off, dropping onto the bed and letting out a long breath. Even if nobody's here, I'm embarrassed about that poor display, letting silly unimportant past events affect how I feel now. Sometimes I have to talk to myself, to convince myself to calm down. It veers dangerously close to cattle territory, but I'm a human being, and being non-cattle didn't save Father.

I do some breathing exercises, closing my eyes and focusing, my mind fixated on the expansion of my lungs alone. Everything else drifts away: the bed beneath me and my clothes and my body, my skin, my guts and everything else. The breath is all there is, and it passes in and out, in and out, until I can open my eyes with predator calm.

I was abused as a child. It's over. There's nothing I can do to change it.

I return to the laptop, hitting *refresh* and staring at the screen.

But there's lots I can do to change *her*.

34

HAZEL

I don't even think about it anymore. I wonder about that sometimes. I wake up, and before I know it, my phone's in my hand. Sometimes, in those little moments, I'll ask myself why I'm doing this right away. But that's my sleepy brain trying to trick me. I *need* to check my phone. My followers always change overnight.

Increasing my following is a vital part of my career. My future career, anyway, since I don't make loads of money yet.

But I will. I know I will. I've got the potential to be an Insta-superstar.

I can hear Jamie in the shower. Birds tweet outside the window, maybe using the bird feeder I bought and assembled myself. There's traffic and I can smell my own sweat.

But I can't *see* anything except for my phone.

I lost thirty-six followers last night.

I haven't lost followers since I was a teenager. It doesn't make sense. I'm doing everything right, everything the bigger influencers do.

I'm riding trends. I do my research. I kill myself in the gym and I drink fucking *cucumber* juice and I've lost thirty-six followers.

I laugh. I don't even care if it comes out crazy and shaky.

"Cucumber juice." I shake my head. "Pineapple juice isn't that bad, no way, but cucumber juice? Less sugar. Less *taste*. How's that for an advert? Maybe I should get a cucumber juice contract. Fuck, fuck, *fuck*."

I used to talk to myself as a girl. Dad was at sea and Mum didn't care and I was a shy little girl, so I talked to myself and I watched TV. I even read books sometimes.

I'm shaking.

I try to think of the horrors in the world, the people without food, without water. I'm lucky. I'm privileged. I'm blessed.

But I can't. They're them and I'm me. Just because bad things are happening a thousand miles away or even next door, it doesn't change how badly I want to bite my arm, in the same exact place: slot my teeth into the previous mark like a promise.

Thirty-six followers. Thirty-six people, actual humans, looked at my page and said to themselves, *This isn't for me. She's not pretty enough. She's not funny enough. She's not engaging enough.*

How much skinnier do I need to be? I haven't got a six-pack. I've got a faint outline. Most people don't like the really fit look though, not with women. But maybe I need to lose a few more pounds, shave a percentage off my body's fat content. Are my teeth white enough? I had braces when I was a teenager and they're pretty straight, but they don't sparkle. Maybe I should get them professionally whitened. What about my clothes? Do I need new clothes?

I know what I could do, *would* do, if I wasn't married. I'd have countless options then. A young woman who's willing to cross a few lines on social media can make her fortune.

I could hunt down Kirk Hope on our shared birthday, laser

in on him, blow him until his balls are gasping for relief and then take a few well-thought-out photos. I could leak some topless snaps of me. I've got enough followers where people would take notice.

I want to tear my hair out. Maybe I'll bite myself later, once Jamie's at work, when he won't interrupt me. I'll probably talk to myself all day. My heart is pounding too hard. It hurts.

I need to remember my marriage. What Jamie and I have, it goes beyond fame.

Jamie's stressed. Work is getting to him. I'm his rock.

Whatever else is true about us – whatever dark alleys cut through our relationship – he's always been able to rely on me. Even when I hate *why* he's relying on me, what he's confiding in me, what I'm forced to accept, I've been there for him. Because that's what a wife does. It's her job as much as it's a husband's duty to provide, and one day we'll have children and I'll have to be even sturdier for him. I have to remember that, no matter how I feel, I have a purpose.

I meant the oaths we took under the star-bright altar. I truly meant them, with as much conviction as a person is capable of feeling.

I'll have to work out a way to fix this without prostituting myself online. And not because I'm better than the women who use their bodies to get ahead in this game. I *would* do that if I didn't love Jamie, if I didn't know how much it would bother him.

Marriage is loyalty. People can say anything they want about my mum and dad, but they've been married for twenty-seven years and they're as loyal as soldiers to each other. Which fitting. Marriage is a war, and I'm a front-line trooper. Whatever we do, we do together.

And yet isn't that just bullshit? Mum and Dad's marriage is a sham: as much as mine and Jamie's is a sham.

The things we let our men get away with...

The shower has stopped. The door to the en suite is opening with a soft creak. I quickly wipe my cheeks with the quilt. I didn't even know I was crying.

I make myself as bright and shiny as Jamie expects me to be. He needs my support. He won't talk about it. But something is really bothering him at work, something big. Maybe there's a merger or a takeover or whatever they call it.

"You all right, H?" He has a towel wrapped around his waist and steam rises from his thick-muscled body.

"Don't I look all right?"

"You look incredible. You always do. I was just wondering about the freaky smiling routine."

I shake my head, tossing my hair.

Please see me, Jamie. Please see how upset I am. Please don't make me tell you. Please, please, I beg you... Please, Jamie, don't offer me solutions. Don't tell me everything will work out. Let me cry and feel like my tears aren't pathetic, even if they are, even if I know they are. Please tell me I'm real.

"Sorry for *smiling*. I was actually going to ask if you wanted egg and bacon for breakfast, but now I don't think I'll bother."

He chuckles and races over to the bed, dropping the towel. We wrestle and we laugh. We kiss. We toy with the idea of having sex, but Jamie doesn't have the time.

As he starts to get dressed, I pick up my phone and stare at my follower count.

Eleven more have abandoned me.

35

BEFORE

The dolls had been perfect once, but now they were burnt and parts of their insides were showing. They were like regular people in that way: like the Comrades and the parents who wished they weren't parents, like the lady in the supermarket who'd forgotten half her shopping list. They wore their smiles and their kind eyes and they whispered their saintly words, and they bowed in the right places and knelt and stooped and laughed, and they were people – people like these dolls were people – and they were all hiding something.

All of them, the little girl thought as she ran her fingernails up and down the dolls' bodies. She was in the corner of her bedroom and it was dark and it was night-time, and she leaned over her dolls and tortured them subtly with her nails, digging harder and harder the louder her parents became.

"Don't pretend there's a point," Constance snapped. "We both know what this is."

"Keep your voice down, woman," Comrade Charles snarled, and he sounded like *Master*, the name he'd earned for these godly displays of rightful rage.

"I'm right," Constance hissed, a little quieter.

Millicent listened closely. She was nine, and some people thought that made her silly and gullible, but no, she was learning. She was a huntress now, and she would hurt them all, every last demon who'd taken his nick of her flesh.

She'd hurt kind in kind, and the severest punishment would always wait for whoever harmed her worst. Kneeling there, she felt certain it would be her father. Who else could scar her as he had? It was *Charles* who insisted Mother never be allowed to mother her. He must've told Philip and Moonie to take her to the Rainbow Room, because nothing happened in the cul-de-sac without her father's say-so.

In the years to come, she would learn her mistake. Somebody could cut her far deeper.

"Would you have us live like everybody else?" Charles said.

"Listen to yourself. You say that like they're cattle."

"They *are* cattle. They live as they're *told* to live. I refuse to stoop to that."

"Oh, God, listen to yourself." Constance hadn't been smoking the pipe and Millicent detected the change in her voice. This was *Strong Mummy*, who Millicent had seen less and less since she was very little. "Nothing you say makes any sense. Good and bad, black and white, blah-blah-blah, Charley. Don't pretend this is about your fucking *cause*."

"I am trying to change the world."

"And that involves fucking your friends' wives, does it?"

"This again? Get a grip, Connie. You sound psychotic."

"I've seen you dancing."

"Dancing? It's part of the ritual, but you'd know that if you spent less time smoking crack, you druggie whore."

Millicent picked up her father and her mother and she mashed them together, and she hit her father hard, harder, until Mother was on top and he was pinned beneath her. "That's how you speak to me." Mother sounded like she was fading. *Hiss-hiss-hiss.* "The mother of your child."

Millicent knew what the *hiss-hiss-hiss* was, but she thought maybe she could think it was a snake. There was a snake in the wardrobe and she had to protect all three of them, and that was the *hiss* and the *hiss* and the *hiss*. It wasn't what she knew it was: the pipe, the sucking, the inhaling, the fading. She was fading, and Millicent wiped a tear from her cheek.

"You can't even go in the garden like we discussed," Father said. "You really are pathetic."

"Call me a crack whore and I might as well act like one." *Hiss-hiss-hiss.* "Mmm, this is scrumptious." *Hiss-hiss-hiss.* "I was right, you know. About this. About this life."

"Sit down, Connie, for fuck's sake. You need to slow down. You're embarrassing yourself."

"You knew how to handle a naïve girl like me. Give me a pipe and then give me *your* pipe, eh, you handsome pervert."

"Connie, you can barely move. Stop it."

"Why? You like it."

He *did* like it. Millicent noted it down. Her mother was using her body to make Charles talk how she wanted, to soften, to take the sharpness off his words. Millicent didn't quite understand it, but she knew she could use it, one day, the same way everything she did was a rehearsal. She was training. Nobody knew how clever she was. Nobody knew how much stronger she was: than her parents, than the Comrades, than everybody.

"You can't say things like that, Connie."

"What? It's bullshit. It is."

"No... it's—"

"You had an idea. But you can't quite put it into words. Which is strange, hmm? Because you *used* to write about it academically. I'm sure it has *nothing* to do with the drugs. And now you've got a lot of mindless goons working at factories because it's *humbling* work. They give you their wages, which don't amount to much on their own, but pay you a nice salary when they're stacked together. You get to fuck all the enthusiastic wives and daughters you want, and poor Connie has to lie around begging for your oh-so-impressive cock."

Her father was growling. No, he was chuckling. His laughter rumbled through the walls and Millicent clasped her hands to her belly and pretended it was her laughter booming bigly.

"When you describe it like that, I sound like a criminal mastermind."

"Oh, you *are*. Now come and *mastermind* me, Master."

Millicent crawled to the other side of her bedroom. She moved like a cat, silently, making her feet and hands into paws and not letting her knees or elbows or body touch the ground. She was even quieter than a cat.

She crawled through the moonlight-blue section of the room, the floorboards glowing like they were coloured-in. She liked to pretend – and she liked to believe – the moonlight was hunting her.

She sat in the corner and hugged her knees and moved her head down between her knees, and she gripped hard so she was covering her ears: flattening her ears. She didn't want to hear the next bit.

She listened to the silence and the echoing bone of her skull, like a seashell, and she could hear the sea, beckoning. She'd get there one day. She'd walk onto the lighted shores and show them all how exceptional Millicent Maidstone really was.

In the afternoons she would often sneak away from the enclosed hell of their cul-de-sac, running through the fields until she came to a small collection of hills that overlooked some houses:

some magic, impossible houses where crazy things happened. She would sometimes bring a book or sometimes just sit there, gazing as mothers pushed their children on swings, as whole families laughed and bounced on trampolines, as a big sister picked her little brother up and wiped at his chin.

She watched this little boy and girl for many weeks, gazing in amazement as they traipsed around the garden together, always watching out for each other. The girl was older, but she was scared of insects, so her courageous little brother would march in there and paw at the air whenever one appeared. Millie doubted he ever got one, but he was trying to protect her.

Or was he just pretending?

Maybe when they went inside he threw her to the carpet and kicked her in the stomach, screamed she was a druggie slut and always would be: dragged her to a hidden room and bent her over and—

Her thoughts stampeded like this, and she lived in the agony of not knowing, of never knowing if the person she saw was a façade or the truth. She stopped going to those houses after a while, certain she'd do something silly and wonderful if she kept returning, like slit the girl's throat and take the boy for herself.

Hazel's already left by the time I reach the front door this morning. She's been hitting the gym like a madwoman these past couple of days.

When I walked in to find her grinning at me from the bed on Tuesday, with tears in her eyes, looking downright mental, I knew Millicent had told her. I knew it was all crashing down.

But then we bantered and laughed and everything was normal. Except she's become even more obsessed with her social media stuff than usual.

Normally, I'd tell her to calm down. She tends to get more worked up about this stuff than she needs to. But this is good for me. I need her distracted. At least until I can get this Millicent stuff sorted. I don't like thinking like this. I wish I could be there for Hazel. And I will be, once this is over.

I type in the security alarm code carefully, priming it. I've been more on the ball with the alarm than usual lately. The last thing I need is an unexpected visit from Millicent goddamn Maidstone.

Still, it's not all bad today. I woke up this morning to a text from Ray.

It's time to see Mr Brown again. Same place. Nine o'clock.

Leaving it until Thursday – four days before I'm due back in Cardiff – is a dick move. There's no way I can head to Wales and leave Hazel here alone with her new friend, Millie. I'll have to think of some excuse to stay in Bristol. Or handle it before then.

I climb into the Range Rover and glance at myself in the rear-view mirror. I look tired and worn out and older than my dad.

I hope Tom Brown's got something for me. I can't go on like this.

"She was raised in a cult." Tom leans against the wall with his arms crossed. It's darker in here than last time, no sunlight shining through. "They didn't have an official name, but the locals called them the Freaks. Not very inventive, I know."

I sit on the floor, legs crossed, with the folder open on my knees. The man is thorough. He's given me names and addresses of the ex-cult members, as well as some info about her childhood and her history.

"Father was a famous academic," I say.

"Infamous, more like. He was born into money but didn't touch it for years. And then, one day, he decides he wants to set up a little getaway in the back-arse of nowhere."

"To do what?"

"Whatever it is cult leaders enjoy doing. Millicent's mother had a criminal history: drug possession. She was seen by the locals from time to time, but then she disappears. I can't find any sign of what happened to her. I probably need to do some more digging. Her father, on the other hand, now there's something interesting."

"Suicide," I say, flipping the page.

"Not just suicide."

"Suicide in suspicious circumstances," I go on, reading. "What's so suspicious about hanging yourself? Grim, all right, but suspicious? People do it every day."

"Keep going."

"What. The. Fuck."

"Yep."

"*He made a noose from his daughter's clothes.*" I shake my head as I read. "*He cut his arm and used the blood to write...* She said that to me. She said I should cut my wrists and write *sorry* on the wall. This was her. I'm telling you."

"Maybe. Or maybe it was some weird cult stuff. We don't know."

"She *said* it to me, Tom."

"That doesn't mean she did it. She could just be trying to scare you."

Or both. But he doesn't have all the information. He didn't see the photos of her victims and I'm not going to risk telling him. He might insist we take it to the police, and then Millicent will release the video of me and Julia.

"What happened to the cult after her dad died?"

"It disbanded. It started falling apart a decade before his death though. Something happened in the mid-nineties that shook things up. Nobody had ever left, but whatever this was, it seems to have dampened the hippie vibe."

"So, what happened?"

"I don't know," he says. "I haven't spoken to any of the cultists yet, and if they've discussed it publicly, I can't find a record of it."

I flip through the remaining pages. There's some stuff about Millicent's freelance writing career, clients she's worked with that might relate to Sunny Skies Recruitment, but the links seem tenuous at best. She has no connection to me or Hazel he's been able to find. At least, nothing that would leave a paper trail.

This is bloody absurd. The last time I heard the phrase *paper trail* was in this TV programme Hazel and I were watching on Netflix, bingeing it one hung-over Saturday, cuddled up on the sofa.

I close the folder and stand up. "Why can't you find the mother?"

Tom frowns. Maybe he doesn't like my tone. I've been losing some of my charm lately. I notice it at work, with the way people look at me, a little more impatient than usual. "She might have changed her name. She might have died in a manner not worth reporting on. These cultists didn't take out obituaries. Maybe she left. Women do that sometimes. They disappear from their lives."

I almost swing on him. A vein throbs in my neck like it's going to explode. Is he talking about Mum? Why the hell would he taunt me with that?

His frown deepens.

He's not talking about my mum.

I'm just pent-up and ready to blow because a serial killer is making my life miserable. She's stealing my money. She's threatening my marriage. She killed her father. And now, on top of this, I've got to deal with the fact she was raised in a cult. Which makes her even crazier than I thought. I've seen documentaries about cults. None of them made their followers *saner*.

"When do you talk to them?"

"To who?" he asks.

I wave the folder. "Who do you think? Her old cult friends."

"We can certainly discuss that, Mr Smithson. But I would require additional funds."

"Ah, right." I clench and unclench my fist. "Of course you would. And there I was thinking we were becoming mates. How much?"

"Two per cultist."

"Two hundred or..." He shakes his head. "Two *grand* per person? That's insane."

"It's the price I've arrived at. You're not my only client. The closest cult member lives in York."

"Elijah Wrigley," I say, remembering from the list.

"Yes, that's right. It would take an entire workday to drive up there, interview him, and drive back."

"And your workday is worth two grand, is it?"

"I may have to do some unsavoury things to these people to make them tell me what they know. You're more than welcome to handle this on your own."

"What, talk to this Elijah bloke myself?"

Every time I say the name, I feel like I should know it.

Elijah-Elijah-Elijah, there's something there, right at the edge of my mind. Maybe I used to know somebody in school called Elijah, or at work? I don't know.

"Why not?" Tom Brown says. "I'm sure a big bloke like you can make him talk. Otherwise you can pay me to do it. But I really need to get going."

"Yeah, yeah, fine."

I head out to my car, letting my head fall back on the headrest. This is progress, at least. There are people dotted all over England and Scotland who can tell me more about her.

I ring Ray as I drive back through the industrial estate.

"Yeah?" he says, voice husky. *Slurred.* He's slashed. From last night, or this morning? "Kid, you there?"

"On my way into the office. Are you all right, boss?"

"Women, eh? Can't live without 'em... No, what is it? Can't

live with—Ah, fuck it. Listen, I can't come in today. I'm heading to London. Know a jeweller there, don't I? Getting her a nice little piece. Then she'll see. Then she'll have to see."

"You're *driving* to London?"

"Nah, I'm on the train. Can't have a tipple on the M4, last time I checked. Ha!"

Okay, at least he's not behind the wheel. Not that it makes it much better.

"*Diamonds are forever...* This one's a keeper, I'm telling you. A nice necklace is what she needs. Something as beautiful as she is."

Fuck me. I wish somebody would jump in front of my car just so I could run them over. She destroys everything she touches. I need to fix this.

"Boss, I know it's not good timing, but I need to take the day off."

"What?" He suddenly seems more sober. "This better be a joke."

"It's—"

"It's a joke, right, Jamie? Tell me it's a fucking joke."

"I had a doctor's appointment. But I can change it. To tomorrow. Tomorrow is the latest they can do."

"Doctor? What for? You're not ill."

"No, it's..." I grit my teeth. I'm going to make her pay for this. "It's a downstairs issue. I've been having problems, you know, performing. The doctor said they can help. It's a very expensive private service and they're booked up for months."

"Ah, I see," Ray says, like I knew he would. In his drunker moments, he's confessed similar issues to me. "You can't blame yourself there. It happens to the best of us. But it'll have to be tomorrow, all right? I'll be in then."

"Fine, tomorrow. And, boss?"

"Yeah?"

Run away from Millicent as fast as you can. She's going to hurt you, bad. Everything you know about her is a lie. Every smile, every damn gesture, none of it is true.

"Have fun in London."

37

HAZEL

I sit in the sauna, staring through the clouded glass door at our garden. I normally love being in here when it's raining. It feels Icelandic, boiling up when it's cold and miserable outside.

But today I keep thinking about my follower count problem, going over and over it in my head. Since Tuesday, I've lost *ninety-seven* followers.

I haven't changed how I'm posting yet, because then I risk losing the audience I'm still holding on to. If I'm going to make a change, it needs to be calculated.

"I need to do something big," I murmur, my voice raw from the heat.

I'm not sure how long I've been in here, but I know it's longer than twenty minutes. The sand timer ran out a while ago and I haven't flipped it back over. I don't want to know. I need to think, and usually the sauna helps with that.

"A stunt." I rub my hands up and down my legs. Saunas are good for selfies too, because they dehydrate me and give me a gaunt, tight, shiny look that's popular online. "A big stunt, but it can't risk our marriage. If I had a talent, that'd be one thing. But clearly nobody gives a fuck about my paintings. Maybe I'll start doing pranks? But what if my followers don't like pranks?"

I bring my forearm to my mouth. I open my mouth and I bare my teeth, staring at my reddened skin.

"No, no."

I need to get a hold of this. Talking to myself isn't good.

I'm not crazy, but when I was a child and I used to talk to myself, it led to some bad stuff.

I talked myself into being bulimic. Was it really bad when it made me look shiny and sharp in my Facebook photos? If the other girls were liking, commenting, praising me, and if the boys wanted me, surely a little vomiting here and there was an acceptable price to pay. And I talked myself into believing dating an older boy, a drug dealer, would somehow make my parents notice I was there. I convinced myself they'd be forced to take an interest. But in the end, I had to break it off. He was possessive and scary.

Because I was alone so much, I was sort of able to pretend my voice was somebody else's. It made convincing myself of things easier.

I feel that way now. Alone. I can't think clearly. Everything's moving too fast.

Life is spinning and spinning and I don't know what to do.

I've worked hard to build my following. If I change my content, they might abandon me. But if I *don't* change it, I could stagnate, become irrelevant, and disappear.

Greta's annoying me, with her one hundred and sixty-two thousand followers. She posted a video yesterday where she broke into somebody's garden and jumped into their pool in her underwear. Never mind the fact the garden belonged to one of her friends and it was staged. It still blew up.

Maybe I need to get Jamie to jump into the pool like he said he would last Friday. But then Greta will say I'm copying her.

I'm meeting with Greta and Trish tomorrow for Friday-night drinks. I don't want to. Greta constantly watches our analytics, waiting for one of us to stumble. She must be enjoying my slow downfall.

Trish is not on social media. She's my oldest real friend and I should probably talk to her about how I'm feeling, the same way I should talk to Jamie. But if I talk about it, it's real. I really am failing. There's no going back.

I collapse against the wall as I suddenly get a head rush, and then leap up when the wood scalds my skin.

"Fuck, fuck, *fuck*."

I stand and grab the door handle, pushing it, and then pushing it again when it sticks.

"How many times have I told him to fix this? *Fix the bloody door, Jamie. Somebody's going to get stuck in here one day.* How many *times*?"

Finally, it bursts open and I stumble into the rain, the cold shocking after all that heat. I sprint across the garden in my swimsuit, my bare feet sinking into the mud, forgetting my slip-on shoes until it's too late.

I run into the kitchen. I don't care that I leave muddy footprints behind me. Maybe I can imagine they belong to somebody else, the same way my voice was somebody else's when I was a girl, and I'm not alone in this big empty house.

Get a job if you're lonely, Jamie said once, during an argument.

I have a job. This time next year, I'll have a million followers.

That was more than a year ago, and I've gained twenty thousand since then – twenty thousand which I'm on the verge of losing.

I slam the door and drop onto my bum, pressing myself as

close to the heater as I can get without burning. I sit here for a long time, thinking, talking through the problem and coming up with no solutions.

Maybe I need to have a discussion with Jamie and explain he needs to be more understanding with how I display my body online. Or maybe I need to learn a skill, like an instrument, or acting, something that translates well to the videos.

Painting is so *static*, and the thing is, the really horrible truth is, I'm not very good at it.

Jamie's lucky I love him so much. He's lucky we bonded the way we did, primal and instant and compulsive. I own him as much as he owns me. We possess each other.

Nobody understands him the way I do. They think they have an idea, but they don't know what lurks beneath the surface. They don't know how crazy he is at heart: the same way I'm a little mad myself, even if I don't like to admit it.

They see the sparkle and the sauna and the custom-built Aga and the swimming pool and the suits and the dresses and the jewellery, but they don't see how broken we are. We were both half-real when we found each other. We fixed each other. We owe each other the world.

My mobile vibrates from the kitchen island.

It's Greta, confirming tomorrow evening, with a stupid amount of emojis.

I text her back: Can't wait, gorgeous xxx

Then I find Millie on my contacts list. We haven't spoken in a few days. I guess she's been busy with work. We've texted a little though, mostly jokes about the sounds Ray makes in his sleep.

On a whim, I press *call* instead of *text*, even though I never ring people.

"Yes, hello?" She sounds adorably surprised somebody has called her.

"Hey. It's Hazel."

She laughs. "I know, silly. I saw your name. What's the matter? I can't remember the last time somebody actually *rang* me."

"I guess I'm in a retro mood. And I wanted to ask you in person. Not in person. You know what I mean."

"Ask me what?"

"If you want to come out with me and a couple of friends tomorrow night? It's nothing mad, a few drinks at a club. To be honest, Millie, I think I need my knightess in shining armour. There's this woman, Greta, and she can be a bit of a handful."

I don't know why I'm telling her this. Maybe it's because she's older, more understanding, fiercer than any of my other friends. Maybe it's because she's a stranger. I really don't know.

There's just something about Millicent Maidstone.

"You really want me to?"

"I'd love for you to come."

"That's..." She pauses. She clears her throat. Is she crying? "That is honestly lovely, H. I'd love to come out with you and your friends. Tomorrow night, yes?"

"Tomorrow night."

"Where should I meet you, and what time?"

"I'll text you the details. And, Millie."

"Yeah?"

I need to be careful I don't go too far. I've done that in the past when I've felt like this. I've said things, done things I didn't mean. I've made friends I later decided I didn't like. I've started relationships I had to end once the initial shine wore off. I've said things – *I love you, I hate you, I need you* – I found ridiculous a few hours later.

But screw it. Millie's a good person.

"You don't need to sound so surprised. You're a really, really lovely woman. I'm happy we met. And I'm happy you've agreed to come out with us. No matter what happens between you and

Ray, I think we're going to stay friends. I don't care how awkward it gets for the men."

"Fuck the men!" Her voice cracks. "I promise I'll meet you tomorrow evening. Nothing, nothing could stop me from being there. This is the most excited I've been in a long time. Thank you."

"Just remember me when you're famous, all right?"

"Famous for what?" she snaps, a bite in her voice.

"For being a bestselling writer, silly."

"Oh." She giggles. "Yes, that's right. Silly me. See you tomorrow."

I wonder why she snapped. I guess she's sensitive about her writing.

"Great," I say. "See you then. Bye-bye."

Placing my phone down, I run my hand along the worktop, cool against my fingertips. I grab the corner of the stainless-steel chopping board and pull it over to me, staring down into it: into my partial reflection, the corner of my lip and a shimmery piece of my eye.

"I see you, Hazel Paling," I murmur, wishing I was back there, gazing up at him the first time he said it. His eyes were like little green fires. "I see all of you. You're never invisible with me. Everything you do, everything you are... I'll always be watching."

38

JAMIE

E lijah Wrigley lives in a small terraced house at the end of a long row. The street is grubby, a rundown-looking place. A kid kicks a ball against a garage, making an annoying banging noise that makes me want to stab the ball to pieces. It's loud even through the closed windows of the Range Rover, even with the hum of the air condition to dampen it.

I rub the bridge of my nose. None of this should be happening. I'm in York. I'm here to see a *cultist*. It sounds like a joke. Getting through work yesterday was a nightmare. All I could think about was driving up here and sorting this.

And of course it had to be on Mum's bloody birthday. It's like the universe is trying to tell me something.

If God's real, He's having a whale of a time up there. I can see Him now, proud of Himself, stroking His big white beard with a big grin on His face.

My son, the Bastard is saying, *instead of celebrating your mother's birthday with her, I shall send thee to talk to a man who might be able to tell you why a lunatic serial killer has targeted you.*

I remember Mum's last birthday before she left, the way we sat around the dingy table in the dingy flat and Mum pretended to be happy. She smiled as she blew out the candles, but even at that age I knew something was wrong.

I knew they were going to break-up. That was fine. I just expected her to take me with her instead of leaving me with Dad. I didn't expect her to run off with her secret Italian boyfriend.

Why couldn't she take me with her? What's *wrong* with me, for fuck's sake?

I let my head fall back. I didn't try last year, or the year before... the year before that, I tried and it didn't go too well. She seemed annoyed at me for even making the effort. But maybe she's had time to think. Maybe she's had time to remember I'm her son.

I take out my phone and scroll to her number. Usually when I do this, I hold my thumb over the green call icon for a minute before closing my contacts list. She doesn't want to hear from me.

The phone rings for half a minute or so – the kid is still kicking the ball against the garage, and it's really pissing me off – and then she picks up.

"*Pronto?*" And then, after a pause, "*Ciao?*"

"You don't have my number saved." I grip the steering wheel and stare at the kid's mop of brown hair. It shifts around like a bunch of snakes each time he kicks the ball. I wonder why he doesn't have any friends. I wonder why he's not in school. I wonder what's wrong with him.

"Jamie?" she says, with a slight English accent.

Not a slight *Italian* accent, but a slight *English* accent, as though she's lived over there her whole life, as though she wants to put England and her life here behind her forever. She doesn't even call herself Penny anymore. It's *Penelope* now. Posher, I guess.

"Yeah, it's me. I wanted to wish you happy birthday."

I can hear people in the background, happy voices raised. Somebody laughs and somebody else claps. Everybody is speaking Italian. There are adults and children, a whole mess of joy on the other side of the phone.

She's had two children since abandoning me, a boy and a girl, little Luca and Flavia. She posts photos of them on Instagram. They're beautiful and happy and nothing like the tragic bastard I became after she left.

The kid picks up his ball and sits against the garage, legs splayed, staring across the street at the terraced houses. He's got a hole in his shoe so I can see his sock, a blue sock, and Mum still hasn't said anything.

"Hello?"

"*Sì*, I'm here. I don't know what to say."

"Maybe *thank you*."

"Yes, of course. Thank you for wishing me happy birthday."

I wish she was here so I could... I don't know, I don't know what I'd do. But I'd do *something*. It would be easier if I knew where she lived, but she won't give me her address. She didn't even give me her phone number. I found it on Dad's phone. Last time we spoke, she threatened to change it if I rang her too often. My own mother.

She's never said why she behaves this way. She's never offered an excuse.

"*Un momento.*" She's talking to somebody in that other world. That happy, happy world. "Jamie, I have to go. Thank you for calling me."

"I love you." A pause, a too-long pause. "Mum, did you hear me? I said I loved you."

"Please don't make me lie." She hangs up.

I don't know what happens next.

Everything goes dark and then I wake up, as if I've just gotten blackout drunk in world-record time. There are tears in my eyes and my hands ache from where I've been slamming my palms against the steering wheel. My ears ring like somebody's kicking a football against the inside of my skull.

I rub my sleeve across my face, cleaning myself up. It doesn't matter. She doesn't mean anything. She's just a woman I used to know. She's nothing to me. Her shiny new life could burst into flames and I wouldn't shed a single tear.

I climb from the car and pace across the street, making toward Elijah's sad little house. But then I stop and change direction, walking over to the kid.

He bolts to his feet, grabbing his ball.

"Stay where you are," I snap.

He freezes, gazing up at me, his leg tapping frantically. "I didn't know it was your garage."

"It's not. Why aren't you in school?"

He shrugs.

"All right then. Why aren't you at home?"

"Can't go home. Can't go to school."

"Why?"

He looks up, his eyes red. He's been crying, like me. We were both crying at the same time, maybe twenty feet from each other, and we never would've known if I hadn't come over here. We never would've cared.

"I said *why*."

"I can't," he whines. "I'm—it's bad. It's just bad."

"I get that. But listen, all right? Are you listening?"

He nods.

"It's not going to get better unless you get the fuck out of there. And the only way you can do that is by going to school. You work your arse off even if you hate it. I hated it. But I worked. Work sets you free. A great man said that. I can't remember who. But it's the truth. Work hard, keep your head down, and one day you'll have a car like mine. You like my car?"

He nods again. "The windows are really dark."

"Because I paid through the nose to make them that way. You're getting bullied in school, right?"

"Yeah. Because we're poor."

"Suck it up. That bully's gonna end up a crackhead choking on his own vomit. And so will you if you sit around waiting for somebody else to fix your problems. Don't be a loser. It's the worst fucking thing you can be." I take out my wallet and grab five twenty-pound notes. "Here. Enjoy yourself today. Get some new trainers. But tomorrow, you drag yourself to school."

He grins. "But it's Saturday tomorrow."

"All right, smartass. Monday, then. But you have to promise, or you don't get the money."

"I promise. I swear I'll go."

"All right." I hand him the notes. He grabs them, but I hold on a moment longer, staring hard into his eyes. "Whatever you do, don't let your parents see this. It doesn't belong to them. It belongs to you."

He takes the notes and shoves them into his pocket, like he's scared I'm going to snatch them away. Then he breaks my heart. He picks up the ball and he holds it out to me. It's old and half the leather's peeled off, but he offers it like it's made of gold.

"Cheers." I take it. "Now fuck off. I've got things to do."

He runs down the street, grinning as he yells over his shoulder. "I've got things to do as well!"

I watch him go and then drop the football, letting it roll away. It's a nice gesture. But I'm a rugby man, always have been.

I walk over to Elijah's house and slam my fist against the door. This bloke better give me some answers. I'm not in the mood to be messed around.

"One second," he calls, his voice weak-sounding. He reminds me of the interns we get at work, the whiners who can never hack it. He opens the door and frowns at me. It's difficult not to notice the purple birthmark that spreads across half his face. "How can I help?"

39

MILLICENT

"Give us a spin, darling," Ray says.

I stand in the centre of his absurdly large bedroom, the afternoon sun blaring deafeningly through the window, in a sequinned dress the colour of gold. The sun catches the gold and it lights me up, up, up, so I'm brimming with so much light I almost think – for a mad confused moment – I don't have to kill Jamie Smithson.

Perhaps I can be Millie, instead of Millicent. Perhaps Hazel truly does desire my friendship.

Ray is a problem, however, with his leather-bound flask and his flushed cheeks and his silly gestures: gestures he imbues with far more significance than they merit. He presented me with a necklace last night, welling up as though he thought I was going to collapse to my knees and choke on his dick for the diamonds.

I spin, indulging him.

He makes some piggish grunting noises. "Now *there's* a picture. You're gorgeous, Millie."

Ray does have his uses. There's no way I'd be able to afford this dress without his financial assistance. This time, I even let him know he was making the payment, rather than swiping the money from his bank account. I allowed him to buy me two more dresses, a pair of shoes, some tights, some lingerie, and a set of hair straighteners.

It's been a very productive day.

I drift over to the bed. "Ray, I want to thank you for buying me these lovely things."

He leers at me, his cheeks glowing with liquor, the same way Mother's face blazed as she melted into the sofa and stayed there for hours and hours. I've encouraged dear Ray in his drinking, it's true. It's his natural state. I see no reason for him to pretend.

It's quite funny to see how readily he has fallen into the abyss. He hasn't even tried to fight.

"You're welcome." He licks his lips. "What say I shut the door, eh, sweetheart?"

"So we can have sex."

His eyes widen and he nods quickly: a boy eager to answer yes before the offer is snatched away. He is a little sprite as he sits there, gazing adoringly up at me. "It'd be so, so good, Millie. I'll treat you right."

"That does sound nice. But I think I'd rather break-up."

"What?"

"I said I think I'd rather break-up. Yes, that sounds preferable to me."

"Break... up?"

"Yes. Separate. No longer associate with each other."

Walking to the door, I scoop up my shopping bags with a deft movement.

"Wait a sec." Ray trails me through his lurid apartment, with its hundred protestations of sophistication, none of them convincing. "Millie, fucking hell. Will you stop? We need to talk about this!"

I pause in the hallway, near the front door and the door to

the kitchen. He cringes away from me when I turn to face him. I'm not showing him my Millie-face anymore, with the quirked eyebrows and the approachable lips and the docile dimples.

I am Millicent Maidstone, and I would rather die than lie beneath him as he grunts himself into oblivion.

"If you wish to talk, talk. But it won't change anything, little lamb."

"Little *what*? Why're you talking to me like this? Millie, we can work this out."

"Work what out?" He can't be serious. "We've known each other for a few weeks. You're nothing to me, and I should be nothing to you."

"But you said you loved me. You said time didn't matter. You said we bonded quicker because we were meant to be together. You said you'd never leave me."

I don't bother to remember if any of this is true. Perhaps I *did* say some words, and perhaps some of them are even the words he's claiming I spoke, but what of it? I created a reality with my speech and I can break it just the same. "Anything else?"

"Can you at least tell me why?" His full-flushed cheeks shudder. Anger has worked its way into his voice, the anger of a man who is used to hearing yes: *yes, yes, yes*, from his employees and his women and a world that contorts itself disgracefully for a fleeting taste of his exempted existence.

"My life is heading in a new direction. I'm making friends, real friends, for the first time in my life. I have plans that do not involve you. You've outlived your usefulness to me."

He gawps as though I've muttered spells in Latin. "This is a joke."

"Is it?"

"This has to be a fucking joke. After everything I've done for you. Do you have any idea how much that necklace cost?"

"Ten thousand pounds."

"What? How did you—"

"I checked your banking app last night. I sold it for much less."

Bovine tears brim in his eyes. He's the same as every other man I've allowed to believe I cared for them. But the sort of man I could love only exists in mind-made fantasies. I despise Ray and his ilk, and I especially despise anybody who thinks jewellery gives him invasion rights.

To be *inside* somebody is the greatest intimacy there is. It's worth far more than a few ounces of metal.

"You sold the necklace?"

"I sold the necklace. Are we done?"

"You sold the fucking necklace."

I walk toward the door. I need to get home and decide which dress I want to wear when I meet Hazel and her friends – *my* friends – later. I need to paint my face in the right way and practise my laughter and straighten my beautiful black hair.

"I knew there was something wrong with you. I knew you were a fucking freak."

I shouldn't care what he thinks, but something is throbbing deep inside of me, pulsing, shimmering: starlight and pain and fragments of memory rock and I don't know what else. That word was thrown at me, at all of us, many times growing up.

Freak, freak, freak.

I spin. "Excuse me?"

"Daddy get too handsy with you, did he? Put you off dick so now you walk around thinking you're better than everybody else?"

"My father never touched me, Raymond." I really wish he'd stop, stop this before he goes too far. There was a room and there was a rainbow and there was a secret knock, and there was a slice of the sky, and I will show them, I will show them all how special I am. "Shut your mouth, Raymond."

"Oh, your *father* never touched you." He grins horribly, strolling over to me, bringing with him the stink of whisky and sweat and prurience. "It was somebody else then. Who? An uncle, a family friend? Because *somebody* did, love. You're fucked."

"Get away from me." I've dropped the bags and my hands are shaking. "I mean it. Step back."

He steps closer. He has me pushed against the door. I can feel his belly against my belly and his chest against my chest and he is way too close.

"Or what?" His hand glides up my thigh. Worms crawl over my skin, and the worms are rainbow-coloured, and there is a purple blotch across this moment in the shape of a moon. "Relax a bit. I can help you relax."

"Please stop touching me."

"But you like it. I can tell you like it."

"I do not like it. I have never liked it."

His hand sends unwanted sensations to the place between my legs, and that is the most confusing part: the piece of this most people will never comprehend. There is a survival mechanism in perversion and it is called pleasure. But not real pleasure, not humane pleasure. This is the body's ape response, nothing more, an excretion in response to stimulation. It's the most foetid aspect of a victim's development.

But no, *no*, I have never been a victim. I *make* victims.

I am the jaguar in the park, with the mask and the gloves and the hair net and the rock and the conviction. I am Millicent Maidstone.

"Last chance," I say.

"You're getting wet." He groans as he grinds his palm against me, as the heel of his hand rubs unpleasantly up and down my underwear, and my body does things, prompts things, over which I have no control. "You want it, Millie. I'm sorry for what I said. I'll be nice, I promise—"

"I said *get the fuck away from me!*"

I whip my hands up and around to clear his attacking belly, and I plunge my thumbnails into his eye sockets and press as hard as I can.

He weeps tears of blood as I bury my thumbs deep. He grunts and he falls and he brings his hands to his face, gasping, panting.

Fuck, fuck.

This was never part of the plan. I've committed assault. A living witness to my actions, to my true self. I can't afford that.

I adjust the hem of my dress. "Fine. Have it your way."

Skirting around him as he spins in a blind circle – as though he's the one in the brand-new outfit and he's putting on a show for me – I walk into the kitchen and grab the biggest knife from the metallic knife block. I pull it out with a *hiss*, a knightess' *hiss*, the same sound swords must make sliding from scabbards.

When I return to the hallway, Ray is at the door, fumbling sightlessly for the handle.

There is a fact about death most people do not know: the dying don't always remember to scream, to beg for help. The shock and the pain and the disbelief that this could be happening to them – to he who is untouchable – sometimes renders them mute.

"I have killed ten men." I stalk forward. "I've told myself things, little lamb. I've told myself they were rapists. They were evil. They would go on to hurt women. And now I see – maybe it is Hazel who has allowed me to see – these have been lies, or half-truths to justify what I've done. That's what emotion has taught me. But you, *you...*"

He grasps at me, as though for deliverance.

I step back and he claws at the air, lurching and murmuring nonsensical cattle words.

"You really are the worst of the worst."

I stab him in the gut.

40

HAZEL

This is such a silly thing to do.

Sitting cross-legged on the floor of my studio, the yoga mat pressing into my thighs, I stare down at my phone as I refresh the page over and over and over. As if it's going to magically leap up, as if my followers are going to stop abandoning me. I try to keep my breathing steady as I stare at the descending number – at least a few every minute – but it comes in gulps.

I'm supposed to be relaxing before getting ready for the girls' night, but instead I'm torturing myself. I know I should stop but I don't feel like I can.

I hate the sound of my OTT breathing. It's so melodramatic. And yet I can't stop it from happening, the tight nerves in my belly making my breath tangled and ugly.

I close my eyes but that does little to help. It just makes me think about why this bothers me so much, the deep-down reason I never talk about.

Dad grins at me from my mind, his eyes glassy with alcohol.

He'd been out with his work friends that night and I was waiting up for him, sitting on the stairs with my arms across my knees. Mum had crushed a pill and passed out hours ago, like she often did. She'd pull a mask over her eyes like she couldn't stand to be alone in the house with me.

Dad brought his fingers to his lips and made a *shh* noise as he clumsily tried to untie his shoes, stumbling back and slamming into the wall. He laughed strangely. I didn't like it.

But I was still happy. Fine, he was drunk. Fine, I could tell he wouldn't be able to remember this in the morning, but he was *looking* at me. He was smiling at me.

"Let me help." I rose from the stairs and walked across to him. Leaning down, I untied his shoes and slipped them off his feet as he grasped onto the heater for balance. "Fun night?"

He murmured something under his breath. I couldn't make it out. "Pardon?"

"So polite, eh? Just like your mother." He burped, covering his mouth. It was odd to see the Captain like this. It fascinated me. He was human after all. "Yeah, yeah, fun night. Good times. Good to get away, to forget for a while, you know?"

I don't think he was aware of what he was saying. The words tumbled out as I placed his shoes next to the welcome mat and stood to help him with his jacket. He was like a child as I pulled it from his arms, twisting to let me help him.

"Why don't you go and sit down, Dad? I'll make you a cup of tea or something."

"Okay, dear. That sounds lovely."

He stumbled toward the living room, tripping on his feet and catching himself on the bannister. He laughed like a teenager and turned to me, his grin even wider, boyish in a way I'd never seen before. I found myself grinning back, even if part of me didn't like seeing him like this.

How old was I? I know it was before I started acting out for attention with bulimia and boyfriends and half-naked social media posts... which failed, because they never noticed anyway.

I must've been around sixteen when I found out my dad was cheating on my mum.

I always wanted to be closer to him, which is probably why I found myself searching his jacket pockets. I didn't even think about it. It was like my hands took on a life of their own as I rooted around.

There were a few receipts in his wallet, and then I found the lipstick-red knickers, bunched into a ball, with a handwritten note inside, *Don't wait so long next time, Captain.*

I reeled and almost fell. I feel silly thinking about how close I was to fainting, but it's the truth. I stumbled my way to the stairs and slumped down, drawing in ragged breaths.

I bunched the knickers into a tight fist and stared down at the note, at how crude the writing was. Mum's handwriting was beautiful, elegant, but this was a scrawl, something a cheap woman would hastily put to paper while her married boyfriend cleaned her stink from his balls in the en suite... of where? Her flat, some dingy hotel?

I went into the living room, no idea what I was going to say to him.

He was curled up on the sofa. He looked strange lying there, knees tucked up, mouth slack, hand hanging over the edge. I'd always seen him as *big*, almost like a celebrity even if he was my father. He came and went as he pleased; he dominated every room he stepped into. He was a loyal, good, *wholesome* man, the sort of man people aspired to be and be with, and yet he was cheating on my mum.

Now his giggling and his drunkenness made sense.

I pulled a blanket over him and stuffed the knickers in my pocket, unsure of what to do.

Now, I open my eyes and let out a breath, trying to make it as long as I can. I rarely let myself think about any of this stuff. I try to focus on the good things, the positives in my life. I have a wonderful home, a wonderful husband. I *had* a budding social-media career until recently.

But I can't stop my traitor mind from skipping back to my mum's reaction when I told her.

I waited a week before I revealed Dad's secret. I wanted to make sure I was right. Maybe there had been some sort of mistake. I wasn't sure how, exactly, I could've got this wrong, but I had to give him the benefit of the doubt.

I followed him, which was crazily difficult considering he drove and I didn't. In the end I went onto his phone and installed a *Find My Phone* app, linking it to my email. Dad didn't know how to work his mobile properly, so he never noticed. I would wait for him to leave the house and then – using money stolen from Mum's purse – I'd take a taxi to wherever he went. Most of the time it was the pub, the snooker hall, his gentleman's club.

But once or twice he went to a dingy-looking hotel at the edge of town, near the motorway, and he'd disappear inside for a couple of hours. I'd wait in the car park, sitting under a tree, pressing my back against the trunk so it scraped against me. I wanted it to hurt. I wanted the pain to blot out what I was seeing.

Dad left fifteen minutes before the woman, and then out she came: probably around twenty, wearing a miniskirt, a leopard-print top, big blocky heels. She looked like trash compared with Mum, nothing elegant about her, and I hated her. I hated her more than I can even fathom. I wanted to hurt her.

I dreamt about what it would be like to push her into the motorway traffic. But of course I wouldn't. I couldn't. But the urge was there, swelling inside of me. *Make this bitch pay.*

I waited for Dad to return to the ship for work and then I laid out the note and the knickers on the kitchen table. Mum had her back to me, fussing over her green tea, swishing about the kitchen in a billowing summer dress.

She turned with the tea in her hand, her eyes flitting to the table. I expected her to drop the mug, to snap, *What the fuck is that?* I expected some sort of emotional explosion, but instead an inconvenienced look came across her face, as mild as if she'd forgotten her reusable bag at the supermarket.

"What are you planning on doing with that, Hazel?" she said as she sat down, taking a dainty sip of her tea.

I waved an urgent hand at the knickers and the note. "They were in Dad's jacket. He's cheating on you, Mum. I saw him go to a hotel and then this woman came out, and she was clearly... She was young, and she was—She's *fucking* Dad. Look, read the note."

My words came out jumbled as I tried to work them into some sort of order. But Mum's perturbed stare was unbalancing me. It was like she was more annoyed at me than Dad.

"How foolish do you think I am? Your father isn't as discreet as he likes to believe. In fact, he's as clumsy as they come."

"I don't understand."

"Put that disgusting thing away," she snapped, nodding to the knickers. "Now, Hazel. I don't want to look at it. I'm offended you'd ambush me with such a petty plot."

"Ambush you. I'm trying to help you. Didn't you hear me? He's cheating on..."

"Yes, yes, you've said that." She sighed, shaking her head. "Your father has hobbies."

I expected her to go on, but she left it at that, hanging like a rotten stink in the air.

"What the fuck is that supposed to mean?"

"Language," she hissed. "God, you always have been such an uncivilised little tramp."

I reeled back in my chair, gripping the table. I wanted to flip it. I wanted to run.

"How is this my fault?" I whispered, sounding pathetic even to myself.

"What do you suggest I do with this? Do you want me to leave him? Do you want to be the daughter of divorced parents? Do you want to lose our wonderful home, our wonderful life? God, what an immature way to look at things. Your father has hobbies and visiting certain hotels with certain acquaintances is part of that."

"Mum—"

She slammed her mug down. Scalding tea swilled over the edge and slapped against her hand, but she didn't react. She stared hard at me, her eyes as icy as her pearls. "You think you're lonely now? Imagine what it will be like when your father only has to visit you once a month by law... a duty he'll most likely neglect anyway. Imagine what it will be like when I have to work at some horrid café simply to support myself. You're looking at this like a child."

"But—"

"Quiet. Listen. Do you know what a prenuptial agreement is?"

Something sunk in my chest. "Yes, Mum. It means you signed a form agreeing to keep your hands off Dad's money if you get a divorce."

"Finally, the girl gets something right. You see... Your father has his hobbies, and I'm okay with that. What I'm *not* okay with is you ruining my good mood and this lovely day. Get rid of that ugly thing. I never want to see it again. I never want to hear about this again."

Hobbies...

That word has stayed with me, bouncing around my head, ever since she used it.

I stand and pace up and down the studio, my phone on the floor, waiting to cause me more pain. I grip my hands together tightly, telling myself I'm nothing like Mum.

But is that true? Has Jamie always been the fairy-tale husband I present to my followers?

"You think you're lonely now?" Mum had hissed, finding my most vulnerable part and prodding viciously at it.

I don't want to think about any of this, but losing these followers is making me think about what else I could lose, and what I'll have to stomach if I want to keep what Jamie and I have. A lovely home, a picture-perfect marriage, enough money so we never have to worry.

I groan and scoop up my phone, shaking my head. My thoughts are moving too quickly to catch. I refresh the page.

Fifty-seven more followers have abandoned me while I've been trapped in the past.

41

BEFORE

She had become friends with the little sprite by helping him look for his poor orange kitten. People said she had done things to him when she was younger, but she never believed them; it didn't make sense. She wasn't sick or broken or wrong.

The pet still hadn't returned, and Millicent thought maybe it had jumped off the cliffs and landed in the sea, and climbed aboard a raft with lots of other kittens and sailed far away, someplace happier with a real rainbow in the sky.

The little sprite – the son of Philip and Diana – danced across the rocks in front of Millicent, a big goofy grin on his face. They shouldn't have been out this far, but the cute pink-cheeked boy could trust Millicent. Of course he could. She was older than him. He was rightly grateful for her attention.

"Whoa." He turned to her and became a silhouette, the sun glistening over the sea and flooding the sky blood-red. Millicent smiled, and it felt real. She was sorry his father was Comrade Philip. "It's so far up, Millie."

"Be careful. I don't want you to get hurt."

He smiled. "I won't."

Millicent smiled back, but it wasn't a very clever thing for him to say. *I won't*, he'd said, as if he alone was in charge of who hurt him, or how he was hurt, or when, and with what tools.

"Millie." He skipped over to her. He had a round face and a big pink smile and his hair was always sweaty. His eyes were far too soft. As light shifted, he became Comrade Philip, wrinkling and decaying. "Thanks for coming out here with me. You're my best friend."

Millicent touched his shoulders, both his shoulders, and she thought about how she could push and run and push him right off the edge, and he'd sail and he'd fly and he would see his orange kitty again.

Why was he so fucking *smiley*? Comrade Philip was a devil, and the devil's son was all grinning teeth.

"You're my best friend too," Millicent told the lad.

She looked up and down and then – when she saw they were surrounded only by nature – she punched the boy in the belly. He grunted and fell. She walked around, judged the best angle, and punched him again.

"*Ahhhh*. I'm sorry."

Millicent bared her teeth like a vampire. "Why are you sorry?"

She'd seen vampires on the TV shows in the electronics shop. Sometimes the owner pretended not to notice if she sat there all afternoon watching the television sets. Then Millicent would do nice things like steal change from ladies' purses and leave the money on the shelf.

"For my dad."

Millicent dug her fingernails into his flesh. "*Why?*"

"Because he's old and ugly and stupid," the boy whined. "He's horrible to my mum. He hits my mum—"

"What else does he do?"

"He tortures animals and drinks their blood and—please, Millie, I can't remember."

"Their heads. Remember their heads."

"He cuts their heads off. He poisons the heads and he feeds them to other animals and kills them. Please, please."

Millicent let him go and stared down as he lay crumpled on the rocks. She'd told him what to say, and the worthless idiot couldn't even do that properly.

He looked up and she began to cry. She sat down, coughing out painful sobs. "I'm sorry, I'm sorry." The tears felt real and the tears felt fake.

"It's okay." The boy wheezed as he climbed to his feet. He rubbed her back with his small hand. "We're still friends."

"Promise?"

"Yeah."

"And you'll say it right next time?"

"Yes," the boy said, voice shivering, his back-rubbing pausing for the barest moment before continuing in mechanical efficiency. "I'm sorry."

"It's okay." She hopped to her feet and leaned down, kissing him on the forehead. "Come on, little sprite. Let's go and see what your mother has made for lunch."

The boy smiled, jumping up. His forehead tingled from where the girl had kissed him. He knew he deserved whatever she chose to do to him: he knew he had it coming. He knew he was to blame for being Comrade Philip's son and doing nothing to stop the pain his father dished out. He didn't blame the girl.

Nobody could blame the girl.

Elijah Wrigley's living room is dusty and full of ornaments. The sofa and the chairs are brown and look about a century old. It stinks of dog, but I can't see a dog anywhere.

I leave my milky tea on the charity-shop-style coffee table and lean forward. "Millicent Maidstone."

When the man frowns, his purple birthmark puckers. He's tall and thin and has scared eyes. He'll only look at me directly for a few seconds before glancing down at the floor. If this was a client meeting I'd already be signing the contract in my head. "You must be the husband."

"What do you mean? You know who I am?"

He picks at his brown corduroy trousers with clipped fingernails. "I tried to warn Millicent you wouldn't like it when she became friends with your wife. But she's a troubled woman. She always has been. She was a troubled girl and she's a troubled woman."

"You need to start making sense."

"Isn't that why you're here? She's befriended your wife, hasn't she?"

"Yeah."

"I told her it was a bad idea, but she became obsessed."

"Obsessed with what?"

"Your wife's... Hazel, right?" I nod. He goes on. "She became obsessed with Hazel's social media page. She stayed with me for a while, you see."

"Why?"

"She doesn't make much money. She stays with some of us from time to time. We let her, out of respect for the old days."

"Out of respect for the Freaks, you mean."

He shrugs. There's no fight in him. He's like a deflated balloon. "Some people used to call us that, yes."

"So she started following Hazel's Instagram?"

"*Following* is an understatement." Elijah takes a small sip of his tea. His hands are shaking. Why are his hands shaking? "She'd spend hours at a time scrolling through her photos, studying them in detail. She kept notebooks about each photo, commenting on what she was wearing, her facial expression... everything. She wouldn't stop. I told her it was unhealthy."

I run my hand through my hair, letting out a long breath. "But she's been fucking with *me*. She's been trying to blackmail *me*."

"Yes, she does that. She's always done things like that."

"But if she's interested in Hazel, why target me specifically?"

"She wants to get you out of the picture so she and Hazel can be together."

"Be together as in... *be together*? I don't think she'll have much luck there."

Elijah hugs his arms across himself. It's like he's waiting for me to hit him, and it makes me want to hit him twice as much. There's nothing more pathetic than a weak man.

Is this why Mum left, because Dad was weak? Or was it because *I* was weak?

"Speak, Elijah. You clearly have something to say."

"I don't think Millicent is interested in your wife in that way," he mutters. "It's something else, something stranger. I think she's convinced herself they're going to become like sisters."

"All through studying her Instagram." I shake my head. "That's madness."

"That's Millicent," he counters.

"And the photos?" Screw it. Let's see how much he really knows. "Why does she carry around photos of dead men?"

Elijah pulls a long thread of fabric from his trousers, rubbing it between his fingers, staring at it like it's the most fascinating thing in the world. "She shouldn't have those."

"What are they?"

"A few years ago, Millicent seduced a police officer and persuaded him to give her access to certain case files... files where men had been killed in particularly gruesome ways. For some reason, these fascinated her."

For some reason. Yeah, because it had nothing to do with growing up in a cult.

"Sounds plausible. But the thing is, Elijah, I don't feel like you're telling me the truth."

He flinches. "What?"

"I lie to people for a living. All damn day, I lie. I lie through my teeth. And you're shit at it. Why don't we cut..."

My gaze moves over the cabinet on the other side of the room. There's a bunch of brown ornaments, wooden skulls, model boats, dice, and there are photos too. People standing on a cliff edge with the sun setting over the sea. People standing in a circle with a younger Elijah holding a drum proudly in his arms. The photos go on like this, dotted between the ornaments, but one has been turned face down.

I lean up to make sure I'm seeing it properly. Yeah, right there, he's flipped one of his photos down.

Why would he do that?

"I'm telling you the truth." Elijah stands and stares down at me like a chicken-shit baby. "I'd like you to leave now. I've told you everything I can."

"Why's the photo flipped over, Elijah?"

"What?"

"That photo, why'd you flip it over?"

"What photo?"

I laugh darkly, rising slowly to my feet. The man's got a couple of inches on me, but I probably have five stones on him. I think about little Luca and Flavia singing *happy birthday* as Penelope blows out her candles, and I think about how different our last birthday with her was, and I think about how I'm really not in the mood for this shit.

"All your photos, proudly on display." I gesture at the cabinet. "Except one. Why?"

He frowns and backs away. I stalk forward, inching around the coffee table, wondering what it'd feel like to hit somebody so hard their nose shattered. I haven't been in a fight since I was a boy. But after the month I've had, I'm ready to get stuck in.

He spins and leaps for the cabinet.

I jump forward and wrap my arm around his hip. He squeals as I tackle him onto the sofa, pressing my knee on his bollocks, leaning down so his eyes bulge and he gasps.

"No more games." I slap him across the face, open-palmed. I'm shocked by how loud the noise is, *whack*, like his skull is hollow.

"Please!"

"Please what? Please let you lie to my face about my wife? Please let you treat me like a gullible prick? I'm getting that photo now. If you try to move, if you *breathe* in a way I don't like, I'm gonna feed you your teeth. Understand?"

He gazes up at me dumbly.

I slap him again, this time with the back of my hand, my

knuckles smashing into his cheek. It's funny the things you notice when you're hitting someone. His birthmark looks like a moon.

"*Understand?*"

"Yes, yes," he whines.

I stand and turn so I'm facing him, keeping him in view as I walk around the sofa and over to the display cabinet. He crosses his arms over himself and closes his eyes, rocking back and forth, like he knows this isn't going to bode well for him.

I pick up the frame and flip it over.

Elijah and a few others stand in the middle of a street. I can make out an overgrown garden in the background, and washing lines criss-crossing between the houses.

My dad's grin is the most surprising part. I've never seen him smile like that. No, maybe I have, maybe since he's gotten ill. But never before he lost his mind. He looks content and happy. Mum stands at his side, her eyes aimed demurely away from the camera, her hair falling across her face. She looks young. She looks beautiful.

And then I remember where I heard the name *Elijah*.

Dad mentioned it when I went to visit him, when I was running for the door as fast I could. I'm sure I remember it. What did he say?

We had some fun, didn't we, Eli, old boy?

Yeah, that's it.

I smash the frame over Elijah's head. The glass shatters and he screams, falling onto the floor, crawling across the room. Then I run around the sofa and collapse on him, driving my knee into his back.

"Time for the truth, Eli, old boy. Or this is going to get really fucking bad for you."

43

MILLICENT

I have killed ten... I have killed *eleven* men and not once have I been tasked with cleaning up.

I start by moving his body, which is a more difficult prospect than I had imagined. He is heavy and the best I can do is drag him into the pantry in the corner of the kitchen, closing the door on his facile eyes. I will deal with him later.

Next – and this pains me far more than what Ray forced me to do – I wrap my sopping new dress in several carrier bags and lay it in the corner.

Standing still for a moment, I let the cool air prick my skin. I must remain calm. I cannot allow this mishap to ruin my plans this evening. I never expected to be welcomed so wonderfully into Hazel's inner circle, and I won't let Ray spoil it for me.

He is... he *was* such a stupid, presumptuous man.

A woman has every right to end a relationship. That doesn't give him the right to push his body against mine, to make me think things, feel things I'd rather keep locked away deep inside of me.

Moving to the under-sink cupboard, I search for some cleaning supplies. Most of the mess is on the wooden floor in the kitchen, where he stumbled after the first puncture. I don't recall much of what happened next, but the crimson pattern of his blood tells the story.

I think he tried to hide in here. Where did he think he was fleeing, out the window? There is only one door in and out of this room.

After rooting around in his disorganised cupboard, I find some bleach and a few old rags. I suppose his cleaner brings their own supplies. I abandon the rags and go into his bedroom, grabbing some of his T-shirts and a few pairs of socks. I'll bring order to the kitchen first and then worry about the carpet in the hallway.

How am I going to dispose of the body? I've never had to ponder this problem before.

I pause in the kitchen, a thought occurring to me. Ray was taking a break from work before returning for the evening, which means people are expecting him.

I lay everything on the counter and walk over to the pantry.

He stares up at me as I reach into his pocket and take out his mobile phone. His eyes are red, blood-red, the red of an apology made too late. The screen is partially cracked from our tussle, but I can still use the lock pattern. I've observed him swipe the clumsy Z dozens of times.

I text his assistant, letting her know he's decided to abscond for the weekend. I don't give any further details and she doesn't ask. It's as easy as that for people like him. They do what they want when they want. And he has the temerity to gaze up at me like I should feel guilty for what he made me do.

I close the door and turn to the kitchen. The blood is congealing between the tiles and sparkling in the light. If it weren't such a nuisance, it would be quite enthralling.

I can handle this. People disappear all the time. He'll have to wait here for a few hours while I fulfil my social responsibilities with my new friends. It isn't fair that I should have to forgo the blossoming of my new life just because he got himself killed.

It's time to get to work.

Walking across the kitchen, I grab the bleach and one of his football T-shirts and I fall to my bare knees.

As I drop his third T-shirt onto the reeking pile in the corner, I hear my phone ringing from deeper in the flat, from his bedroom. I sigh and spin in a slow circle, studying my work. Most of the blood has disappeared and the floor has begun to sparkle, as though new-made, like me: ready to start afresh.

I don't want to answer my phone before this work is complete, but what if it's Hazel? What if she wants to meet sooner than we planned?

I grab a pair of his socks from the counter and pull them onto my feet. The last thing I need is to leave a trail of bloody footprints through the rest of the flat.

I walk into the bedroom and pick up my phone, answering without glancing at the screen. I don't want to waste any time. Our last telephone conversation was so fun and intimate and downright lovely.

"Yes, hello?" I'm breathless from exertion and excitement.

"Millicent?" he says, and darkness envelops me.

I drop onto the bed. "I told you not to ring me. I told you never to ring me. *Never.* Do you have a death wish?"

"He knows," Moonie whines, ever the coward, except when he's locked in a room where anything is possible.

"Jamie came to visit you." I make myself take slow, slow breaths. "Or was it his man?"

"It was Jamie."

"And you told him the story I gave you."

"I did. But then he saw a photo of me and Philip, and he made me tell him. He knows, Millicent. He knows everything."

I fall onto the bed and I laugh, and the laughter makes my belly tight and it makes my throat hurt, but I don't care. I keep laughing. Elijah croons down the phone, calling my name, but I laugh and laugh and laugh. There is no mirth in the noise. It is jagged, as though there's glass in my throat, and it feels that way.

I am being eviscerated from the inside.

Sitting up takes considerable effort. The room is suddenly spinning. "You kept a photo of you and Philip? That was a very, very, *very* silly thing to do."

"I'm sorry. He made me tell him—"

"I'm sure he slapped you around a little. You fucking coward. Yes, I'm sure he scared you. But listen close, Moonie, listen very closely. Are you listening?"

"Millicent, please—"

"I said *are you listening?*"

"Yes," he moans.

"Do you remember the video I recorded?" He says nothing. There's nothing he can say. "No? Very well, let me nudge your memory for you. You became very friendly with a girl – aged thirteen – in an internet chatroom, and you thought it would be a good idea to meet with this girl—"

"Please—"

"Interrupt me again and I will drive up to York." He whimpers and falls silent. "You spoke to her in a... shall we say, quite *forward* way. You said some saucy things to her, as the Victorians would phrase it. I hired that girl. And I paid that girl to wear a microphone. I was recording the whole dirty exchange in *H* fucking *D*. The whole world is going to learn what you really are, Elijah Wrigley. Your friends, if you have any, everybody in your shithole street, the postman, your employer... everybody. And you know why, don't you? Tell me why."

"Please," he begs.

"Because you're a fucking idiot *who can't follow simple instructions.*"

I jump to my feet and bring my arm back, almost hurtling my phone across the room. At the last moment, I stop myself, reeling backward. I need my phone.

All he had to do – all any of them had to do if Jamie or his hired goon came knocking – was relay the fiction I'd given them, concerning my obsession with Hazel's social media page. Like all the best stories, it is rooted in fact. I *have* become somewhat obsessed with her page. But not in the sinister way I instructed them to tell it.

I can still hear Elijah, bleating from the phone, his voice faraway and tinny.

I end the call and open my email app, and then navigate to my drafts. I have fifty-two emails saved here, a whole armoury of blackmail ready to fire off should the need arise. I navigate to the correct one and double-check all the recipients are present.

I don't hesitate to click *send*. I should've done it years ago. But I've always liked playing with dolls, and I enjoyed letting him flounder and fall into his pathetic pill addiction, getting twitchy and paranoid as the years wore on.

It's over now. It's all over.

Jamie knows.

"He knows. With his pretty green eyes, he knows. He knows."

I pace the bedroom, my phone clutched in my hand, the same way I clutched the rock in the park before this whirlpool sucked me in. Things were much easier then.

Fine, I didn't have the light. I didn't have meaning.

But I never felt like this. I never felt anything, except in those ephemeral pulses surrounding my earlier kills.

I need to compose myself. Jamie can't do anything with the information. I still have what I have: the video, the power.

But do I truly have the power if he knows my motive?

It's like he's inside my mind, crawling behind my eyes, laughing at me.

He's mocking me. I know he is.

"I don't want to feel."

Hazel would laugh if she could see me now, if she could hear me talking to myself. Hazel, with her shiny skin and her shiny life and her kind smile and her kinder eyes, with all the love in the world bursting from every enchanting inch of her, she'd laugh at me. She'd hate me, if she could see how mad I truly was.

I refuse to meet her like this, oscillating on the precipice, unable to think without reliving the shape of his back, the broadness of his shoulders, the back of his head... his footsteps.

Clip-clip-clip, so loud on the concrete.

I run through the flat, into the kitchen, over to the pantry.

"You don't mind, do you?" I say, reaching into Ray's pocket.

I take out his leather-bound flask and unscrew it quickly. I stare at it for a moment, my nose curling as the acid stink rises into the air. This is Mother. This is my legacy. This is who I am when you scratch away my fringe and my smile and my Millie.

I toss my head back and guzzle every last drop.

44

HAZEL

"I'm starting to think you made this so-called friend up," Greta says, a look of wicked delight in her face as she takes a sip of her champagne.

I try to laugh, but it comes out strangled and weird-sounding. I can't stop thinking about my follower count. That's the selfish truth. And I know it's only a matter of time before Greta mentions it, because she watches our accounts like a prosecutor waiting for us to make a mistake. Matters have hardly been helped by my best friend, Trish, cancelling because she took a last-minute shift at the hospital, meaning it's just me and Greta until Millie arrives.

"She'll be here," I say, reaching for my glass.

We sit at the corner of the bar, steadily filling up with students and business types. It's a beautiful place, with big round oak tables made from recycled materials, the beers and ciders served in jars, and soft jazz playing in the background.

It makes me want to take out my phone and snap a quick photo. But of course if I did that, Greta would leap on the chance to aim a snide dig at me.

The last time I checked my follower count I didn't even

bother to work out how many I'd lost. It's in the hundreds though. I know that much. And it keeps going down, down, fucking *down* every time I check.

Greta watches me over the top of her glass, looking glamorous and victorious. Her bleach-blonde hair falls to her shoulders in casual waves, and her dress is runway-gorgeous. She wears the low cut confidently, drawing the gaze of most of the men – and some of the women – who pass by.

"Hmm," she says.

Just *hmm*, but it makes me want to smash my glass over her head.

The night wears on and the staff begin to clear away the tables and chairs to make room for their pop-up dance floor. I don't even know how many drinks I've had, but the room seems less steady than before, shimmering. The music gets louder and my mouth is filled with the taste of Sambuca and Jägermeister from the shots we did a while ago.

Greta has been talking at me – not *to* me – for what feels like a century about her latest post. "I just can't believe how it flew. It was like—*poof*. I let it out into the world and then it was, like, oh my God... Can you believe these numbers? I had to double-check."

I feel like I did when I confronted Mum about Dad's cheating, the same feeling of powerlessness falling over me. It's the feeling that has pricked me many times with Jamie, any time I confronted him about that awful thing he does, that awful thing I wish he didn't do but... But what? But I'm too afraid to tell him to stop, too pathetic, too comfortable with the life he gives me?

I don't know if it's the alcohol, my plummeting social-media career, or the fact that Greta refuses to shut the hell up about her own success, but I feel like I'm on the edge. I feel like I could slap her and be fully justified.

"Will you excuse me for a moment?" Greta says, in that faux posh way that grates on me even more tonight than usual. "I have to use the little girl's room."

I nod and take another sip of my drink, and then another. I keep sipping until the rosé is gone, swirling around my belly. I regret mixing drinks already. I know I'm going to have the mother of all hangovers tomorrow.

"Boo!"

I jolt when somebody yells in my ear, spinning with too much panic coursing through me.

Millie grins at me shakily. It doesn't take a genius to figure out she's been pre-drinking. Her eyes are glassy and her normally-neat hair is jagged, her fringe wavy across her forehead. Her dress is messy around the hem, like a girl who doesn't feel comfortable in her school uniform.

"You *bitch*. You almost knocked me off my chair."

She tries to bow, but it becomes a stumbling dance. I hop from my barstool and grab her by the shoulders, steadying her. "Let me get you a glass of water." She just looks at me. I raise my voice over the hammering music. "Water, Millie?"

"Water?" she yells, so loud several people snap their heads to look at us even over the music. "What in the name of all that is holy would I do with water, my sweet Hazel? Fine, I will take water... but please mix in some whisky, and maybe some wine too."

I laugh, shaking my head. "I think you've had enough already."

"Oh, a few drops here and there. Nothing to be dramatic about. Where are your friends?" A childlike grin spreads across her face, infectious despite how unhinged she looks. "Is it just going to be the two of us? What a wonderful surprise."

"No, Greta is here." I lean close to her ear so I don't have to shout as loudly. "She's just in the toilet. She'll be out in a second."

"Fine, fine. Yes. Fine. That's fine."

I'm sure I detect some anger in her voice, but then Greta arrives and I quickly introduce them. Greta pulls Millie into one of her OTT hugs, making a fuss of her like she's a prized poodle. "I was starting to think you didn't exist. So, Millie, tell me something very, very, *very* important. Do you like shots?"

"What sort of self-respecting woman doesn't?" Millie yells, and Greta lets out a fake-sounding peal of laughter. I find myself laughing along with them, even if I don't find it funny, even if I wish I was back at home with Jamie so I didn't have to deal with this.

I wish Greta would just come out and say whatever insult she's saving, but it seems she's decided to keep quiet for the time being.

The night spins on and on, as we get more shots and then go to a different club to dance. The music is far louder in this one, and that, combined with the alcohol surging around my body makes it so I don't have to think about Greta or my digital life. I lose myself in the simple act of dancing, the three of us cordoning off a section to ourselves.

There's something primal and carefree about letting loose like this, grabbing Millie's hands as we swing around together. She giggles and let's herself fall back. I laugh and grab onto her tighter, making sure she doesn't fall as we flow together. She breaks off and spins into an adjacent group, ignoring their bemused looks as she leaps up and down, weaving her hands through the air like she's trying to catch falling leaves only she can see.

I'm not sure how many songs we dance to, how many shots we drink, but I know I'm pretty drunk because one second I'm in the club and then the next – like magic – I'm leaning against the wall of the smoking area.

I've got a cigarette in my hand with no idea who gave it to me.

I take a long inhale, the nicotine rushing around my body, making the world sway. I look around and find Greta pushing her way through the tight-packed bodies, clutching her handbag with one hand and holding her phone with the other. She talks into the camera, her voice raised, not caring when people glance at her like she's crazy.

Normally I respect her ability to go live without caring what people think, but any reminder of social media makes my belly swirl right now. I stub out the cigarette on the wall and walk toward the club's entrance, meaning to disappear onto the dance floor.

"Wait a sec, Hazel." Greta grabs my arm and spins herself around so we're both in frame. Instinctively I plaster a fake shiny smile to my face, aiming it at her phone. There's no way I'm going to make my situation worse by being grumpy on Instagram live. "Here she is, my lovely followers, the poor lost soul I was telling you about. Hazel Smithson needs *all* our help in these tough times. You see, her posts aren't getting the attention she desperately wants…"

I squeeze my hands into fists, somehow maintaining my smile as humiliation flows over me. I try to tell myself it doesn't matter. I expected her to do something like this. But it stings.

Especially when my gaze flits to the stream of comments.

Who?
Kiss, you sluts.
Who the fuck is that redheaded bitch?

She looks gormless.
Imagine begging for followers.
LOL, this is sad.

"Greta," I murmur, trying to keep my voice level. "I don't think—"

She throws her arm around me, squeezing me close to her as she lets out a vicious laugh. "Don't be silly. Every newbie needs a helping hand. Go on, Hazel, *beg* my followers to go to your page. They will. I know they will. But you have to *beg*."

Tears make my sight blurry, filling my eyes, even as I keep the pretend smile fixated to my face.

Go on, beg for us.
Move the camera down and maybe I'll follow your shit page.
Are they going to kiss or what?
BORING.

"Just say pretty please." Greta titters, and I wonder why the hell I'm even friends with her. But *this* is the reason. To leech off her follower count. She's just never been this cruel before. "Or maybe you should start an Onlyfans instead. What do you think? Would you like to see Hazel Smithson's sweet naked—"

Suddenly a hand darts out and grabs her phone, tossing it over the wall that separates the smoking area from the street.

Greta gasps and I turn to find Millie standing there, a dead look in her eyes, her lips peeled back in a sneer.

"What the fuck do you think you're doing?" Greta yells. "That phone cost more than your rent."

Millie moves forward slowly, eyes narrowed. "Apologise."

"What?" Greta looks around at the gathering crowd, her mouth falling open. "For helping her? For giving her a shoutout?"

"Apologise. To. Hazel." Millie leaps forward drunkenly, almost stumbling as she darts her hands toward Greta.

Seeing her move so violently snaps me out of my daze and I leap forward, looping my arm around her waist.

"Millie, stop," I hiss in her ear when she lashes out like she's trying to scratch Greta's face off. "You'll get arrested. Fucking hell. *Millie*. You've had too much to drink. Come on."

I pull her toward the exit, straining under the pressure as she bucks around, like a wild animal trying to get to her kill. I never expected her to react like this. I never dreamed she'd do something so violent, so... what? So *uncivilised*. It doesn't seem like her, but then again, she was drunk when she got here and we've been necking shots ever since.

"I'm taking you home." I grab her shoulders and make her face me. "Millie, calm down. I'm taking you home. Okay?"

She gazes at me with wide eyes, tears pricking the edges. "What did I do?"

Is she joking? It *just happened*.

"You broke Greta's phone and you tried to assault her."

"I didn't hurt her?"

"You're in no state to hurt anybody. Come on."

"You owe me a phone!" Greta yells after us as I lead Millie through the doors and into the club.

Millie leans heavily on me, her head on my shoulder, forcing me to basically carry her. I'm worried the bouncers are going to stop us from leaving, but they just glare at us as I drag her onto the street and around the corner, sitting her down on a bench.

"I'm sorry, H," she says, hardly able to force her words out past her slurring. "I didn't mean to... I've ruined it... I'm sorry."

I sit down next to her, taking out my phone. My heart's going a million miles per hour.

Then I laugh. I sound crazy, deranged. "I can't believe you

did that. Did you see her face? Nobody's ever done anything like that to her before."

Millie giggles as her head comes to rest drunkenly on my shoulder. "She's not allowed to talk to you like that. Nobody is. You're my best friend."

It sounds childlike, ridiculous. And yet it touches me.

"All right, drama queen," I say, bringing up the taxi app on my phone. "Just try not to attack the driver, all right?"

J ust helping one of the girls get home, Hazel tells me in a text, and I'm left wondering if it's Millicent. But that can't be right. Millicent isn't a girl or a woman or even a human. She's a monster who killed her own father, who slit his wrists and hanged him. She's slaughtered countless since then. She's evil, right down to her bones.

And now I know why she chose me.

Come home soon, I write. I miss you, H xxx

Something about Elijah's news has made me understand how badly I need my wife. No other woman would give a damn about this side of me – not Lacy or Sadie or any of the others I seduced and stalked. None of them would care about how badly I'm hurting.

Hazel's the only thing in my life that isn't a lie.

The flames flicker in the metal pit. We last used the fire a couple of months ago, before I'd ever heard the name Millicent Maidstone. We drank wine and we laughed and we made love right here in the garden.

We *made love*. We didn't fuck, screw, bang. It was romantic. We didn't have to worry about our neighbours seeing us because

I've worked my ass off for this house, for this detached house in Clifton, with its high fences and its desirable location. We've got privacy here.

She wants to take it all away, for a sick twisted joke.

Or maybe my life is the joke.

I stare at the photo, the only one I've bothered to keep. It was taken at my ninth birthday. Mum was called Penny back then, not Penelope, and she wore tracksuits and trainers instead of the elegant dresses she displays on social media. Her hair is tied back and she's smiling, really smiling, with her hand on my shoulder. She looks genuinely happy.

Was she faking it then? Or did her doubts come after?

They must always have been there, festering beneath her smile, until they finally exploded and she drifted away in the night.

Dad isn't smiling. The mean old man stares at the camera.

I remember how seriously he took the task of setting the timer. It was so strange. I knew he hated me, hated Mum, hated this life he'd fallen into. Why did he care so much about this damned photo? Maybe there was some love there, a flicker. I don't know.

I look pathetically happy, beaming like a naïve little prick. I had no idea the only bright spot in my life – the only person who made living with Dad bearable – would abandon me in less than a year.

I wish she'd told me the truth instead of leaving me to wonder and suffer and hate myself. What sort of a person inflicts that on a child?

I throw the photo into the flames.

As it crackles and the edges begin to curl, I think about the look on my father's face when he told me Mum was gone. He didn't look sad or regretful or anything really. He didn't have any emotion on his old, old face. Even then, he was ancient. People would confuse him with my granddad. He said she was gone and she'd never be coming back and then he switched on the radio.

I should've screamed or cried or *something*. But I sat at the table and he looked at me, sighed, and then he went into the kitchen and put some bread in the toaster.

One jam and one margarine? he said.

Yeah, I replied.

All right.

I knew better than to cry in front of him. If I did, he'd get angry. He didn't like it when I showed weakness. When I was a child, I thought it was because *he* felt weak, and he didn't like to be reminded of that. But maybe it's just he was a cruel bastard who'd use any excuse to give me a slap.

The photo disappears into the flickering fire, the paper melting away, our faces melting away.

I kept waiting for Mum to come back. I accepted what Dad said when he told me. I'd be an idiot to call him a liar to his face. But I didn't believe him, not at first. I was sure there was more to the story.

And then I found the letters in Dad's bedside drawer. I don't know why she didn't take them with her. Maybe Dad stole them from her and she didn't know where they were. Or maybe she wanted to leave behind some sign, a little hint, about where she'd disappeared to.

She'd started a pen-pal relationship with a man in Italy, bonding over a shared love of classical cinema. The early letters were all about film. They were short and innocent and straight to the point. But then they became sexual, disgusting and horrible to read. This was my mother. She wasn't supposed to talk like this. She wasn't supposed to *think* like this. I know it's naïve, but I was a kid.

I stowed the letters away and I never looked at them again.

As the years wore on, Dad found other girlfriends. I learnt a lot from watching that ugly old bastard. He wasn't even remotely handsome. He wasn't kind. But when women were around, he had this switch he could flip, making them laugh without trying, making suggestive comments that somehow didn't seem crass when accompanied with his cheeky smile. When he smiled, I could see what he looked like when he was young.

I sigh and turn to the house: my big proud fucking house.

Please come home, Hazel. Please come home and hold me and tell me it's going to be okay. Please tell me I'm not broken.

I walk over to the poolside chair, lying back and looking up at the starry sky.

I used to sneak into my dad's bedroom when he and his girlfriend were asleep. It didn't matter which girlfriend, only that there was a woman in the bed. I'd creep across the room and gaze down at her, at the shape of her in the dark.

I'd stare and I'd convince myself it was Mum, she was right there, she hadn't walked out, she'd never leave me. She was *right there*, and I could reach out and touch her if I wanted. I could climb into bed with her, even if I was too old, and she'd hold me and stroke my hair and tell me I was a good boy.

If I'd known the truth, would it have been any different? Maybe I wouldn't have felt the need to sneak into those houses, driven by... by what? What the fuck was I driven by? Was it the need to take her back, to make sense of the pain she left me with? I don't know. I don't think it can be that simple.

I didn't do any harm. I didn't *hurt* anybody. I would never hit a woman.

I run my hand along my jaw, massaging the tenseness. I need my wife to come home. Even if I can't tell her everything, I need to hold her like I did on our wedding night, after the sex, when she was pressed close to me.

It's like you're going to fall through my skin, I told her.

Oh, Jamie. That's the most romantic thing you've ever said.

I grinned, kissing her sweaty cheek. *Don't sound so surprised.*

I should've kept us like that, innocent and happy in bed together, with the smell of champagne and roses in the air.

Why did I have to cheat on her, again and again and again?

What the fuck is wrong with me, to risk an angel like Hazel so cheaply?

When she gets home, I'm going to talk to her about moving. We can start fresh somewhere, and I'll be better. I'll value what we have.

It's me and Hazel against the world. I hope it isn't too late.

46

BEFORE

Charles Maidstone smoked his pipe and the smoke drifted around his face and clouded it. He could hear them upstairs, Millicent and William, and he didn't know how to feel about the girl's doting.

It went against everything he'd taught the Comrades: family was a word-made construct, not physical reality, and now Millicent was singing William a lullaby. And even if a lullaby was made of words, it was something else too, something primal and vital. It had no place here, and yet love whelmed in the house, the sort of love his essential nature had starved them of, the Comrades and their children, ever since he became Master.

Perhaps he had loved Constance to some degree, because he'd valued her dying wishes. She'd died giving birth to the boy, and she'd made two requests.

Call him William. My father was called William. And Charley, oh, Charley... let her love him.

She was dying and that was rotten, but he told her no, and she screamed *yes* as a flare of withering life awoke inside of her, and they argued and it was too dreadful, even for him, far too evil to argue with a woman who'd given birth to his son and who was dying because of it.

Charles was still a wealthy man by inheritance, and he'd accumulated more wealth since then, through the Comrades and their dedication. It wasn't cheap to bribe and blackmail Constance's death record into nonexistence, but it was necessary, because if there was no sign of her death, no collection of human-made words to proclaim his dear Connie gone, then perhaps she was still here: perhaps she was in William.

Millicent's voice rose higher and the girl sounded happy, and she was twisted and she was wrong and her father knew it, but she sounded happy as she sung to the boy. And surely he, Charles, must've felt *something* good at the sound of her lilting voice, at the joy rioting around in each note, because he'd caused her so much pain and now here she was, submerged in hope.

She had found a reason to close away the dark parts of herself, a reason to exist: a way to look at her reflection and see a girl who may one day become a woman who'd inspire pride in those around her. He must've cared, a little, when he heard his children bonding, at least for a moment, a bare breath.

Or perhaps it is easier to wish it were so, to remake Charles Maidstone into something like a human being, not the monster who raped and molested and abused and encouraged others to do the same.

But truth and untruth are not rigid states, and sometimes fiction is the warmest fact.

47

HAZEL

M illie's flat is small and cheaply furnished. There's a suitcase on one side of the bedroom, neatly pressed against the wall, and her laptop is open on the desk in the corner. A Word document is open. As I pass, I read, *We care about the safety of you and your family, which is why we at Ludovico Tyres only use the most durable...*

I walk into the kitchen, trying not to feel sad by how cramped and depressing everything is. I'm not sure where I imagined Millie living – a duchess' manor maybe – but it wasn't down a grimy alley above an electronics shop.

I take the water into the bedroom, placing it on the side table. Millie's stripped her dress off and she lies sprawled in her underwear, her chest rising and falling softly.

"Millie, can you drink some water for me?"

"Hmm."

"Just a sip."

I help her sit up, then bring the water to her mouth. She dribbles half of it down her chin and then falls back with a gasp, rolling onto her side and tucking her knees to her chest. At this angle, I can see the tattoo on her hip bone: *13/03/95*. I still have no idea what the date signifies.

I take out my phone, meaning to arrange for another taxi to come and pick me up. I didn't know how long I'd be here, so I told the first taxi not to bother waiting.

There isn't much else I can do. She needs to sleep it off. She'll feel better in the morning.

"Millie, I'm going to..."

I trail off as my gaze comes to settle on her memory stick. The pendant lies against her back, flipped around, tempting me.

Millie is articulate, kind, caring, interesting. Tonight wasn't the greatest display of those qualities, it's true, but who hasn't made mistakes when they're drunk? And part of me was thrilled to see Greta put in her place for once.

If my instincts about her are right, I bet her writing is as amazing as she is.

I know I shouldn't, and I probably *wouldn't* if I wasn't a little drunk myself. But what harm can it do? I'll take a quick look and then replace it.

"Millie, I'm going to have a look at your writing, on your memory stick, okay?"

"Hmm," she grunts.

"I'll just read a page or two. Okay? You don't mind, do you?"

"Hmm."

That's good enough for me. I know she's self-conscious about her work, but I think it's silly. And it's not like I'm some big-time reader or anything. She has nothing to worry about. I'm not going to judge her.

I take the memory stick and fiddle with it. It detaches and I take it over to the laptop. I slide it into the USB slot and the file explorer appears.

I expect to see *Avenging Angel by Millicent Maidstone* or

something. Or maybe a file marked 'Novel Work'. But instead there's a list of files and dates, going back to two thousand and five. I scroll down to the first entry and then stop when Millie makes a murmuring noise.

I close the file explorer and spin in the office chair, waiting to see if she'll wake up. But she's just talking in her sleep, muttering words I can't make out. I think I hear *Sprite*, and I wonder if she's asking me to get her a can of lemonade. But then she quietens down.

I turn back to the computer and open the file explorer.

I click the earliest entry.

"What the fuck?"

I double-click the image and it fills the screen.

The man's face is hardly a face anymore. His head is hardly a *head*. It's like he's been ravaged by a jungle cat. An emerald-green shard of beer bottle lies next to the mess, the jagged edge of it stained with his blood. Gore spreads down his neck and chest.

I click away from the photo, swallowing acid bile, cocktails and vodka and disgust mixing together.

What the hell is this? Research?

There's a Word file in the same folder titled 'Little Piggy Deserved It.'

I open it to find a newspaper article.

Vicious Slaying by Unknown Killer, Police Have No Leads.

I read, my belly churning, as the author details how Lenard Fitzgerald was walking home after a late shift at his warehouse-picker job when he was ambushed on an unlit, unmonitored passageway between the street and the train station.

'He was a lovely man,' wife, Natalie Fitzgerald, said when questioned about the killer's motive. 'I can't think why anybody would do this. We were planning on starting a family. He was always ready to lend a helping hand. He volunteered at the youth centre twice a week. I'm stunned anybody would want to hurt him.'

Red annotations mark the edges of the article. Millicent has left comments on the text.

Lying slut, one reads, the arrow pointing to Natalie's statement. *He made her say that. Lying fucking bitch slut cunt cunt CUNT. He RAPED HER. He's a rapist. He's a monster. I had to do it.*

I had to do it. I *had* to do *it*. I had to *do* it.

No matter how many times I read the sentence, it doesn't make sense. Surely Millie didn't kill this man. Surely... but why else would she have these photos and this article?

I read the article again quickly, checking for the time of death, then freeze as Millie grumbles from behind me.

Turning, I see she's lying on her back, the whites of her eyes showing through half-closed eyelids, flickering as she lets out a sleepy moan.

Who are you, Millie? Who the fuck are you?

Once I'm sure she's asleep, I turn back to the laptop.

The man was killed at three o'clock in the morning. I right-click the photo and click *Properties*. I won't be able to tell when the photo was taken, but I can tell when it was added to the memory stick.

She added the photo an *hour and a half* after the murder.

There's no other way she'd have this picture.

She killed him. Or she knew the person who killed him.

But she admitted it in her notes. *I had to do it.*

To be sure, I do a reverse image search of the photo, and of course there are no results. It doesn't appear anywhere online. The police wouldn't release a photo this gruesome.

I go through the other files. My hands are shaking and I have to focus hard to click where I want.

The rest is the same: photos, newspaper articles, evil comments implying these men deserved to die.

Millie isn't writing about an avenging angel. She *is* one... no, that's not right. She *thinks* she is, but she's wrong.

Most of the newspaper articles mention how loved the victim was. Girlfriends and wives and mothers – and boyfriends and friends and children – talk about how much they miss the dead men. They talk about how hard their lives have become since their loved one was killed without explanation, without reason, savagely torn to pieces in the night.

The last victim – killed a month and a half ago – had a girlfriend.

'I think he was going to propose to me. He was dropping lots of hints. We were so in love.'

I click off the folder, scrolling through the rest of them. They all have dates except for one, titled *Before*. Before what? I don't want to click on it, but it's like something else has taken over.

"What are you doing?"

I leap to my feet with a scream, raising my hands. What can I do against a person like this? How could I be so wrong? "Nothing."

"It doesn't look like nothing." Millie rises from the edge of the bed. She trembles a little, but she seems more in control now. Maybe finding me on her laptop has sobered her up.

"I was arranging a taxi. My phone died."

She can't see the laptop screen. I'm stood in front of it. She has no way to know I'm lying as long as I stand right where I am.

"Your phone is a part of you. You wouldn't let it die any more than you'd will your heart to stop beating. Please step aside."

"Millie." Tears prick my eyes. "I don't want to—"

"*I said step aside, you self-indulgent bitch!*" she roars, and she isn't Millie anymore. I don't know what she is.

She marches over to me, stumbling from side to side. I shouldn't be scared of her. She's drunk and she's so skinny I can see her ribs through her bare torso. Her hip bones jut out. And yet terror grips me. I'm going to be sick.

She moves to grab my shoulder.

I slide out of the way, back-stepping to the door.

She glances at the laptop. "Oh, Hazel. What madness would prompt you to betray me like this?"

"I didn't see anything. You woke up before I could take a look."

"Then why are you looking at me like that, little lamb?"

"Like what?" My voice trembles as she walks toward me with slow footsteps and a fierce glint in her eyes.

"Like *that*," she snarls, baring her teeth. "I'm sorry but—"

I leap forward and push her in the chest, aiming the heel of my palms right at her centre. I hit the place between her breasts.

She grunts and collapses.

I run through her flat, throw the door open, run down the stairs.

Don't fall, I shout in my head, over and over. *Don't fall. Don't fall.*

I want to stop and take my heels off, but there might be glass in the alleyway. I'll cut myself and then she'll use the broken glass to slit my throat, to slice me to ribbons like she did to those men.

I run down the alleyway and burst onto the street, ducking my head and running, running as fast as I can as I reach into my handbag and take out my phone.

I need to call the police. I need help. I wish Jamie was here.

I don't know how long I run for before I finally stop.

Minutes, hours, both very long and too short. She could be right behind me.

I stop outside a kebab takeaway, leaning gratefully against the lit window. There are a few people inside, loud and drunk.

I look down at my phone to find Millie has sent me an email: many emails. She's still sending them as I watch, new notifications coming in one after another.

`Jamie is not the man you think he is`, the subject heading reads.

`Jamie never loved you.`

`Your marriage is a lie.`

She wasn't following me. She stayed behind to send these emails, these pathetic tricks to try to stop me ringing the police. Or maybe she *was* – is – following me and she sent them from her mobile. But she can't have been running fast if she was busy with her phone at the same time, as well as being drunk.

And there are people in the kebab shop. She won't attack me in front of them. Will she?

I don't know anything about her. I met her *two fucking weeks* ago.

I move to click Emergency Services, but then another email comes in. I can't ignore the subject heading.

`I'm posting this video if you do anything stupid.`

I laugh, and it hurts. The laughter hurts.

She's a lunatic. She has nothing.

I open the email and I watch the video, and I think about what my followers would think if they saw it, and I think about how Mum would nod matter-of-factly like of course I got cheated on, of course her stupid daughter got cheated on, and I think about the humiliation I'd suffer, every day of my life, the looks of pity I'd get if this video was released.

And I know Millicent fucking Maidstone has got me right where she wants me.

48

JAMIE

I sit with my head in my hands, thinking of the first time I saw Hazel.

There was an employment event at university and she was walking ahead of me, swaying her hips, and there was something so... Dammit, I have to be honest with myself, especially after everything I've learned.

There was something Mum-like about her.

She was far younger than the women who usually captivate me, but it was in the way she moved, the way she held herself. I remember when I was very young, following Mum through a crowded high street, her hand slipping from mine as she disappeared into the fray. I remember the way she walked: the way she held herself, almost as though she was glad she'd let me go and she wouldn't have to deal with me anymore.

Fear like that never leaves a person.

I ran through the crowd, bumping into strangers' legs, panting in my desperation to get back to her. But she just kept walking. I never found out if she was trying to ditch me. Maybe she was toying with the idea and then thought better of it, but that's the impression it left on my young mind.

When I saw Hazel, it was like I could take back that piece of my life, that fear, and make it mine. I didn't have to be the scared little boy anymore.

I didn't think like this at the time. Maybe I've *never* thought like this. But I see it now.

I watched her from afar before I ever worked up the courage to introduce myself into her life. And when I did, the way it happened... I never expected it to go down like that. I thought she'd hate me. She *will* hate me if she ever finds out the truth, all of it, not just the pieces she knows.

I can't believe my love for Hazel is that simple. It can't be, can it? I saw a shade of my mother in a crowd, I followed... I claimed. Can our whole marriage really be reduced to something so weird and pathetic?

I've never shared this with Hazel, with anybody. I can't even imagine telling her.

Hey, H, do you know what first attracted me to you? You reminded me of my mum when I thought she was going to abandon me outside Poundland.

No, I have to keep this buried deep, the same way I keep so much of my messed-up psyche stifled.

It doesn't matter now. None of it does. I'm going to take Hazel far away, someplace Millicent and the past can never hurt us.

It's going to be a fresh start.

I bolt to my feet when the door bursts open, forcing a smile to my face. "Finally, you're home... Woah, H, what the *fuck*?"

She springs across the hallway, throwing her handbag at me. I duck and then she's on me, scratching, screaming, slapping me across the face. The door swings on its hinges behind her and the lights of the taxi disappear, leaving us in semi-darkness.

"Hazel, stop, *stop*."

She's goddamn hysterical, raking her nails down my cheek

when I try to grab her wrist. "How could you? How fucking *could* you?"

Oh, no. Please no. Not this, not tonight, not when I was going to convince her to leave with me. "Calm—"

I roar when she scratches my neck again, gouging her fingernails into my skin. I've got no choice but to spread my arms and bear-hug her, squeezing her arms against her body. She struggles, spitting in my face as she calls me every name under the sun, a prick and an arsehole and a monster and a liar.

"I hate you!" she screams, bringing her knee up in a vicious slam against my balls.

I grunt and fall backward, the air sucking out of my belly. Women'll never know how painful this is. I don't give a shit about childbirth.

"H, wait," I gasp.

She runs past me and up the stairs, slamming the bedroom door with a shudder that moves through the house.

I chase after her, panting. It can't end like this. Why did Millicent tell her? I didn't break any rules. I was playing her sick game.

I run down the hallway and push the bedroom door, trying to turn the handle. It rattles in the frame, locked. "Hazel." I slam my fist against it. "Open the door. We need to talk about this. What did she tell you?"

I can hear her opening and closing drawers. "She showed me photos, Jamie!"

The wardrobe creaks in a way I'm familiar with, something I keep promising to get fixed. *Creak*, and that means she's gone, the love of my life.

I've ruined it. I've ruined everything.

"What photos?"

"Of your little dates. In the cinema. At bars."

"They were client meet—"

Something smashes against the door, the reverberation moving up my arm. *"Don't fucking lie to me! She showed me the video. Silky, silky, silky! You're pathetic!"*

No, no, no. Please no. Please, Hazel. It's me and you. I love you. Please don't let it end like this. "I'm sorry." My words crack with a sob.

She throws the door open and folds her arms, glaring at me, her eyes red from crying. But her lips are razor-straight and there's no pity behind the tears. She looks like she hates me. "Are you seriously going to try waterworks, you cheating fuck? Do you actually think that's going to change anything?"

"Millicent isn't what you think—"

"She's a killer and you're a cheater. I don't want anything to do with either of you. Clearly this is your mess. Clearly I don't know what's going on in my own marriage. I'm going to stay with Trish."

"Hazel, please."

I follow her when she paces away. The sight of our bedroom causes more tears to stream hotly down my cheeks. The lamps are lit, a soft yellow glow, and it's late. I should be holding her in bed, stroking her hair to help her fall asleep. Or making her a snack to soak up the alcohol. Or something, anything other than what's happening.

She shoves clothes into her suitcase. "Stop crying, Jamie."

"Let me come with you."

"To Trish's?" She laughs bitterly. "I don't think you'll be welcome when I tell her what you've done, when I *show* her."

"Somewhere else, anywhere else. You don't understand. You don't know who she is. She's been blackmailing me. She's killed people. She's—"

"I. Don't. Care." Hazel glares at me for a moment before shoving another handful into the suitcase. "What we have – what we *had* – I thought it was pure, perfect. I didn't think anything could touch it. The way we met, what we've been through, what we agreed... It was never this. It was never supposed to be this."

"I can be better. I promise. I can change."

"Change? Change? I didn't know you *needed* to change. You've had your dick inside another woman. There's no coming back from that. You were never meant to fuck them, Jamie. Never. That was the deal. They were never supposed to know you *existed*."

"Julia wasn't one of them," I rush to say. "She was just a whore."

"Oh, charming. Okay, if she was a *whore*, I suppose it's all right. God, you're such a pig. I can't believe I ever loved you. We're getting a divorce. I want you to know that."

"She knows, H."

"I know. She showed me the photos."

"No... about me, about what I do. She knows. That's how she's been blackmailing me. That's how this started."

"Why would you think I care now? This is none of my business. You're both sick. Whatever this is between you, I want nothing to do with it. I bet you've been fucking her too, haven't you?"

"No." My belly churns in disgust. I hate that I was ever attracted to her. "Never. I wouldn't."

"Why, she doesn't look enough like your mother, hmm?"

"That's not fair."

"Fair would be pushing you off the fucking Clifton Suspension Bridge, so shut up about *fair*."

"Give me a minute to explain—"

Sudden darkness.

The lamps have switched off. The hallway light has gone dead. The house seems quieter.

"What the hell?" I can barely make Hazel out by the light

from the window, pale through the curtains, the faint outline of her frown and the glint of her hateful eyes. "Power cut? I wonder if any of the other houses—"

"This is her, H."

"What?"

"This is Millie. I'm sure of it. That bitch. That psycho bitch."

"Jamie, don't overreact—"

"Did you shut the door?"

"I don't know. No, I don't think so. I was a little distracted by you being a cheating piece of shit." Her silhouette trembles. "Do you really think it's her?"

"Lock yourself in the en suite and call the police. I'll go and check."

"I can't call the police. She'll release the video. I'll be humiliated."

"Would you rather be humiliated or fucking *dead*?"

"You'll be humiliated too. The whole world will learn your twisted little secret. I won't be the only one to suffer."

"Just hide," I say, hardly recognising my own wife. She's never spoken to me like this before. "I'll keep us safe."

"Sure. Because you've done such a great job so far."

49

BEFORE

Diana – Comrade Philip's wife – was weeping, and it was because her son was dead.

"Umberto!"

She was inconsolable as she gripped onto the railing of her porch, unable to stand, unable to believe life would ever get better, because her son was dead and life would always be tinged with darkness. Her son had fallen off the cliffs and broken his little sprite's bones and his head had exploded and he was dead. He had fallen off the cliffs, the silly boy: the silly beautiful little sprite.

Millicent watched from the top window, with precious William in her arms, so cute with his glistening green eyes, the brightest eyes she'd ever seen, emerald-green: they shone and they stared up at Millicent with such adoration she sometimes wept. William agreed it was right, what had happened, what Umberto the little sprite had received: the punishment.

"You shouldn't smile," Charles said, pacing into the room, with his tangled beard and his tangled soul and his eyes hazy from the pipe, from both pipes: the wooden and the glass.

"I wasn't smiling, Charles," Millicent told him. "It's very sad.

I feel awful for her. I hate the sound of crying. That's why I hold William so often. You know how he gets otherwise."

Charles scowled, but it was true. William cried far less when he was in his older sister's arms. That was a problem for him, like the death of the little sprite Umberto was a problem. Comrade Philip was just as torn up about Bertie's death as his wife. And Charles was just as torn up about this troubling relationship Millicent and William had formed, almost a *sibling* relationship, which was wrong, which disproved – which tried to disprove – what he had created here.

There were no brothers. There were no sisters. There were cattle and non-cattle. Why then did he feel sorrow for Philip and Diana? They should not have doted on the little sprite, for he belonged to all of them and none of them.

Charles was a hypocrite. It was as simple as that. But he would never think of himself in those terms.

He would fix this, and he would fix it in a way that would cure both his problems at the same time: he would use his vast funds to arrange for Diana and Philip to be given new names, complete with believable histories, and these identities would sustain them in their new life. If they refused he would set the Comrades on them for daring to question him, for he was not only Comrade Charles. He was Master.

William would go missing and it would be a tragedy, but it was only a tragedy by conventional standards. Charles would do a good thing. He would give his only son as a gift.

What nobody but Charles and a select few of his loyal Comrades understood was how *right* this was, on a fundamental level, because he knew, and some of the others knew, that Millicent was broken. It was Millicent who had pushed the boy off the cliffs. They couldn't prove it and the little demon was too shrewd to give anything away, but everybody knew it.

This was how this wicked man thought about his own

daughter, designing ways to steal the only gleaming moments of happiness she had ever experienced.

So it came to pass one evening, when the cul-de-sac was quiet and stroked by moonlight – and the moonlight was very blue and very real and it cast shadows across the moment – Diana and Philip transferred their belongings to a second-hand Nissan Micra.

Charles carried William to the car and handed him over to Diana, and Diana flinched, but she knew better than to question Master's decision, even if this decision was questionable and this bundle of pink-cheeked flesh could never replace her little sprite, not her Bertie, but Master said it, so it must be so, and it was so.

Her name was Penny now, and Philip was called Frederick, and the child would become Jamie.

Millicent watched from the porch, something shattering and burning in her chest, and it scorched and it went deep inside of her, to a place that would never be remade.

The shape of his back, the broadness of his shoulders, the back of his head... his footsteps.

Clip-clip-clip, her father's footsteps were so loud on the concrete as he carried her brother, her sweet William, her green-eyed angel to the second-hand car.

Millicent waited for him to cry, he with the glistening green eyes, because surely he'd cry: he *had* to. He only fell silent and content when she was cradling him.

Why wasn't he *crying*?

It wasn't fair. If he cried – like she was crying, with tears burning down her cheeks – they'd know it wasn't right and he had to stay with his sister.

But he refused. Millicent hated him.

"We're dead to you." Charles stared at Comrade Philip – at Frederick – with intense eyes above his scraggly beard. "Do you understand? Forget we exist. You know what happens otherwise."

Frederick glared at Charles, and Frederick was old and his wife was young and he was half the terror in the Rainbow Room, and he glared at Master before lowering his eyes like cowed cattle. "I understand."

"What do you understand?"

"You have recordings of me, Master." His young wife stared at him in disgust, as she held the unwanted child and hated this man she'd tethered herself to, and who she was desperate to get away from. "Confessions. And you'll release them."

"That's right." Charles smiled kindly, maliciously. "Now go on your way."

The family climbed into the Micra and they drove from the cul-de-sac and down the street, and by the time they reached the motorway, maybe they could pretend they were a family and not three unconnected people in a second-hand car with rust creeping up the doors and rust creeping into their thoughts when they considered the future laid out before them: laid out like a road, the road over which they glided, a road they did not want to travel.

"I loved him," Millicent whispered when her father walked up the porch steps.

"There is no love." Charles lit his pipe and his eyes glowed in the tobacco flame. "There is no hate. When will you understand, little lamb?"

"But I *loved* him."

"Pathetic." Charles grunted, walking inside.

Millicent watched him go, fists clenched, and she knew what she had to do.

She'd wait. And then she'd make him pay. She'd make them all pay.

This date would forever be scarred into her memory, and when she was old enough to act upon her genius, she would scar it into her flesh. She would never allow herself to forget.

Why didn't he *cry*?

She closed her eyes and she saw it again. She heard it again.

The shape of his back, the broadness of his shoulders, the back of his head... his footsteps.

Clip-clip-clip, so loud on the concrete.

Once upon a time I believed I could find the light, that ungraspable quality which has danced beyond my reach all my life. I believed with every ounce of my predator's being somewhere, somehow, I could step into the golden glow and close my eyes and allow the lighted power to illume my eyelids like a blazing blood-red firework.

But here we are: in the dark.

I press myself against the wall beside the bottom step, the knife gripped in my hand. My mind is hazy from the alcohol, layer upon layer of intoxication causing my perceptions to waver.

I call to her: the apex predator within, the huntress. She pushes through the clouding alcohol and heartache, and she is ready.

I don't remember the drive over here particularly well. I remember a *crash*. I remember my forearms juddering with an unseen impact. I am on autopilot now, existing in this moment alone. The past falls away and the future collapses in upon itself.

I should have gutted him when I first learned of his location.

Elijah and Philip – Elijah and *Frederick* – feared Father so intensely they followed his edict even after his death. They did not communicate, which they must desperately have wanted to do. Only the other knew how evil he was, how rotten.

After they'd summoned enough daring to seek each other out, I forced Elijah to tell me where Frederick and William had gone. That pill-addicted degenerate hasn't been able to lie to me for years.

I found, I followed, and I waited. I did not know what I was waiting for: a sign, any sign. And then I discovered dear old Frederick was losing his mind, as though God or the universe or some other arcane force had decided to grant him the mercy of forgetting.

But there was something else to my delay.

I, the most effective predator who has ever lived, was frightened. Yes, yes, scared right down to my core. Perhaps it's the alcohol that allows me to reveal myself to myself, but it's undeniable. I did not want to face Comrade Philip.

But I *did* face him. And I wasn't scared. I won. He raped me. They gang-raped me. He sodomised me. And now he's a sad old cunt who can't even feed birds on his own. So I win, old man. I fucking *win*.

The stairs creak as sweet William, as the man who has never spoken his true name descends. I grip the knife tighter and silence my breathing.

I wish I was sober. If my head wasn't so groggy, and if my body wasn't behaving so disobediently, this would be easy work. I'd gut him effortlessly and then perhaps I'd go upstairs and see if Hazel is home. I could reason with her, make her see she's got it wrong.

She does love me. She *said* she loved me.

Creak-creak-creak, my little brother descends glacially.

I cannot see him, but I'm sure he's scanning every twitching shadow.

Sweet Hazel, you have posted far too many photographs. A comprehensive geography of your home exists online. You did not prime your alarm. You did not even shut your door. It was pathetically simple to slink in and drift over to the fuse box, to flip the switch, to kill this grand house the same way I shall kill its owner: one of its owner's, at least, and perhaps I will gut you too.

She deserves it for looking at me like I'm mad.

Mad Millie, mad Millie, they used to sing when I was a child, those cattle folk who called us Freaks.

Jamie – William – he of the glittering green eyes, the emerald soul-seeing eyes, walks to the bottom of the stairs. He has a cricket bat in one hand and a torch in the other, aimed at the wall in front of him: an undulating meteor of yellow. He moves the light one way, and then begins the movement that will reveal me.

I judge the distance and I leap at him, bringing the knife up in a punching arc.

Instinct makes him spin at the last moment, smashing the hilt of the cricket bat against the blade.

I push against the bat, biting with the blade, but Jamie is stronger than me and he drives me against the wall. My belly empties of air and conviction when he brings his knee up, cruelly, impressively, causing vomit to try to explode up my throat.

"Drop it," he growls.

I flail, aiming for his face. I will puncture those cherubic cheeks, those cheeks I once squeezed and kissed and loved.

Why didn't he *cry*?

He ducks and leaps back, swinging the cricket bat in a semicircle of devastating impetus.

I crouch and the bat crushes the wall behind my head, and I dive at his belly.

Wet fleshy noises shimmer in the air, and the scent of his blood rises, as I drive the blade into the spot above his hip bone. He gasps, but he doesn't collapse. He dislodges the bat and knocks me on the top of my skull.

Liquid agony seeps over my head and down my cheeks, the force of the blow sending me to the floor. He grunts and I feel him moving to strike again.

I stab him in the foot. He's not wearing shoes and *now* he remembers how to cry, shaking sobbing noises cracking in the back of his throat.

Too late, little brother. Much too late.

I pull the knife out and aim at his other foot.

The bat slams against my neck. My fingers loosen and the blade slips from my grip. I have his blood on my hand, greasy and hot and alive, soaking my fingers from where I punched him with the blade.

We dive on the knife, caught in a whirling dance of bloodlust, utterly lost to the song of murder.

I am smiling. I don't care what happens now.

Maybe this is the light. Maybe the light is pain and purpose.

He pushes against me, aiming the tip of the blade at my heart. "Crazy—fucking—bitch."

"I was happy." I gnash my teeth on his lip, smiling as his blood washes into my mouth, seeping between my teeth, becoming part of me. "When I found you. And I learned. You were like me. You do. What you need. To do."

My arms strain with the effort of forcing the blade tip away, but he is strong. Of course he is strong. He is my William.

"Nothing like you." His words come out distorted and half-real through his shredded lip. "Just. Die—"

I bite him again, and in the same instant I lash the knife down. I'm not sure what I catch, but it is flesh, glorious flesh.

The blade sinks and more blood spurts and then sweet

Jamie rolls away from me, gasping as the knife slams against the wooden flooring like chattering teeth: like my teeth chattered when I sat in my bedroom alone, thinking of how relieved I was Philip was gone, and yet how certain I was I'd brave the Rainbow Room a thousand more times to be reunited with my William.

"Where are you going?" I laugh, rising to my feet and then collapsing against the wall. He hit me very hard, and blood is streaming from my matted hair down my forehead. "*Jamie! William!*"

I chase him down the hallway, into their pristine kitchen.

He's at the garden door, swaying in his effort to stay upright.

"Where are you going?" My voice doesn't sound good, and then I feel it, in my gut: the place where he stabbed me. Somewhere in our scrimmage, he has invaded my flesh with metal. I didn't feel it then, but I do now, faintly, throbbing from some far-off place. "You can't run—"

I stumble and grab onto the kitchen island, pulling myself toward him, the blade's handle going *clip-clip-clip* against the obsidian surface.

"Go to Hell." He pulls the door open.

He stumbles into the night and I stumble after him, the world spinning with grotesque speed beneath my feet. He limps toward the rear of the garden, and I look past him and see a trowel buried in the flower bed.

Oh, little boy. You've never bled like this before. You're not thinking clearly. You passed a dozen knives in the kitchen. Or are you so scared of me, so desperate to be separated from me, when I'm the only person who ever truly cared for you?

I cared for you, and you betrayed me.

"You should've cried," I scream, or I want to scream. It comes out pale and fading. "Why didn't you?"

Jamie reaches for the trowel and the predator in me roars,

forcing energy into my limbs. I stumble-run across the garden and fall into the knife thrust, collapsing against him as he spins.

He stabs me and I stab him, and we stay like this: pinned against each other, gazing into each other's eyes.

So pretty, I whisper, but my tongue is submerged in hot sticky blood.

He grits his teeth and twists his implement, and I twist my blade. We waltz across the garden. A gleeful part of me sings and cavorts deep inside.

I am dying, but so is he, and, and, yes, I am *feeling*.

I feel. I am alive. I am dying but I am alive.

"You're... insane."

We collapse against his oh-so-impressive sauna.

"Yes." I spit to make room for speech. "Yes, yes."

He lurches and his forehead crushes into my nose. A spider's web of agony spreads, erupting, pulling my sensation to the point of impact.

He pushes me and I fall into the cold dark sauna.

He stands at the door, inhuman in the moonlight, his shirt soaked and his face smeared crimson and his eyes gleaming like precious gemstones. His hand slips on the door and the force almost sends him hurtling to the earth. He rights himself and reaches again for the handle.

I leap forward, even as my body protests, even as the vitality drains from me.

I grab his wrist and tug him inside.

He falls and I pirouette with him, and perhaps this is what it would be like to have a brother, a sweet younger brother who grew big and strong and could dance with me on my wedding day: a marriage to a good man, a man who wouldn't use and deride and hate me, a man who wouldn't take me to worlds where rainbows rend the sky.

I land atop him as he collapses onto the floor, wedged in the narrowness between the seating and the wall.

His hands are vapour at my hips, so weak. "Get... off."

"I love you," I whisper.

"Fuck you."

"I love you."

"I hate you."

"I love..."

I cough and something shatters inside of me, and then darkness is falling, complete darkness.

I smile. This is it. I feel it.

The darkness seeps away and light spreads, blistering light, impossible light, and the light is me and I am the light, and I am Millicent Maidstone, Millicent fucking Maidstone, and nobody can ever hurt me again.

51

JAMIE

I kick my legs, soaring higher on the swing. I love how she laughs as she pushes me. She's so happy. That's why I don't jump off right away. Jumping off is my favourite part, but I live for Mum's laughter.

I open my eyes and stare at the dark sauna ceiling.

Millicent is a dead weight on top of me and the door is open. I can hear wind and music playing softly from one of the adjacent houses. I don't hear any sirens.

My eyes fall closed and I open them, and then they close again.

I'm fading.

Fuck's sake, I'm going to bleed out right here, with this psycho's bloody lips smeared against my face.

Get off, I roar, but no words come out.

Why can't I speak?

Get the fuck off of me.

Hazel and I will go to Italy and find Mum.

I'm sorry, I'll tell her. *I didn't know I wasn't your son. I didn't know that's why you resented me. I forgive you. I don't blame you.*

Please let me be a part of your life. Look, Mum, look... I have a wife and a job and a house and a car. I'm happy. Please be happy for me. I love you.

Yeah, that's what I'll do when I get out of here. Hazel will forgive me. She has to.

"Jamie," Mum says, standing at the sauna door.

I try to lift my head, but I can't. I need help. I don't want to die.

Mum, help me.

"I have to think of myself, Jamie." She's doing an impression of Hazel for some reason. I don't know why. I don't want to die.

Please don't let me die, Mum.

"You've ruined it all. You have to see I have no choice. I'm going to call the police and an ambulance. But you have to do something first. You have to die. Can you do that for me?"

My eyes open and close, open and close, and one second I'm soaring higher on the swing and the next I'm staring into the dark.

"We made vows. I took them seriously. I honoured them. I'd never dream of disrespecting our vows the way you have. And even deeper than the vows, you *promised*. I think I was very understanding. You can't say I wasn't. But you went behind my back anyway. So you have to die. It's the best way to secure my future. I would say I'm sorry, but the truth... oh, God, the truth is I'm not."

I kick my legs and Mum laughs and she's happy. She's laughing. She *must* be happy.

"You fucked another woman." I think it's Hazel. But if Hazel's here, that means I don't have to jump. I can keep swinging. I don't have to jump... Mum is laughing, and it's the most beautiful sound in the world. "There's no coming back from that. Not for us."

I love you, I whimper, and I jump.

I soar and I touch the sky and then I'm in the grass. Mum leaps on me with tickling hands, and we laugh and hug and I wrap my arms around her. She hugs me close.

I close my eyes. I smile.

52

BEFORE

I have decided to tell this story with the distance of language because, simply, it is too painful to remember it all as something *I* did, as a childhood *I* was subjected to. It is much easier to make me a *she*, an other, excised from my true self the day I killed my father. I have spent the time since these sad early years learning how to make them pay for what they did, blackmailing and torturing, threatening, possessing.

I can't bring myself to remember it in full vivid terror. It comes in bursts, fired at my mind like weaponry, and that's why I've written it down; maybe I can push it away forever, dampen it so I never have to think about what they did. It belongs to the page now.

I don't like to pity myself. I've always looked down upon people who indulge in such unproductive behaviour. And yet when I look back at that childhood – at the abuse and the rape and the gaslighting and the pain and the molestation and the neglect – I can't help but feel something.

Something.

Not the light: the gasp before the kill, the ephemeral ascension. This is something mundane and human. I want to wrap my arms around her, the little girl, myself, and tell her everything's going to work out in the end. I want to steal her away and let her develop in a decent place, surrounded by loving people.

I think I could've been different.

There were times when I valued the closeness of my mother's body over the call to the wild: the whispering that I should stab or steal or hate. But then she would turn on me, laugh at me, call me sick names that made me feel worthless.

There is so much I could write about if I was willing to delve into the true perversion of my upbringing. I could paint these pages with the most grotesque torture methods, the most depraved sexual acts imaginable, committed against a girl too young and naïve to know she was doing anything wrong. Everything men and women can do to a child, they did to me.

But no, no... you see, by thinking of the past in distant terms, I can imagine things happened in a distant way, and with that little mental trick I can remake reality. Father was a foolish idealistic sadist but he was right about a few things.

Reality is nothing but what we make it, projections of our minds sending neurons fluttering like autumn leaves, and we choose which ones we catch.

I don't have to be pathetic. I don't have to hate myself.

I don't have to wish things had been different. If I believe hard enough, they already were.

53

HAZEL
SEVERAL MONTHS LATER

I t's my twenty-third birthday and I've just surpassed two million followers.

I stand in the art gallery, aware everybody is acting awkward about being near me while trying not to act awkward. They're behaving like I'm famous.

And I am. Not Insta-famous. I'm famous-famous.

The gallery is displaying *my* art, and not as part of a larger event. Every single piece in here is mine.

I sip champagne and study the painting in front of me.

Droplets of rose-red flare across the upper part of the work, joining the nature-greens and the big swathe of sun-yellow. It's an abstract nature scene, with lots of vivid colours and personal expression in the piece. It's the painting I was working on when this all started.

I didn't know what was really going on between Millie and Jamie. I didn't know Jamie had once been called William, and he and Millie were brother and sister. That came out a few weeks after their deaths.

Lots of ex-cult members have started to speak up now Millie isn't there to stop them. One of the cultists has been arrested for meeting with an underage girl. Penelope – Diana – is being bothered in Italy, which is a shame, but also: fuck her for abandoning Jamie. She was the one who screwed him up to the point where he'd cheat on me.

After their deaths, I also learned Millie murdered Ray in his flat. One of his neighbours smelled something and called the building manager to investigate. I learned she caused some property damage the night she drove to our house, smashing into a bus stop, driving over somebody's garden, almost causing a car crash when she pulled out in front of a red light. She was so drunk it's a miracle she even made it to our house.

I guess she really wanted to kill. Or die.

Maybe I'm a little fucked up – I know I am – but what infuriated me most was learning Millie was behind my follower count plummeting. The lunatic had hired some low life on the Dark Web to mass-report inactive accounts, getting them banned from Instagram so it seemed like I was being abandoned. She orchestrated it to make me feel alone, pathetic, needy... and I'm guessing it's because she wanted to swoop in like the predator she was and make me rely on her. She was using me the same way Jamie did, to justify some evil aspect of themselves.

I hope they've got adjoining rooms in Hell.

I take another sip of champagne, focusing on the bubbles instead of my rage. I hear somebody approach me in high heels and turn away at the last second. I *intimidate* people now. It's crazy. It's awesome. I'm proud, and I'm not ashamed of being proud.

It came to me as I stood at the sauna door, looking down at Millie and Jamie, both of them bleeding and near death. I think Millie might already have been dead. I'm not sure. It's kind of hazy. *Hazy Hazel*, Millie called me once. I guess she was right.

What I remember very clearly is the plan that unfolded in

my mind. I had a choice. I could get a divorce, because there's no way I'd forgive Jamie for what he did to me. So, a divorce, and all the problems and humiliation that comes along with that.

Or I could let Jamie bleed out. It wasn't like *I* was killing him. I was just waiting a few minutes to dial 999.

I am the sole survivor of Millicent Maidstone, one of the most notorious serial killers of all time.

I knew how to market the hell out of the experience. I knew the right selfies to take, the right filters, the right hashtags, the right posts. I knew how to imply I was on the verge of committing suicide, and that faking a drug addiction was a good idea, and that people would cheer me on when I announced I was clean and doing well.

I was ready to take on the world again, *yaaaaaas queen*, and *#Iwontletthemkeepmedown*.

I always had it in me to be this person, but I was never able to use my skills to their full extent. Marriage held me back. I *wanted* to be held back, as long as our marriage was what I thought it was. But it wasn't. And now I'm soaring.

I'm working with a top ghostwriter to get a book deal. A big publisher is very interested. I mentioned maybe we'd want to hold off until the police's cases are complete, so the book would cover everything. Using Millie's memory stick, the police are retracing her wanderings across England, piecing the murders together.

The lady laughed, like I was telling a joke. *Darling, you can write more than one book about this.*

I laughed and pretended I'd been joking. I told her of course. I'd write a whole library of books about this experience.

Make-up, fashion lines, perfumes, meditation guides, diet and workout apps... I'm going to squeeze every last drop of fame and money from this as I can, and then, once it's dried-up and not useful to me anymore, I'll have enough followers and clout to catapult myself into superstardom.

I refuse to feel guilty about using this situation to my advantage. The alternative was to hide away and let other people make money and careers from what happened to me. This way, I'm in control. I'm taking it back, everything Jamie stole from me when he broke our vows and the promises we made.

I can't even feel guilty about leaving Jamie to bleed out. He knew what he was signing up for.

Total devotion. Unwavering commitment. Forever.

When I woke to find him standing over me in my university bedroom, I should've screamed. I should've leapt up and scratched him.

But I didn't.

He was staring at me, seeing me, really seeing me. I'd never been looked at like that before. His glistening emerald eyes pinned me in place, and then he smiled.

He could tell I liked it. I read surprise in his expression, but not a lot of it, not enough for him to stop.

I see you, Hazel Paling. He moved to the bed, getting so close I could feel the heat of him. *I see all of you. You're never invisible with me. Everything you do, everything you are... I'll always be watching.*

I know something's wrong with me.

Kissing this man, this intruder, yes, it was definitely the wrong thing to do. It probably says a lot about me that we had sex right there, the best sex of my life, before I knew his name or who he was.

But he knew *my* name. He knew I needed attention, real attention, not the kind everybody else pretended to dish out. He'd first noticed me at an employment event in university, following me for a while, reading my hungry need to be seen.

Later, when he came to me and confessed he'd followed a woman home, I made him swear they'd never see him. They'd never know he existed. He'd never kiss them. He'd never touch them. He'd definitely never *fuck* them.

I see now how twisted this arrangement was. It was the same thing Mum did with Dad's cheating, pretending it didn't exist, lying to herself and saying it didn't matter as long as he kept it separate from their storybook life.

But I was dead wrong.

What Jamie did was sick, and *I* was sick for allowing it to happen, for allowing my fear of abandonment to lead me down this dark road. I should have slapped him across the face the moment he told me what he'd done, his puppy-dog eyes pleading with me to accept him for who he was.

I feel more anger trying to burn up inside of me, but it's not aimed at Millie, not even at Jamie. It's aimed at myself. These last few months have taught me that relying on other people is one of the stupidest things a person can do. Mum tethered herself to Dad, even when he cheated on her, and it made her bitter and resentful. I relied on Jamie – telling myself we had the perfect marriage, that the façade was the same as the reality – and it led to me getting cheated on, used, ignored.

We never had a perfect marriage; we didn't even have a *good* marriage.

We had a perverted connection formed when he stalked me. We had some underwhelming words spoken at a gaudy wedding. We had fear of being alone and complicity in the evil things my husband did. That's all.

I take another sip, calming myself, and then I hear footsteps walk up behind me.

"Hazel."

I may not be a teenager anymore, but hearing *Kirk freaking Hope* say my name sends a shiver up my spine. I've been tagging him for years on our shared birthday and he's never responded. This time, it was *him* who tagged *me*. He must've seen my earlier posts. Or maybe one of his PR people told him about me.

Whatever. It doesn't matter. He's here.

I turn with my most alluring smile. I'm dressed modestly, glamorously, and sexily all at once. It's a combination that should be impossible, but my stylist – my *stylist* – is incredibly talented.

Kirk offers me his pearly-white smile. He's wearing a tuxedo and his blond hair is tousled just so. All around us, dozens of cameras capture the moment.

THE END

ACKNOWLEDGEMENTS

If I tried to list every single person I owe thanks to – who contributed to this novel's existence in even minor ways – I'd add at least one hundred pages to this book's length. Which is to say if I miss anybody, I am very, very sorry.

I have so much gratitude for my editor, Morgen Bailey. Working with her was an absolute pleasure and she made my twisted story so much better.

Everybody at Bloodhound Books has been professional, welcoming, and all around amazing to work with. Betsy and Fred, the wonderful cover designers, my proofreader, the super-conscientious Tara, social-media guru Maria... all of you have my deepest thanks. This would have been a very different novel if I'd gone it alone, 15k shorter and with much less depth. I'm so grateful to be able to work with such an honest and supportive team.

Keri Beevis, Patricia Dixon and Heather Fitt deserve a special mention, as always. Without them it would be a much lonelier bookish world.

I thank my dad, Raymond, for being the silent hero people rarely write books about. I thank my mum, Betsy, for always laughing at my jokes. I thank my brothers, Ben and Jake, for laughing with me in the gym and (Ben) asthma! I thank my dogs, Loki and Gizmo, for being cute and unmanageable and perfect. I thank my friends, James and Marshall and Kane and Joey, for making me laugh and letting me go a little crazy every now and then.

Lastly, most importantly, I thank my wife. Krystle, without you I never could've written a single page, let alone a whole book. You inspire me more and more every day.

A NOTE FROM THE PUBLISHER

Thank you for reading this book. If you enjoyed it please do consider leaving a review on Amazon to help others find it too.

We hate typos. All of our books have been rigorously edited and proofread, but sometimes mistakes do slip through. If you have spotted a typo, please do let us know and we can get it amended within hours.

info@bloodhoundbooks.com

Lightning Source UK Ltd.
Milton Keynes UK
UKHW040748131021
392136UK00001B/172